ALSO BY AMY YORKE

The Wilderise Tales
The Good and the Green
The Bright and the Blue
The Ancient and the Amber
The Silent and the Silver

The GOOD and the GREEN

Book One of the Wilderise Tales

Amy Yorke

GLASSLOOK
PRESS

*For anyone in need of a good hug
and a warm cup of tea*

WILDERISE
HEROT'S HOLLOW
Weldan House
FOSSHOLM
Gull Bay
SUDPORT
SALLIN SEA
LANDSEND
LOEGRIA
ARCAS DYRNE
Castle

Pronunciation Guide & Glossary

CHARACTERS

Alison Lennox: AL-ih-son LEN-nox
Rinka: RINK-a
Nolwynn: nole-WEN
Lady Sibba: LAY-dee SIB-ba
Gwenla: GWEN-la
Keir Ainsley: KEER AINS-lee
Weyland Gilroy: WAY-lend GIL-roy
Lydiach: LID-ee-ahch
Mezec: MEZ-ek
Aras: AIR-as
King Derkomai: KING DER-ko-mye

PLACES

Wilderise: WILL-duh-rise
Loegria: LOW-gree-uh
Arcas Dyrne: AR-cuss DERN
Landsend: LANDS-end

Sudport: SOOD-port
Herot's Hollow: HAIR-uts HOL-low
Sallin Sea: SAL-lin SEE
Weldan House: WELL-dun HOUSE

OTHER

Korrigan: KOR-ih-gen
Spriggan: SPRIG-gen

Fulling: FUL-ling. The full-height races of the world: humans, elves, orcs, dwarves, mermaids, sirens.
Halfling: HALF-ling. Not a separate race; rather, the offspring of a Fulling and Quarterling or Eighthling.
Quarterling: QUART-er-ling. Races that come up to knee-height on humans: korrigans, hobgoblins, goblins, selkies.
Eighthling: EIGHTH-ling. The smallest races: fairies, pixies.

Prologue

In a harshly lit room full of identical beds, the early-morning stillness was broken by a terrible scream.

A commotion followed: a rush of chattering people in white coats, mostly elf and human; the squeaking of a cart with a bad wheel; the whirring of a 'lectric pump; the pop of a glass bottle; the scent of something like vinegar on a breeze from a swiftly yanked curtain.

Alison held her father's hand while he slept through it all. She gave it a squeeze. *It's not for you,* she thought. *Not today. Not yet.*

Her mother had gone to the flower shop down the street. The daffodils in the vase on the bedside table were wilting, she said. Alison could see no flaw in the perfect yellow trumpets gently nodding over the side of the glass. But she didn't blame her mother for trying to find some way to be useful.

Alison had gone through that phase and many more in the past six months. First, before the reality of her father's diagnosis set in, she worried for herself. Her father would likely recover, but with too much time away from her new job, she wouldn't. Then when the treatment began, her worry was replaced with something like hope but stronger. Alison's youthful faith in the power of modern medicine gave her a certainty in his healing that seemed hopelessly naïve upon reflection, but it had been a source of comfort to her father all the same. Now that it was clear the treatment had failed, all Alison could feel was anger. Anger and clinging desperation to keep the man tethered to this world in spite of whatever forces conspired to rob her of him.

"Ali? Shouldn't you be at work?"

Alison startled at her father's strained voice. She hadn't felt him wake.

She squeezed his hand (so small, so cold) and knelt to pull a pillow from beneath the bed to help him prop himself up. He was so light now, she could lift him into place herself. "It's early still," she said.

"Don't be late on my account. I'm feeling better today."

He said this every day, and Alison wondered if it was ever true, or if it was something he said to give her permission to leave.

"Ali?" he asked, reaching for her hand. His pale blue eyes, eyes that looked exactly like hers, were soft and filled with tears.

"I'm here, Papa."

"I'm so proud of you. My clever daughter. You know that, don't you?"

"Yes, Papa," she said. "I know."

Chapter One

AN UNEXPECTED LETTER

There was a kind of magic to the city at twilight. The glow of the 'lectric streetlamps, the whine of the underground rail-wheeler carrying its hurried passengers home after a long day. The entirety of Arcas Dyrne took in a collective breath, one final gasp before the long exhale of night.

Inside the lobby of the Looking Glass Tower, a crowd gathered for the evening post. The room was an imitation of finery–granite rather than marble, brass instead of gold. People-minders and pencil-pushers rather than executives and tycoons.

Alison tapped the heel of her boots–leather, not wyvern hide–as she waited. To her mind, there were few greater joys than the arrival of a wanted letter. But there were also few greater frustrations than waiting for it to come.

"The second time this week the pigeon's been late," said a dwarf in a tattered suit. "Lord Arleas will have that bird by its iridescent neck if it doesn't watch out."

Alison nodded. The image was crude, but she wouldn't put it past their elf landlord.

Just then, a rush of cool night air swept through the lobby, lifting Alison's cloak to her knees. The Halfling night manager burst through the double doors with a fat stack of letters in hand. The crowd made way as he dashed for the post boxes and frantically began stuffing the cubbies.

Alison pushed her way to the front.

"Ah, Ms. Lennox," said the Halfling, looking up at her through tiny spectacles. "I'm afraid I'm not up to the Fulling floors yet. The bird only just left."

"May I?" asked Alison, gloved hand outstretched.

"Oh–I don't know if that's–oh–"

Alison grabbed the stack of letters and flicked through them. Bill, bill, love note with a lipstick kiss on the envelope, bill, and then:

"Yes!"

There it was. A plain cream envelope with her name in the bottom left corner.

The rest of the letters slipped from her hands, but she didn't notice at first. Only once the Halfling had returned to clean up her mess did she realize her error. Blushing, she knelt to help him.

"Something good, ma'am?" he asked.

"I rather hope so," said Alison, shoving the rest of the letters back into his hands, and she was off.

Alison made it as far as the stairwell before she could wait no longer. She ripped open the envelope, hands trembling.

Feax's Golden Tonic will bring the light of the sun into the mane of any elf, human, dwarf, or orc who dares possess a bottle. You must take care: the shine is so bright it could blind a fairy! (Not for use by Halflings, Quarterlings, or Eighthlings. The Elfscyne Corporation is not responsible for any unintended fires that occur as a result of using this product.)

"It's a bloody ad." She crumpled the paper into a ball and tossed it towards the bin, missing by a good six inches.

There was nothing left but to drag herself up the stairs; the lifts were busy carting the day-shift dwarves down to the building's subterranean levels. By the third flight of stairs, she was winded. By the seventh, she was nearing collapse. She had thought the climb would get easier over time, and it had. But a human body just wasn't meant for this much climbing.

An elf from an upper floor passed her by with a smirk. Alison muttered a curse under her breath. It had no power, but it did make her feel a bit better.

The apartment was tiny–"intimate," Lord Arleas had said when he showed it to her the first time. It was fortunate that she was not much bigger than a Halfling, he joked. She laughed along, wanting to make a good impression on her new landlord, until he asked her if she had any pixie in her blood. Her ears went bright red at the suggestion, and Lord

Arleas must have realized he went too far because he quickly changed the conversation to the generous sizing of the cupboards.

Those very same cupboards were flung wide open now, and an orc was rifling through them.

"I can't find the rosemary," the orc said without turning. "Don't tell me you used it all."

"I know you aren't accusing me of cooking," said Alison.

Rinka flashed a toothy (well, fangy) smile at her flatmate. "I thought perhaps it was good for a spell or something like it."

Alison's last foray with the old magic, from a book titled *Old Magic, New You*, had been a literal bust. They were still finding glass shards between the floorboards months later. "I haven't tried any spells since–"

"Believe me, I remember the last time. But you're sure you haven't used it?" The orc dropped two large fistfuls of potatoes into a pot of boiling water with a splash.

"Quite sure," said Alison.

"Has the post come?"

"Only just. Mr. Theo hasn't finished sorting it yet."

Rinka must have picked up on the defeat in Alison's voice. "Still nothing from *The Evening Times*?"

Alison shook her head. Her poetry contest entry titled "A Korrigan's Courage" had thus far gone unanswered. Not that the twenty-gold prize would have done much for their situation. It would have pushed them a few months further away from eviction. No more.

"Ah, here it is," said Rinka, producing a small glass jar containing sprigs of a bluish color. "The knockers must have moved it again."

"I think they prefer the term 'hobgoblin' outside of the mines," said Alison.

Rinka pulled a large chicken carcass from the icebox and began ripping off its limbs with her bare hands.

Alison slunk down into a chair at the tiny kitchen table. "I'm just going to have to get the promotion. They've promised it to me for ages now. It has to be soon."

"And you're sure the head number-cruncher salary will cover the difference?"

"Number-checker," Alison corrected. "It's an eight-gold salary increase. I've seen it in the numbers."

Rinka delicately placed the rosemary sprigs on top of the bird parts she had just dismembered. "Eight gold. So precise. Those dwarves have it all figured out, huh?"

"It's humans that run the numbers. At least we're not greedy with the coin like some elves we know. Well, one elf in particular."

"Don't get me started on Lord Arleas," said Rinka. "A six-gold rent increase. It's more than half!"

"It's less than a quarter."

"Well, you're the number-cruncher after all. But it's still a lot."

"It is," Alison agreed. Their elf landlord insisted the increase was necessary to bring new modern amenities to the building—'lectric 'frigerators to replace the iceboxes, a long-talker on each hall, and a furnace to replace the failing boiler—but the other buildings in the neighborhood had managed on increases much smaller. Rinka suggested they move to one of the more reasonable buildings, but those had years-long waiting lists. Alison had only landed this apartment by showing up on the very day the previous occupant (her colleague's grandmother) had died, and even then it had taken a bit of a fib about her familial relations to appease the elf.

"I've tried asking Mr. Winklebottom for a small raise. Not even enough to cover the entire increase, but enough to help. But he said the price of meat's going up too, and no one wants to pay more when they can barely pay the rent. I'm not sure he'll be able to keep me on much longer," said Rinka.

"At least he lets you take home what they don't sell. We won't starve," said Alison.

"Not this week at least," said Rinka.

There was a knock at the door.

"Ms. Lennox–" gasped the night manager as Alison opened it. He must have climbed the stairs himself. "There was another letter for you, ma'am. Evening, Ms. Rinka," he said, tipping his hat to the orc.

"Just Rinka," she said. She threw open the oven door, causing Mr. Theo to jump back in surprise.

"Of-of course, ma'am. Meant no offense. I hope you ladies have a good night."

"Thank you, Mr. Theo," Alison called over her shoulder. She was already fetching the letter opener.

Rinka finished basting the bird and joined Alison at her desk. "Well?"

"It's not from *The Times*," said Alison.

"What is it?"

"I think it's some sort of joke."

"Let me see it."

Dear Ms. Alison Lennox,

I'm writing to you regarding your first cousin, twice-removed, Ms. Frances Lincoln. I am sorry to be the one to tell you that Ms. Lincoln has passed away. As I'm sure you are aware, Ms. Lincoln had no direct living descendants. As such, her estate passes to the next living kin, and you are she. All assets and possessions are hereby awarded to you as the sole heir. The deed to her home is enclosed. Again, my condolences for the passing of your beloved relative.

Regards,
Mr. Lagulind Thornchik, Solicitor

"Deed to her home? All assets and possessions? It's the answer we've been waiting for!" Rinka's gray features lit up with glee.

Alison slowly placed the letter down. She began to stroke her dark hair in its braid as the orc danced around the room in the periphery of her vision.

Rinka kept talking, but Alison didn't hear her. There were only two words in her mind: *passed away.*

The pain she felt was all too familiar. It had been eight years since her father had died, long enough that not every mention of death brought the grief back to the surface. And even when it did, it was easier now to push the feeling back down than it had been in the beginning.

Yet still, the ache was there.

Ms. Frances Lincoln had no children to mourn her as Alison mourned her father. Alison wondered if anyone mourned her at all. That thought was sad too, in a different way. "Sorry. What did you say?" she asked Rinka once the dizziness of the reminder of grief had passed.

Across the room, Rinka's face fell. She must have noticed Alison's shift in mood. "How unbelievably unkind of me. Did you know her well?"

"No, not at all," Alison said.

"That's wonderful! I mean, very sad. Very sad indeed for poor Ms. Lincoln." The orc frowned unconvincingly. "But for you–for us–it's wonderful news. When you sell it–you are going to sell it, right? You'll have enough to, well, not to buy this place. But enough for you to stay here. And me, if you'll have me. I'm sorry I can't pay more, but I could also clean for you, in addition to the cooking, and I could run the errands–"

"Let's take a look at this deed first. Maybe it will give us a sense of how much it's worth," said Alison.

Alison read the tattered scrap of parchment aloud as Rinka smashed a clove of garlic with her fist and stirred the paste it made into softened butter.

Know Ye that on this day, the eighteenth day of September, in the twentieth year of the reign of our Sovereign Lord Typhon, King of Loegria and Wilderise, that I, Fraser Ainsley of Herot's Hollow in the County of Merelor do hereby bestow for good and valuable considerations to Fiona Lincoln of Herot's Hollow in the County of Merelor and to the heirs of her body fifteen acres of land lying to the northwest of the property of Jodoc of Herot's Hollow being bordered by Orchard Lane on the south and for six chains and three rods hence before being bounded by the property of Niall Ainsley of Herot's Hollow and then thus continuing for two furlongs and three chains to and including the Winterburn Stream and being bordered on the east at the old oak tree and all usages, houses, gardens, fruit trees, woods, meadows, pastures, waters along with any royalties or rents made thereof. In faith and testimony whereof I do set my hand and seal, Fraser Ainsley.

"I've never heard of Herot's Hollow. Wait," said Alison, piecing back together the torn envelope. She sighed heavily. "It was sent from Wilderise."

"The kingdom across the sea?"

"Well, it's technically not its own kingdom. King Derkomai rules there as well. Only it's…"

"It's wild," said Rinka. "I've seen it at the picture show. What about the land, though? Something something rods and furlongs? What does any of it mean?"

Alison shook her head. "I'm not sure. I know the Dyrne Common is seventy acres, and this is for fifteen."

"More than half of the common!"

"Less than a quarter."

"Less than a quarter of the common! That's a lot of land, Al."

It was. Maybe it would be worth something, even in Wilderise. "I'll have to meet with a real estate broker. I'm not sure how to sell it from here."

"You're not going to go there? You don't want to even see it?"

Alison didn't share the orc's curiosity. Wilderise was a barren land with little civilization to speak of. There was nothing there but farmland and woods and mountains. Certainly no jobs number-crunching or number-checking, no rail-wheelers or manufactories or 'lectrics. She doubted they even had sound or picture shows outside of Sudport. Alison didn't have much; it was hard to have a lot when her lifespan was less than a fiftieth of that of the elves, and humans would never be the titans of industry that the dwarves were. But she had a path here, a path her parents had sacrificed everything to put her on, and she was so close to breaking through that she could feel it.

"What use do I have for however many furlongs of land? It's most of a day just to Landsend by rail-wheeler, and then another day over the Sallin Sea, then who knows how long from Sudport. And there's no way Mr. Rosales will give me the time off." The inheritance was good fortune, a shortcut along the road and nothing more. She was sure of it.

Rinka pulled the chicken from the oven and dumped it onto a pair of plates. She then drained the potatoes, coating them with garlic butter. It smelled heavenly. Alison's stomach growled in appreciation.

"Well, if you're sure. Still, it seems a shame to let it go without even seeing it for yourself."

As she devoured the orc's home cooking, she turned her mind to more interesting ideas. What would she do with the coin once she had it? It was hard to guess what the property might be worth, but it had to amount to a couple hundred gold at least. It wouldn't buy her a place in Arcas Dyrne, not even a broom closet like the one she shared with Rinka. But perhaps invested in the right venture, it would turn into more over the course of a few years. And maybe in that time, if she was earning the number-checker salary that she knew she deserved, and maybe with a poetry contest win or two, she would build up enough to buy a spot in one of the new buildings the dwarves were erecting. The buildings with tall golden spires and the latest 'lectrics in every room, just minutes away from the theater district. And there would be a new restaurant at street level serving only the finest fairy fare.

Not that Alison didn't appreciate Rinka's chicken. But she had always enjoyed the finer things in life. From a distance, at least.

"Thank you for dinner, Rinka. I'll wash up–no, I insist," she said as the orc made a move for her plate.

In her mind, she wasn't running the lukewarm water in the sink over dirty plates. She was miles away uptown, running a piping hot bath in a clawfoot tub, the air scented heavily with lavender and jasmine.

Chapter Two

THE FEE TAIL DETAIL

Do you have the need for a home? Or perhaps you long to get rid of one? Or indeed, it could be both! Whatever your real estate needs, you can trust Lady Selelas. With over six hundred years of real estate experience, you can't afford not to trust her. Give her a ring today!

Alison clipped the ad from the morning paper and placed a call with the long-talker across the street. With an appointment scheduled for Friday, all that was left to do was secure time off from work.

It was short notice, and her boss Mr. Rosales would say no at first. Alison had little experience with absences, but she had watched her fellow number-crunchers request time off enough to understand the game that had to be played.

"I'm so sorry for the late notice, sir, but my dear cousin Frances has died. I was wondering if I could take off Friday and next Monday to attend her funeral? It's in the country, you see."

Mr. Rosales was a gruff human man with a piggish face and a belly too large for his suspenders. He puffed on a cigar, filling the room with so much smoke that he had to wave his hands to clear his view of Alison.

"Two days off? And with less than a week's notice? I don't think we could manage that, no. Were you close to this cousin of yours?"

"Very close," said Alison. Any guilt she might have felt for this ploy was assuaged by Mr. Rosales's callousness. She pulled her handkerchief from her trouser pocket. "It's been very difficult to hear of her passing, and all alone in the countryside…" She dabbed at her big blue eyes, which were actually watering a bit from the smoke, and let out a choked sob that was half a cough.

Mr. Rosales shifted uncomfortably in his wingback chair. "Right, well, be that as it may. Two days is far too many. There are numbers to be crunched, my dear."

"I understand," said Alison, looking at the floor. "I never want to let you down. To let Andsaz Industries down. Perhaps if I only went to the funeral on Friday? I could take the night rail-wheeler and be back before Monday."

"Hmm," said Mr. Rosales. He pressed his fat fingers together. "Well, you'll have to work extra hard this week to make the time up. And don't think I won't be checking."

Alison suppressed the urge to squeal in delight. "Oh, thank you sir! Thanks so much. Don't worry, sir. I'll crunch more numbers this week than ever before!"

Maybe she was overselling it a bit. Still, Mr. Rosales seemed pleased that he had managed to "win" their negotiation.

"See that you do," he said.

❧

By the time her appointment with Lady Selelas arrived on Friday, Alison had read the deed a hundred times. She could make no more sense of it now than the first time she had read it, but at least she nearly had it memorized.

The elf's office was in a beautiful old building downtown. It was a large and lovely structure of green marble and glass stretching towards the sky, taller than the surrounding buildings by ten stories at least. The doorways and windows were crowned in soft gold embellishments; delicate, almost organic spirals recognizably elvish in origin. This was, after all, the kind of building only elves could own. The rest of the races of Loegria had been priced out centuries ago.

Lady Selelas had her office on a lower floor. Her ad had claimed she'd only been in business for six centuries; she was young, by elvish standards. And she was involved in residential sales rather than big property sales to the dwarven industrialists who built the buildings of Alison's fantasy. Still, to have any office in a building like this was impressive. Alison hoped the elf wouldn't laugh her out of it once she had seen the property Alison now owned.

An Eighthling staffed the reception desk—a pixie, to Alison's surprise. Despite what people said, Alison had always taken the stories about pixies leading one astray as superstitious nonsense, and she took it as a good sign that Lady Selelas held a similar view.

"Ms. Lennox? Head right in, ma'am. Lady Selelas is expecting you," said the pixie in a sweet and childlike voice.

Lady Selelas's office smelled of cedar and the feverfew oil given by the apothecaries for headaches. The walls were lined with shelves overflowing with books, with piles more on the floor. A breeze from an open window blew papers and scrolls from atop the desk, blanketing the only spot where the wooden floors had been visible.

But the elf herself was nowhere to be seen.

Alison had almost turned back to the door when she glimpsed something near the window.

Lady Selelas climbed into the room in a fluid motion, her silken robe and silver hair trailing behind her. She glided over to Alison without disturbing a single scrap of paper.

"How do you do?" she asked, bowing slightly and reaching for Alison's hand. "I'm Lady Selelas of the Ash Woods."

The elf pulled Alison's hand up to her lips and gave it a soft kiss.

Alison was mesmerized. The only other elf she had known personally was her landlord Lord Arleas, but his beauty was cold and cruel. Lady Selelas was as bright and warm as a summer's day.

"Were you just outside?" Alison couldn't help but ask. The office was on the twenty-third floor of the building with no visible balcony in sight. Had she been walking along the window ledge? Though Alison did not fear heights, it was too much imagine even for her.

"Ah, yes. I like to take a walk sometimes when it's warm. To feel the sunlight on my skin, the wind in my hair…"

The elf's eyes closed as she spoke, and Alison closed hers too, almost feeling the sensations Lady Selelas described. And almost forgetting that the elf had been teetering on the edge of a twenty-three-story drop.

"Now," said Lady Selelas sharply, clapping her hands together and breaking their shared reverie, "tell me, what are your plans for the home? Is there land as well? Were you thinking of letting it and collecting rent?"

"No," said Alison, reaching into her leather satchel for the deed and the letter. "I'm thinking of selling. The property is in Wilderise, you see."

"Ah, I do see. Let's just look at this deed then–"

As soon as Alison placed the old paper in the elf's hand, she made a wistful sigh.

"I'm afraid it cannot be," said Lady Selelas.

Alison was confused. Could she really have read the deed so quickly? And if so, what was wrong with it?

She didn't need to trouble herself coming up with a question. Lady Selelas had moved alongside her almost imperceptibly, and she was pointing at the relevant passage.

"'Fiona Lincoln and to the heirs of her body.' It's a fee tail after all."

"What's a fee tail?"

"It's a type of land conveyance." She paused and looked into Alison's puzzled eyes. "It's how land is passed down over time. The original owner of the land Fraser Ainsley gave it to your ancestor Fiona Lincoln. But not just her. 'The heirs of her body.' That's how you've come to own the property. You must be an heir of Fiona's."

"I'm not sure how. I have this letter as well–"

She passed the letter to the elf, who read it instantly.

"Ah yes. Ms. Frances Lincoln was the last of her line, so they went back through the line of inheritance until they found someone with living issue. That's you, Ms. Lennox. And only you, apparently. You're the last of your line."

On her father's side, Alison supposed, considering her still-living mother hadn't been named an heir. Not that she planned to endure a conversation with her mother to confirm the fact. Or to hear, for the hundredth time, her disappointment that Alison had still not managed to find so much as a suitor, let alone a spouse. It seemed like a thing that she would do if the occasion arose on its own, and it most certainly had not up to this point. Would her entire ancestral line die with her?

She put that thought aside. "I don't understand what that has to do with my selling the property."

The elf looked at her kindly, like she was talking to a child. "You can't sell it. You can't mortgage it or borrow against it. You could let it, as I mentioned. Or you could sell an interest in the property during your lifetime, but it's a risky investment few would be willing to make. It would only be a good deal if the land was very productive and if you survived for a long time. Because once you leave this life, the property passes either to your heir or to an heir of the original owner if you have none. There may be a human out there willing to make the deal, but certainly no elf would."

She paused to see if Alison was understanding. She was, but only just. "And I'm afraid I'm not familiar with this part of Wilderise, at least not for the last three centuries or so, so I can't say what condition the property is in with any certainty. I'm sorry to be the one to tell you."

Lady Selelas took a seat behind her desk. Alison's eyes could barely register the movement; it was so smooth. The elf had been kind enough to explain the situation, but it seemed she had nothing else for her.

"There's nothing else I can do?" asked Alison.

"I'm ever so sorry. I'm probably not the best suited to help you with the letting, if you decide to go that route, but I have a colleague in Sudport I can recommend. Let me see if I have his card." Lady Selelas tossed aside piles of papers haphazardly. It was such a strange juxtaposition—a being of near-infinite grace surrounded by utter chaos. And yet, there must have been some order to it. She produced a single dark square of paper in mere moments.

"Tell Lord Ilcas I sent you."

Lady Selelas stood and bowed again. Alison, who had never stopped standing during their strange meeting, left the room in a daze.

"Did she have good news for you?" the tiny voice of the pixie asked as Alison came back into the reception area.

Alison wasn't sure what to say. The news hadn't been what she was hoping for. But she was surprised to find she didn't feel all that disappointed. An idea was forming in her mind.

A crazy idea.

"Not exactly," she said to the pixie. "It turns out my property is a fee tail—I can't sell it, but I don't know how I'm supposed to take care of it either. I'm going to have to find someone to rent it, but I don't have the money to hire someone to take care of everything for me. How much do I owe the good lady elf today?"

"Consultations are free, ma'am. And perhaps there's one more answer Lady Selelas did not share with you."

Alison thought she saw a design in this arrangement. Lady Selelas had a duty to provide advice in line with the laws of the land. The pixie was under no such restriction.

"Go on," said Alison.

"You could do nothing. Pretend you never received the letter. There's seldom much of a choice for those in your situation, and King Derkomai's enforcement of the law doesn't reach far. Just look at all the crumbling ruins in the countryside. But you didn't hear it from me. And, as I'm sure is very clear to you, Lady Selelas would never recommend a course of action that could end in legal trouble for her clients. Even if that trouble is quite unlikely."

Alison wondered about the pixie's legal education, but she still thought the advice was well-intended. It would be the easiest and safest course of action. Continue on as if nothing had happened. Keep working hard, keep her head down, and finally get the promotion she deserved. Hold on to the apartment she had worked so hard to get and even harder to keep. And maybe by the time she reached old age, she would have a fraction of the things she always hoped for.

But it wasn't enough. Something about her life wasn't enough. She had been afraid to admit it to herself. What would her father think if he were still here? But now that she had had a taste of something different–something bigger, even if just in theory–she found she couldn't turn away from it. Maybe it wouldn't be the shortcut to the penthouse she was hoping for. But Rinka had been right–she needed to see it for herself.

Chapter Three

A-JOURNEYIN'

It took more than a week for Alison to hear back from Mr. Lagulind Thornchik, Solicitor.

Dear Ms. Lennox,

I received your letter regarding your cousin Ms. Lincoln's affairs. Answers to your questions are below.

1. *I'm afraid we don't have a long-talker in our office, or indeed in the town of Fossholm at all. There are few in Wilderise. I hope the simple letter suffices for correspondence.*

2. *Ms. Lincoln did have some coin to her name at the time of her passing, but perhaps not as much as you would hope for. I'm enclosing a banknote for fifty gold. This is all that remains after paying for the care*

home where she spent the last years of her life, and after the management fees for the estate owed to my office.

3.   *As for the state of the property, I have not had the occasion to visit, nor to visit the town of Herot's Hollow as of late. I am told by an associate that the home on the property is in fine condition, but that the lands themselves may be in some state of disrepair. I don't believe Ms. Lincoln was able to arrange a land manager, so they may have been neglected for a time while she was in care. I am confident a fine young human lady such as yourself will be able to get them into tip-top shape in no time.*

Please feel free to write again with any further questions. I would be happy to assist you if you were to become my client.

Regards,
Mr. Lagulind Thornchik, Solicitor

"What does that last part mean?" asked Rinka as she read the letter. The orc was still in her butcher shop uniform, a navy and white outfit that looked a bit like a sailor's attire, except for the bloodstains. She handed the letter back to Alison and went into her room to change.

"It means he wants me to pay him for more information," Alison called after her. "And I also think he took most of Frances's money, by the sound of it." Alison had arrived home first, for once. She had shed her work trousers and changed into a lounging gown made from soft linen.

She sat on their small, tattered couch, feet tucked into the dress as if it were a cocoon.

"Still, fifty gold isn't nothing. It's enough to…to…"

"To cover the rent increase for eight months, assuming Lord Arsehole doesn't raise it again in that time. But it's not enough to do something about land in a 'state of disrepair.'"

Rinka emerged in a pink dressing gown. Her features were surprisingly delicate for an orc, aside from the large and sharp teeth, but her body was made up entirely of their characteristic muscle. It made for a funny sight, particularly when she was performing domestic duties. "I had an idea today while I was cleaning a boar. You get a tenant to do the work for a discount. Then once the place is back in order, you kick them out for someone who can pay what it's worth."

"Rinka, I'm surprised at you."

Rinka shrugged as she retrieved a cut of ham from the icebox. "It's what Lord Arleas is doing to us, isn't it? I don't like it either, but maybe that's what we have to do. Think like the elves."

Alison had considered it, though she didn't want to admit it. Maybe if she found someone who didn't want to stay long, she wouldn't have to kick them out. But she was hoping there was another solution.

"I've been thinking about something that you said." She handed Rinka the pepper grinder. "You said I ought to go see it. And I've decided that I shall. Perhaps after I've seen it, I'll know better what to do."

"Oh, I'm so glad! When will you go? Will Mr. Rosales let you have the time off?"

"He's not going to like it, but he's just going to have to. I know it might delay my promotion again, but with any luck, I'll be able to make more in rent than the eight gold that would have been worth. I'm hoping to go soon. I've heard spring is lovely in Wilderise."

"Oh, it truly is!" Rinka looked up from the ham she was pounding against the counter and stared wistfully into the distance. "Of course, the picture show I saw wasn't in color. I bet it's even prettier in color. Bright blue skies, just like your eyes. Grass as green as a newborn orc. Sunsets as red as the blood of the animals. Truly incredible. I'm so envious."

Alison's stomach turned a bit at her last analogy, but she understood the spirit. "You should come too, Rinka. You deserve a vacation more than anyone."

Rinka returned to pounding the ham. "Oh no, not me. Mr. Winklebottom would never agree to that long off, and there are only so many butchers in town that would take an orc. No, I'll stay right here, but I wouldn't mind if you send me a letter or a postcard or two. Let me live through you."

"Of course I will. I'm also going to leave a bit of the coin, just in case. Enough to cover my part of the rent coming up and the increase. In case I'm delayed."

"You mean in case you fall in love with it out there and never come back."

It didn't seem likely to Alison. She'd never cared much for the countryside, not even the much closer countryside outside the boundaries of Arcas Dyrne. There were too many unfamiliar sights and sounds, and most importantly, smells. The city didn't exactly smell like roses, particularly in the summer, but it was what Alison knew. The scent of manure and good earth freshly tilled and so many varieties of plants and animals made her nauseous. And the distance from all the modern conveniences concerned her. What if she needed to call someone on a long-talker? Or what if she needed a doctor or a rare medicine from the apothecary?

No, Alison would be happier to spend no more than a week away. It would be a pleasant change of pace, and then she'd be back to normal, but hopefully with a bit more gold in her pocket and more prospects for her future.

❧⦿⦿⦿☙

Mr. Rosales's office door was locked when Alison finally worked up the courage to approach him.

"Did you need something, Ms. Lennox?" Ms. Varma, the number-checker with the office next door, had spotted Alison's attempt.

Alison entered Ms. Varma's office instead. It was identical to Mr. Rosales's in every way, except for the cigar smoke. "I was hoping to speak with Mr. Rosales. I was planning to request some time off to take care of–"

"You can stop right there," said Ms. Varma. "I don't need to know why. How long?"

Alison studied a scuff on one of her loafers, unable to meet Ms. Varma's gaze. "A week?"

"A week?" repeated Ms. Varma. It was a question.

"Yes, ma'am. You see, I–"

"Again, I don't need to know. You've been here for how long now? Seven, eight years?"

Alison lifted her eyes from her shoes to the golden paperweight on Ms. Varma's desk. It was shaped like an anchor. "Nine, ma'am."

"Nine. And in all that time, have you ever taken a full week off?"

Alison's gaze had settled onto a fine silver watch on Ms. Varma's wrist. "No, ma'am."

"Well, I've got good news for you, Ms. Lennox. I'm not Mr. Rosales. He runs a tight ship. Incredible number-crunching rates, no one is denying that. But do you know who has the lowest turnover rates in the office?"

Alison's eyes traced the folds of Ms. Varma's deep plum sleeves to the high collar of her blouse and finally dared to take a peek into the number-checker's eyes. They were warm and kind as they met Alison's. "You?"

"That's right, I do. And you know why? Because I let my people live their lives. They've been watching you, Ms. Lennox. You're going to be up for this job soon. And I hope when you get it, you'll remember what I'm doing for you now and how it felt. See you in two weeks."

Alison couldn't believe it. "Two weeks, ma'am?"

"Yes, two. After nine years without a full week off, you've earned it. Send me a postcard if you like. Or don't– up to you."

Alison fought back the urge to hug the woman. A handshake was more professional, and so that's just what she offered. "Of course I'll send you a postcard. Thank you, ma'am."

❧ⓒⓖ☙

Alison's trunk was a scrappy old box that had once belonged to her father. The leather was scratched and peeling in places, and the brass was tarnished and water-stained. And it was heavy. Even when empty, it would have been cumbersome for Alison to move on her own. Luckily for her, Rinka was more than willing to help her to the station.

Alison stood with her on the platform awaiting the rail-wheeler to Landsend. A cool breeze blew through the open station as a different rail-wheeler arrived. Alison tightened her wool cardigan to her. Winter's last chill was in the air.

"And you know where you're going once you get to Landsend? And after, the way from Sudport?" asked Rinka, wringing her hands.

Alison patted the pocket of her cardigan. "I've got my maps, and I can always ask for directions if I need to."

"Good, good," said Rinka.

Alison could tell her flatmate had something else to say. She waited.

Finally, Rinka spoke up. "I'm so glad you're going. I know you've taken care of the rent, but I don't want you to worry about me. I hope you find something good there. Something that makes you happy. And write me lots of letters!"

"Rinka, I'm only going for two weeks. And it takes the better part of one for a single letter to travel anyway. I'll be back right here before you know it. Who knows? Maybe I'll make enough in rent to move us to an apartment with its own bathroom."

"Oh, that would be something. I'm afraid I frighten poor Mr. Everwick every time I go to have a bath."

The station attendant made an announcement over a tinny-sounding 'lectric system: Alison's rail-wheeler was arriving at the platform. It was a great steaming monster, an engine made from black dwarven iron followed by a dozen red cars with glass windows cracked open.

"Oh," Rinka groaned. She was practically vibrating with energy.

Alison knew what was coming.

The orc pulled her into a big hug, practically knocking her off of her feet. Alison's face smashed into Rinka's muscular chest, squishing her cheek almost beyond recognition. Once she had shifted enough to enable breathing through her nose again, Alison returned the embrace. Two years ago, they had been strangers. Now Rinka was her dearest–and maybe only–friend.

When Rinka let go, Alison felt the blood that had been constricted flow freely again. She smoothed her cardigan as Rinka lifted her trunk up the steps. On board the rail-wheeler, Alison was hit with a wave of nerves. Was this plan of hers insane? What if Mr. Rosales fired her once he'd found out where she had gone? And what if there was nothing for her on the other end but a bottomless pit of wasted coin and wasted time?

Rinka pulled her from her despair with one more hug. And then the orc was off, her cloak of brown wool trailing behind her as she leapt from the platform in a single bound.

Smoke rise and sunset,
Lamplight's glitters glow,
Valley wide and starlit,
A-journeyin' I must go.

Alison jotted down a verse in her journal as the view of Arcas Dyrne receded out the sleeper car window, the sun's last rays casting just enough light on her page for her to see. Sometimes, a phrase would pop into her head unbidden, and she tried to capture the moment in her journal before it left her. It wasn't a purely artistic pursuit. Although "A Korrigan's Courage" had seemingly failed to win the contest in *The Evening Times*, she was certain that with enough persistence, she could turn her hobby into a profitable venture.

The night rail-wheeler to Landsend tore through the darkening countryside, leaving the city and the bulk of civilization behind. It roared through smaller stations in its express overnight service to the far northwestern corner of the island of Loegria.

Alison's car had no lighting of its own. It was a third-class sleeper, the lowest class and the only ticket Alison could afford. She sat on her bunk, one of the four suitable for Fullings in the cabin. The sun was gone at last, and Alison's bunkmates had already changed into their nightclothes. The lady dwarf above her was softly snoring.

Alison tucked her journal under the flimsy pillow. It was hours before she usually slept, but there was little else to do in the darkness. She stumbled to the front of the train and retrieved her heavier nightgown from her trunk. It was even colder in the rail-wheeler now that the sun had gone down.

Alison changed in the shared bath at the other end of the car. By the time she had returned to her bunk, she was wide awake from the movement.

She tossed and turned on the thin mattress, trying to find a position where the springs within it did not poke into her side. The old orc in the bunk across from hers had begun to snore, loud, throaty snores that woke him intermittently with a gasp. Every now and then, the rail-wheeler squealed against the rails as it turned. None of the noises would have bothered Alison if she had just been tired. She was accustomed to far more noise from her lifetime in Arcas Dyrne.

Alison finally settled onto her back and lost herself in a daydream. She imagined a home made of brick in a field of grass. It was two stories tall with a pleasing symmetry and simple design. At the front, there was a circle of gravel for greeting the horse-drawn carriages of visitors. It was the kind of country house that still existed out here beyond the confines of the city, in the moonlit land the rail-wheeler was passing through. Alison sat up on her elbow and tried to get a glimpse through the window, but she could make out nothing distinct among the darkened moors.

She laid back down and imagined a different house. This was a grand house made of stone with crimson banners hanging from the parapets. The home of King Derkomai, Loegria's draconian ruler. This was a place she had visited once as a child with her father. It was the Solstice Festival, and Alison had begged for weeks to go. The king's castle and the summer palace he'd built on the surrounding land was a short voyage from Arcas Dyrne, but Alison's mother did not care for their ruler or his extravagant parties, and so they had not been since Alison was born. But Alison's pleading finally won out, and she and her father had taken a crowded rail-wheeler out of the city along with half of their neighborhood. Even in the crowds, Alison felt dizzy when they reached the castle grounds. The view was too much for her. The land was too empty, and she could see much too far in the distance. She tugged on her father's hand and began to whimper.

He swept her into his strong arms and held her against him, pulling her from the crowd and blocking the view. "Start slowly. Look at the ground until you feel steady, and then slowly look up little by little. Look back down if you have to; there's no shame in it. Here. Give it a try."

When she was back on the ground, she did as he had instructed. She looked at the reddish-brown dirt of the path until her head stopped spinning. Then she followed the stones of the garden wall up to a tree where she picked up the trail among the branches. She turned slowly from there into the open space. The change made her lose her grip again, but instead of looking back the way she had come, she focused on the stone walls of the castle. They were good and solid, and the towers were not unlike the manufactories she knew.

"That's it," her dad had said. "Well done, Ali-cat."

As she drifted to sleep, she felt the warmth of his smile and the touch of his hand on her cheek.

Chapter Four

ACROSS THE SALLIN SEA

The rail-wheeler pulled into Landsend Station just after dawn. Alison had been the last in the cabin to rise, and by the time she went to wash up, there was no hot water left. She rinsed quickly, making sure the water didn't touch her hair to keep away the chill.

Landsend Station was more similar to Arcas Dyrne's North Station in appearance than she had imagined, with an almost identical open-air platform laid out in much the same way. But the land beyond was wildly different. The station sat at the top of a hill overlooking the "city," if you could call it that. Landsend was more of a village, nestled in between the Howeberg Hills and spilling out over the water of the Sallin Sea. Alison had no need of her first map; she could see the path to the harbor clearly from here.

The greatest challenge would be getting her trunk down there. For what she was sure wouldn't be the last time, Alison wished Rinka had come with her. The path to the harbor was entirely downhill, at least, and Alison briefly considered chucking the trunk off the end of the rail platform and seeing where it ended up.

But there were carts for hire just outside of the station, and that seemed the more prudent idea. She began to drag the trunk across the pavement in front of the station, but she was stopped by a large orc in suspenders and a newsboy cap.

"I've got it, ma'am. I've got it." He scooped up the trunk as easily as Rinka had and ran it over to the strangest cart Alison had ever seen.

The back was like a miniature carriage with a bright red canopy and two large wheels with shining dwarven steel spokes. But the front was strange. There was no room to hitch a horse or even to place an engine, not that she expected to see one of the new motor carriages the wealthiest elves and dwarves were riding around Arcas Dyrne out this far. Instead, there was a single wheel even bigger than the wheels at the back. The orc secured the trunk to a rack behind the cabin and gestured Alison inside.

"Where to?" he asked.

"The docks," said Alison. She climbed into the carriage, curious to see how it would move. "What a strange cart you have here."

The orc laughed as he climbed over the large wheel and sat on a small saddle Alison hadn't noticed. "I bought it off of a dwarven merchant sailor from the far East. He called it a high-wheel carrier."

"They're quite literal with their names, the dwarves," said Alison.

"It's a good thing an orc didn't name it. It would've been 'the Bone Crushinator' or something."

Alison began to laugh, but she was caught short by the high-wheel carrier rocketing into motion. The carriage was open in front, affording her a full view of the orc's legs as they turned the pedals. "Of course! It's like a pedal-cycle. I've never seen one with a carriage at the back. Is it very difficult to ride?"

"Not at all," said the orc. "It's as easy as riding a pedal-cycle."

And he must have been telling the truth because he tore through the roads of Landsend like he was being chased by dragonfire.

The carriage rocked back and forth as he weaved through traffic–locals on foot carrying their shopping, the occasional horse and carriage, and more pedal-cycles than Alison had ever seen in one place. They whizzed past shops and homes, layered terraces of descending streets and alleys with buildings of roughly the same make, two stories of sun-bleached plaster with tiled roofs and square windows. The salt smell of the sea grew stronger as they grew closer to the harbor, and a flock of seagulls soared overhead.

The orc–his name was Hyruk–chattered away as he rode. His feet barely touched the pedals; the hill took care of their locomotion. He pointed out various destinations as they blew past them: a fountain for watering horses, the shop of the best butcher in town, and a dwarven blacksmith who had cheated him on the price of a dagger. Alison found him easy company.

Before long, they had reached the harbor. The docks were made up of long boardwalk after long boardwalk, each stretching further out over the water than had been apparent from the rail station. There was a great bustle of people of all races coming and going, though the greatest number by far were human.

"Heading to Sudport, ma'am?" asked Hyruk. He slowed the high-wheel carrier to a crawl to allow a line of people carrying crates of fish to pass.

"Yes, I am. How did you know?' asked Alison.

"It's about the only reason a fine lady such as yourself would be here in Landsend."

Alison laughed. "I take it you haven't seen many ladies, then."

The orc pulled the cart to a stop at the end of a dock and dismounted its saddle. When he looked Alison in the eye, she could tell he was quite serious. "I've seen a lot of folk. And almost none of them as warm as you. If that doesn't make you fine, I don't know what does."

Alison blushed from the compliment and nodded. She wanted to say something, but she wasn't sure what, so she kept her silence.

Hyruk retrieved her trunk from the back and led her onto the boardwalk. "Looks like we're just in time. The daily ferry is about to depart. It's not the fastest ride to Sudport, but it's certainly the smoothest. Will you be in Wilderise long?"

"Two weeks, maybe a day or two less to allow for travel," said Alison. "I should like to ride with you again on my return."

"Of course. I'll make sure I'm down at the docks when the ferry arrives."

Alison flicked him a silver–a very generous tip, especially out here. He caught it in his large fist, winked, tipped his cap, and was on his way.

Alison was disappointed to see him leave and even more disappointed that she had no time to explore Landsend. Still, she was eager to reach her inherited property, and there would always be the return trip.

The ferryman had already taken her trunk aboard before she'd even paid for her passage. The Loegrian work ethic was well at play even this far from the capital. Alison climbed aboard the great steam ship, the largest boat in the harbor by far. Almost as soon as she was aboard, the boat ramp was withdrawn, the whistle blown, and they were on their way across the channel.

❧

Alison had been on a boat exactly once before: a cruise on the Eabrun, the wide gray river that bisected Arcas Dyrne. The cruise was a gift from Alison's father for her mother's birthday more than a dozen years earlier, back when Alison was a miserable and sullen adolescent. She had fought with her mother earlier in the day and spent most of the journey

within the boat's interior, trying to get a handsome crew-
man to notice her by doing nothing more than staring at
him blankly. She was unsuccessful.

The ferry was nothing at all like the river yacht. Hyruk
had been correct about the smooth ride; Alison could hardly
feel the motion. She kept checking over the railing to make
sure they weren't standing still. But sure enough, the boat
was cutting through the current with speed. The captain an-
nounced they would arrive just before sunset, roughly ten
hours later.

It was a fine day to be out on the open water. The sun
had come out from behind the clouds for what felt like the
first time since fall, and a warmer breeze was in the air. Alison knew it wasn't truly the start of spring, and the higher
altitude and latitude of Wilderise meant she could still be in
for a chilly trip, but it did nothing to dampen her joy at feeling the sun's warmth on her skin. She walked a lap around
the entirety of the top deck, whistling as she went.

On her second pass, she saw a small figure bent between
the horizontal railings. At first, she thought it was a child
and rushed to pull it back in before it fell overboard. But as
she approached, she saw it was a Quarterling woman. Her
hair was long and golden, braided much the same as Alison's in a wide plait down her back. Her face was soft and
lovely to behold, if a touch greener than expected. Alison
recognized her kind at once–she was a korrigan.

Alison had never met one in person, and she desperately
wanted to know what the woman thought of her poem. But
it certainly wasn't the right time to trouble her with such

nonsense. As Alison watched, the korrigan leaned out over the railing as far as she could reach and was violently sick.

"Are you all right?" asked Alison. She crouched to the ground to look at the korrigan directly.

"Hold on," said the woman and threw up once more. She turned back to Alison, wiping her mouth on the sleeve of her silken dress. "Right. I know what you're thinking. How can a korrigan be seasick? Don't we love the water? And it's true; I've made my home in the walls of a well, but the sea is something else. Don't know how the sirens do it with all this swaying."

"To be honest, I can barely feel the movement," said Alison. She handed the small woman her handkerchief from her pocket, which she gratefully took.

"Count yourself lucky then. I'm not sure if I'm going to make it to Wilderise at this rate."

"It might be better if you come inside. I'll see if I can find a bucket for you."

Alison flagged down a member of the ferry's crew, who was glad to offer the korrigan a bucket as it meant less mopping for him. Most of the wooden benches within the cabin of the ship were occupied already, but Alison found a space for them near the middle.

The bench's seat was around the height of the korrigan's shoulders. Alison was about to offer to lift her, but the korrigan's wings fluttered behind her, and she landed on the bench with a thud. Standing on it, she was the same height as Alison sitting down.

"They're so lovely," Alison said, looking at the korrigan's wings. They were clear but slightly iridescent in a swirling pattern like mother-of-pearl.

"Thank you. Have you never met one of my kind?"

"I haven't had the pleasure. We don't get many of the fey folk in Arcas Dyrne. I don't think many of them like being so far from nature, and the city isn't the most accessible to even the Halflings, let alone the smaller folk. I'm Alison, by the way."

"Nolwynn, and the pleasure is mine. I've just come from Arcas Dyrne, actually. Well, nearby. I was summoned to court."

"To King Derkomai's court?" Alison had never met any-one who had been summoned for an audience with the king. Nolwynn must have been a noble of some kind.

"The same," said Nolwynn with a sigh. She took a seat and kicked her legs over the side of the bench, keeping a watchful eye on the bucket. "The king wished to express his displeasure with the actions of some of my people. The crown has been sending expeditions further into the reaches of Wilderise, and they've been increasingly encountering the fey folk. And yes, some of his men and women have been bewitched by our songs. But we don't sing to lure them. We sing for ourselves, and we can't help that they en-joy it. And if we happen to enjoy their company, I truly don't see the harm. The idea that we lure them to their deaths is preposterous. So far this year, we've saved two men and a horse from drowning when they fell through the ice."

By the end of Nolwynn's story, Alison wondered how she'd made it out of the court alive. And seeing how animated the korrigan had gotten telling it, Alison found herself glad she hadn't shared her poem. It had featured a drowning, albeit a justifiable one.

The greenish hue gradually left Nolwynn's face, and soon they were able to abandon the bucket. Alison spent the journey in her company, exchanging tales and sharing a meal of tough bread, rubbery cheese, and something that might have been pheasant. They braved a turn outside to see the southbound ferry passing, and once more when land was spotted ahead.

"I haven't asked you where you're going," said Nolwynn. "Further than Sudport?"

"I'm heading to a town called Herot's Hollow. I'm hoping to catch the postal carriage if I'm not too late."

"Herot's Hollow is quite near where I'm heading. My folk gather near Fossholm. There's a winding river there that spills into a great waterfall and then joins a lake just outside of town. I believe the stream through Herot's Hollow feeds that very river."

Alison had grown accustomed to the aquatic nature of Nolwynn's conversation after spending the better part of the day with her.

"Are you taking the postal carriage as well?" asked Alison.

"I hadn't planned to. The ride is a bit strenuous, but it is the fastest way to the hill country. Although I wouldn't mind getting home, come to think of it. I'll join you. There's almost always room for a Quarterling. We'll need to hurry for you though–the Fulling spots fill quickly. I'll lead us there directly once we drop anchor."

The korrigan was as good as her word; they were the very first in line to leave the ferry. As the shoreline came into view, Alison became suddenly still.

The rugged landscape of Wilderise was as dissimilar to the gently rolling hills and valleys of Loegria as the tiny hamlet of Landsend was to the grand city of Arcas Dyrne. Sudport was nestled in an alcove surrounded by tall gray cliffs, great stone shoulders pressing inwards. The sun setting over the inlet cast long shadows enveloping most of the town, though it would not be truly dark for more than an hour. The town itself appeared even smaller than Landsend had from this distance. The buildings were smaller too, and far less uniform than their Loegrian counterparts. It looked as though they had been added onto over a great period of time and with no great care for aesthetics.

"Beautiful, isn't it?" asked Nolwynn.

"It is," said Alison. And she meant it.

Chapter Five

HEROT'S HOLLOW

Not only did Sudport look nothing like Landsend, it felt different as well. When Alison and her korrigan companion rushed first off of the ferry, Alison had expected a crowd to follow behind. Yet when they reached the end of the boardwalk and stepped onto the cobblestone of Sudport's high street, they were alone.

The other passengers were disembarking, but they didn't seem to have any particular hurry about it. No one in Sudport seemed to be in a rush to get anywhere. Couples strolled along the boardwalk, arm in arm, taking in the sunset. Each sidewalk Alison and Nolwynn passed was crowded with café tables full of patrons sipping dark wines and getting lost in conversation.

"Do you think the porter is far behind us?" asked Alison. She had requested her trunk be sent along to the post office.

"Quite far," said Nolwynn. "I doubt we'll be able to take the carriage tonight anyway. There's an inn down the street suitable for your kind. You can have their porter bring some things to you for the night once the trunk makes it to the post office."

Alison wasn't fond of the idea of a stranger going through her personal effects, but the way Nolwynn said it made it sound quite ordinary. "You won't stay at the inn as well?"

"I will, in a way. There's an entrance to a large underground reservoir nearby."

"Can I ask how you breathe?"

The korrigan stopped in her tracks. Alison worried momentarily she might have offended the woman, but her face seemed more thoughtful than angry. "I don't mind you asking, but it's hard to come up with an answer that you would understand. I guess it's a little like drinking water, only into our chests instead of our bellies. It's the most wonderful feeling, the comforting chill. A sensation of fullness too, like after a good meal."

Alison shuddered. "You're right. I'm not sure how a chill can be comforting."

"Oh, I know how to explain this one! I heard it from another human once. It's like the cool touch of a pillow on your cheek on a warm summer's night."

That was a sensation Alison knew well. Arcas Dyrne was sweltering in the summer. It wouldn't be long after she returned that she'd have to face the heat once more.

The korrigan started them moving again. When they arrived at the post office, the one person still on staff for the night was tending to the pigeons that handled local journeys. He was a human with a warm smile and a gentle nature who was pleased to give good news, for once: there was one last spot for a Fulling on the next night's journey of the weekly postal service into the hill towns.

Nolwynn led Alison to the inn, which Alison was charmed to find was an ancient stone structure that had been added onto quite recently with modern brick. The korrigan would be dropping in on some relatives in town while they waited for the carriage the next day, so they bid each other goodbye until the following evening.

❧

Alison had planned to spend the day wandering the streets of Sudport, maybe making it down to the thin strip of rocky beach she had glimpsed during their rush from the ferry the previous evening. But the prospect of coming back up the hill tired her just thinking of it, and so she resolved to spend the day at one of the many nearby cafés, sipping tea and writing postcards to Rinka and Ms. Varma from work.

The postcards took her less time than she anticipated, and so she brought out her journal to work on a new verse.

In the space between where the sentinels rise,
Their craggy forms shadow the view,
Of cobbled street tapestries and mariner's guise,
While under their watch, life springs forth anew.

She crossed out "mariner's" and tried several other possibilities: "innkeeper's", "traveler's", "wanderer's". She liked "wanderer's" the best, but the verse didn't feel complete.

There were still more hours to fill, so she left her table at the café and wandered down the hill a bit–but not too far–to a bookshop. When she entered, the wooden door creaked on its hinges and a little bell chimed from the movement.

"Can I help you?"

The bookseller was a dwarf, a stout, strong man of about the same height as Alison, though he probably had three or four stone on her of pure muscle. He appeared to be young, maybe younger than she was, with a closely cropped beard and hair pulled into a loose bun.

"The poetry books, please."

"Right this way," he said, leading her from the relatively open space of the front room into an adjoining area cramped with dozens of shelves. The dwarf was forced to squeeze his shoulders together to fit through the aisles.

"Here you are. Poetry. Sorted by era, then author's last name or only name."

"You have orcish poetry here?" she said incredulously. Few but the orcs went by single names.

The dwarf turned and gave her a serious look. "Don't tell me you aren't familiar with the works of Fanguk."

"I'm afraid I'm not," admitted Alison.

"Whatever else you choose, take this as well." He handed her a bright green book with a tan leather spine. Then he bowed and left her to browse on her own.

Alison flicked through the pages of Fanguk's collected works–titled *Born of Blood, Bored of Blood*. It seemed to tell the story of an orcish warrior who hung up his battleax in favor of a simpler life on the open sea. Alison didn't need to make another selection; this marvel of a book would occupy her for hours.

After paying the dwarf and thanking him for his recommendation, Alison returned to her café and spent the remaining time until the postal carriage left alternately giggling, gasping, cringing, and crying over the orc's poetry. She left early for the post office in order to package it and send it to Rinka with her postcard.

❧

The postal carriage left at sunset after the traffic on the country roads had died down. The other passengers were all human, a husband and wife and their young son. The boy was already asleep before they'd left Sudport, and the man and woman whispered to each other things that made Alison blush.

"Young love," sighed Nolwynn.

Alison settled back into the carriage, pulling her woolen cardigan around her tightly. The postman had told them it was good they were leaving tonight. It looked like a late winter snow in the mountains would be there soon.

The journey was rough going. Unlike the more relaxed pace characteristic of everything else Alison had witnessed in Sudport, the postal carriage was on a mission. It sped through the night, jostling the passengers and cargo around the carriage like numbers in a lottery machine. They rarely stopped except to change the horses; the letters and packages were thrown to waiting postal workers more often than not. On more than one occasion, they made everyone get out to walk uphill to save the horses the burden. The man carried the boy, who never woke up until the morning. Nolwynn said that if all children were that easy, more people would have them.

The view in the morning as they came down the mountain was worth the hassle. There were endless green fields touched with frost bordered by dark hedges and even darker forests. Creeks and rivers of the clearest, deepest blue Alison had ever seen wound through the landscape. Dotted throughout were the tiny shadows of buildings and the pinpricks of steeples. Every now and then, when the breeze hit them just right, Alison could hear church bells.

Nolwynn pointed out her home, Fossholm, and the waterfall above the town. Alison's eyes couldn't make out the details at such a distance, but she told Nolwynn it was exceptionally beautiful all the same because it was true.

And then she pointed to Herot's Hollow. It was mostly obscured by another hillside, Nolwynn explained, but the town itself was one of the larger ones in the area. All Alison could make out was the sharp cut of a valley and a dense forest on the northern edge.

By midday, she had lost sight of it at all. The hill country had been appropriately named–the carriage went up and down so many times that Alison felt more like she was at sea than she had on the ferry. By the time they had reached Nolwynn's stop of Fossholm, the shadows were once again lengthening.

There was no time for a long goodbye. The postman had to be on his way.

"Thank you for your help and kindness. I promise I'll write, and often," said Alison.

"If you change your mind and end up staying, I wouldn't mind checking out that stream." Alison had shown her the deed during the second part of their journey together.

"You're welcome anytime," said Alison as the postman closed the door to the carriage.

Not long after, the family was let off at a lane to a country home, and Alison was once again alone for the rest of her journey.

The hillside kept Herot's Hollow hidden until at last the road meandered into the valley and revealed the town.

It was…intimate, in the words of Lord Arleas. There were maybe a dozen stone buildings, most of them connected in rows lining a narrow river. Each of them was topped with a thatched roof frosted in snow, and each had multiple chimneys billowing smoke into the darkening sky. There appeared to be only one river crossing, a bridge constructed of the same stone as the buildings and the walls. Yet the appearance was far from uniform. It was broken at intervals by twining brown vines and clumps of empty branches where spring would soon break.

Alison was lucky; the village postman had not been waiting at the end of the road, forcing the driver into the town to deliver the letters and packages to the village. And even more luckily, the post office was next door to the inn.

She bid the driver good night and thanked him for the journey. Then she dragged her trunk twenty paces to the inn's front door.

Light flickered through the leaded glass of the inn's windows. The building was made of the same gray stone as the rest of the village, but there were wooden beams and an iron hook holding up a sign: *The Sheep's Heid Inn.* The muffled sounds of laughter and the clinking of glasses filled the air.

It seemed the entirety of the small village was within the inn's walls. They sat at wooden tables of varying heights with no two chairs alike. They gathered by the roaring fire to hear the music of a flamboyantly dressed bard plucking a darkly-hued mandolin. They crowded around the bar, which tapered in steps, with a harried Halfling behind climbing up and down a series of ladders to reach bottles on shelves that reached to the ceiling.

Alison dropped her trunk to shut the door behind her, and when she turned back around, a pair of hobgoblins were carrying it over their heads toward the bar. She followed behind them, impressed by the length of their pointed ears and the strength of their thin arms. A few of the patrons–particularly an orc young enough to have been refused service in Arcas Dyrne–watched her as she approached the Halfling barkeep. She pulled her dark braid in front of her as if it would offer her some defense from their stares.

"A room for the night or the week?" asked the Halfling. He was standing on a platform behind the Fulling section of the bar, peering down at Alison with beady eyes.

"Just directions, actually," Alison replied.

The Halfling frowned for a split second before quickly recovering. "Of course. Where are you headed?'

"A cottage on Orchard Lane. It belonged to my late relative, Frances Lincoln."

The Halfling gave no answer. Instead, he climbed down from the platform and up a ladder behind him, retrieving a large brass key from the wall.

He handed it to Alison, who looked at him blankly. "It's across the bridge and down the lane, third gate on the right, but you won't be staying there tonight. This key is for the room up the stairs, second door on the left. It's three silver for the night, or a gold for the week. I'd recommend the week."

"What's wrong with the cottage?" She handed him three silver. How bad could it possibly be?

"You'll see when you get there. The hobs have taken your case up. Dinner is included. Do you want it now?"

Alison hadn't noticed the hobgoblins carry her trunk away, but sure enough, it was gone. She nodded to indicate she'd take her dinner, but her mind was still on what the Halfling had said about the cottage. She prepared to ask him for more information, but he had already disappeared into a small door to a back room.

Alison guessed she was meant to have a seat, but there weren't many options. The only empty table was near the open hearth directly across from the bard. It was clearly meant for Halflings or smaller, but Alison could make do. She pulled out the chair, which wobbled on uneven legs, and waited, idly jotting down notes in her journal.

A hobgoblin brought her dinner: a hearty stew flavored with an aromatic Alison didn't recognize but which imparted a pleasant bite, a hunk of dark bread that was delightfully chewy, and a wonderfully soft cheese that Alison finished all too quickly. The hob offered her the choice of her beverage, and Alison selected a strong local ale which hit her much more quickly than the lighter beers that were popular in Arcas Dyrne. By the time the bard came to join her during his break, her head was buzzing.

"Staying a while or just passing through?" he asked. He wore a cloak of a deep scarlet that stood out amongst the browns and grays of the other patrons' attire, and his hair and skin were fair and finely groomed.

"I'm here for a week or so. I've just inherited a cottage."

The bard's eyes lit up. "Your accent. You aren't from Arcas Dyrne, are you?"

Alison had heard it in his voice as well; he was from somewhere near her. Maybe the west side of the city–the nicer side. She was a little disappointed by this. While it was nice to speak to someone from home, she hadn't been gone long enough to be homesick, and she had been hoping to find out more about what was wrong with her cottage.

Instead, Alison caught him up at length on the happenings around town. His name was Nigel Smalls, and he was pleasant enough to talk to, if a little loud and energetic for Alison's state of mind, which was growing ever more tired by the passing moment.

When at last he had excused himself to resume his playing, Alison prepared to call it an early night. But she was stopped before she could slip away by a lovely elf who looked to be the same age as Alison, which meant that she was much older.

"Lady Sibba," she said, reaching out her elegant fingers to clasp Alison's in a peculiar handshake. She was livelier than Lady Selelas had been but just as beautiful; the contrast of her dark brown skin and golden hair was particularly striking.

"Alison Lennox."

"A pleasure. Are you a visiting scholar? I noticed you writing in your book."

Lady Sibba brushed a golden curl behind her pointed ear and leaned forward, casting a furtive glance at Alison's journal.

Alison smiled. "Oh no, I wouldn't say that. I'm…well, I wouldn't say I'm much of a poet, either. Truthfully, I'm a number-cruncher, but I dabble a bit. I'm here in town because I've inherited a cottage."

Lady Sibba gave Alison the kind of soulful and melancholy look that only the elves could pull off without doubting their sincerity. "I was very sorry to hear of Frances's passing. She was a dear friend of mine these past thirty years or so. Did you know her well?"

"Unfortunately, I didn't have the pleasure of knowing her at all. I had been planning to stay tonight at the cottage– do you know why the innkeeper told me not to? He wasn't clear on the details."

The elf leaned closer to Alison, so close that she could smell a hint of a fruity wine on her breath. "Mr. Rainey can be a bit dramatic; it doesn't hurt his bottom line to do so, if you catch my meaning. But in the case of Frances's cottage,

I'm afraid it has been empty for some time. She was taken into a care home in her final years, and with no living relatives that she was aware of, the house has fallen into some disrepair, I suspect. Though I haven't been able to see it–well, that's immaterial. Some in the town are in a bit of a state regarding the vine situation. I, myself, don't really understand the fuss–"

"I'm sorry, the vine situation?" Alison wished she had taken less to drink. Lady Sibba spoke quickly, and it was hard to keep up with what she was saying through the warm haze of the ale.

"You'll see on the morrow. It's hard to miss. It does grow quickly, that's for sure, even in winter. And there are thorns, though I believe the rumors of poison or enchanted sleep are greatly exaggerated. I'm a scholar, myself, and not just a schoolmarm as some around here would like to think, and I can't see the point in worrying when there just isn't any concrete evidence–"

"Poison?" Alison held onto the word in her mind, trying to commit it to memory. She began to jot it into her journal, but the elf waved her hands to stop her.

"No, as I've said, I've seen no concrete evidence that the thorns bear any kind of poison. I will admit that it's odd the way the vine crumbles to ash when cut, Mezec says so too, but it makes for easier cleanup, that's for sure. The key is to be vigilant, that's what Weyland says, though I'm sure it doesn't hurt that he's the one selling the hatchets and machetes…"

Alison couldn't follow along any further. She excused herself from the elf's presence, which the elf barely seemed to notice, and dragged herself up the stairs. She fell into the bed fully dressed and passed out. It may not have been an enchanted sleep, but it was something close.

Chapter Six

THE VINE

The ale had been a mistake but not a terrible one. Alison's head was heavy though thankfully not pounding, and her stomach was queasy but not ill. She would feel better with something to eat.

She quickly rinsed off with the cool water of the wash basin and changed into a blouse and trousers in the muted earth tones those in the village seemed to prefer. She donned her warmest cloak and followed her nose down the stairs and into the village street.

The cloak had been unnecessary. It was a bright and warm day, almost as warm as when she had left Arcas Dyrne. The dusting of snow she had glimpsed the previous evening had already melted, leaving the cobblestones glittering in the sunlight. The town was out in force, undoubtedly enjoying the change in the weather as much as Alison did.

Alison's nose led her to a bakery across the street. There, she enjoyed a scone dotted with the most fragrant raspberries and redcurrants she had ever tasted and topped with a melt-in-her-mouth dollop of whipped cream. She washed it down with a piping hot cup of tea at a table outside. When she felt quite refreshed, she returned to the inn.

The hobgoblins had fetched her trunk for her. The Halfling innkeeper–Mr. Rainey, Alison suddenly remembered from her conversation with the elf whose name she had forgotten–offered to have the hobs carry it to her gate for just two copper, which Alison happily paid. She bid the Halfling farewell and followed the hobgoblins.

As they crossed the bridge, Alison realized she had been incorrect that it was the sole crossing; there was another bridge further uphill where the crystal-clear water of the river came down from the mountain. The hobgoblins then led her down a narrow lane away from the center of town. The stacked stone walls extended down the lane on either side, concealing the land beyond save for the occasional tree and glimpse of hillside. The space between the gates increased as they walked, though it was only a few minutes until they reached the third gate on the right.

The hobgoblins dropped the trunk to the ground where it stirred an eddy of ash and dust. The smaller of the two tilted her head at Alison. "If you need us, we'll be back at the inn," she said with a smirk.

Looking at the gate, Alison understood what she meant.

The vine that twined around the iron gate and as far as Alison's eyes could see beyond was unlike anything she had seen before. The vines that had climbed the village homes and shops had been brown with the first sign of green sprouting forth, but this vine was a plum color so deep as to almost be black. It was incredibly thick, as wide around as Alison's thumb and even wider in places. Alison could see the scars where it had been cut back from the road repeatedly, by the looks of it. And then there were the thorns, great sharp triangles as big as Alison's fingernails which dripped with some dark sap that Alison hoped wasn't poison.

"The vine situation, indeed," she mumbled.

"You're going to need a hatchet," said a voice.

Alison couldn't place the sound. She turned around in the lane, but there was no one to be seen.

"Up here," said the voice again.

Alison looked up, but the only thing she could see was a tabby cat sitting on top of the wall.

"Like I said–" came the voice, but it was the cat's mouth that moved.

Alison screamed.

"What is it? What's wrong?" said the cat. It stood up and turned in a circle, sniffing the air and looking for a threat.

"You can talk," said Alison. "That's what's wrong."

"Oh, this again," said the cat. "A city girl too, huh? Frances was surprised as well. I don't know what your lot did to the city cats, but a rightful cat can speak. I've been teaching Dinah–you know Dinah, I assume?"

Alison looked at her hands to remind herself she was real. Then she looked at the vine. No good, too weird. Back to the hands. Then she looked at the cat. It was waiting to hear her answer. That was weird too, but at least when she was talking to it, it wasn't saying anything. She could almost forget for a moment that it could speak at all.

"I don't know Dinah. Who is she? Did you know Frances?"

"Oh, of course." The cat stood and stretched, arching its back and bending so that its chin nearly touched the wall, and then it reversed the stretch so that its head was up and its belly down. It was a very cat-like gesture, which made sense because it was a cat. A talking cat, but a cat nonetheless.

"Dinah is Frances's pet. Or she was, I guess, before they took Frances away. I told Dinah it was quite undignified, but Dinah seemed to like their arrangement. As for me, I'm Willow. I was a dear friend of Lady Willana's before she passed, and now I keep the company of her widow Gwenla. Are you coming to stay in Frances's cottage? Dinah will be so pleased with the companionship. She's always preferred humans to cats."

It was a lot to take in. Willow was a cat, and she also seemed to be the creature that knew the most about the cottage and its previous owner of everyone Alison had met so far. She seemed trustworthy and friendly enough, if Alison could turn off the part of her mind that was screaming that she was hallucinating, that the vine had already gotten her, and she was in the enchanted slumber the lovely elf had mentioned.

"I'm coming to stay for a time, yes. If I can manage to make it inside," said Alison after a long pause.

"I can help you with that. What you need, as I was saying earlier, is a hatchet. I don't suppose a city girl like you has packed one in that old trunk of yours. So you'll need to see the blacksmith. I can take you there."

Alison looked down at her trunk.

"No one's going to bother it out here," said Willow. "I mean, look at the thing, for one. And for another, the doors out here don't even have locks. It's safe. Follow me."

The cat walked along the top of the wall, clearing the gap made by the gate in a single acrobatic bound. She carefully avoided the vine in the places where it had managed to grow down on the side of the wall nearest to the road.

"It would be good of you to clear this up too, once you have the hatchet. Aras usually takes care of this part of the wall–that's his property up ahead." Willow pointed to the property on the town side of Alison's with her tail. "But this section of wall is yours, and I'm sure he wouldn't mind the help. The lambs will have him busy soon."

Alison nodded. "Do all animals talk?" she blurted out. She was feeling queasy imagining what was in the stew she'd had the night before.

"Only the intelligent ones. Cats, corvids, wolves. Dogs understand but don't speak themselves. I've heard that whales sing and the octopi reply, but that may just be a children's story. We're a long way from the ocean here."

Alison nodded again. "And what's with this vine?" She felt very dumb asking, but she couldn't find a way to compose her thoughts more eloquently. Not while she was adjusting to talking to a cat.

The cat paused. "That I don't know. None of the people around here do either. It showed up one day years ago, after Lady Willana had passed but before they took Frances away.

It never seems to go away, not completely. It's gotten worse lately. Gwenla is organizing a meeting in the town hall. She'll invite you to go, I'm sure. She says it's going to eat the town up at this rate."

"Is it poisonous?" asked Alison.

"I'm afraid I don't know that either. I haven't been willing to try it and find out. Gwenla and Aras wear thick gloves when they cut it; you'll want those too."

As they walked, Alison peppered Willow with questions about the vine, which she largely couldn't answer, and the town, which she largely could. They came back to the bridge but didn't cross it, instead walking up the street on the same side of the river until they reached an open plaza.

"That's the schoolhouse and the church and the vicar's house there before the graveyard. And that's the town hall across the way–that's where the meeting will be. This is where the market is held on Tuesdays. Do you have enough food for tonight? You might need to stop by the inn. There won't be anything in Frances's larder."

Alison hadn't even thought of what she would eat. She was accustomed to never being more than a few minutes' walk from everything she could possibly need or want. Living out here, even temporarily, would take a lot of planning and hard work.

At last, they had made it to the blacksmith. The building appeared to be the standard stone and thatch of the rest of the village, but it was open on the side facing away from town. There were several fireplaces and furnaces, bellows and anvils, and a wide variety of strange tools whose function Alison could not fathom. Pounding away at a piece of red-hot metal on an anvil overlooking the river was the largest human Alison had ever seen.

Weyland Gilroy, the village blacksmith, must have been part giant, or maybe even troll. He had two feet on Alison easily, and she wouldn't have been surprised to learn he was three times her weight. He had a great red beard that matched his long red hair which he wore pulled back. His face was great and red as well and dripping with sweat.

When he saw Alison, he said nothing. But when he saw the cat rubbing at her ankles, he stopped his work and smiled.

"Hello, Willow," he said. The cat purred and went to greet him, accepting what Alison was sure was a highly dignified chin scratch.

Willow introduced Mr. Gilroy and Alison. His greeting for her, even brokered by Willow, was perfunctory at best.

Alison allowed Willow to handle the purchase. She obtained not just the hatchet but a small knife, a hammer, a box of nails, and leather gloves that reached up to Alison's elbows. Mr. Gilroy tried to sell Willow a set of tools for the fire, but she was certain that Frances's would still be in the cottage.

Alison thanked Mr. Gilroy for the tools, but all he gave her in response was a grunt.

"Don't worry about him," said Willow as they headed back into town. "Strelka makes most of the tools these days. She's his apprentice, only I didn't see her today. She must be up at the mines securing the delivery from the dwarves. I usually deal with her. Weyland hasn't been the same since King Derkomai released him."

"Mr. Gilroy was a prisoner of King Derkomai?"

The cat gave a tiny growl. "That foul beast. Not a prisoner but a slave. He won't talk about it."

Alison had never heard someone speak so contemptuously of the king. It wasn't expressly forbidden, but it certainly wasn't encouraged. Still, Arcas Dyrne had been mere miles from the king's palace. Maybe Herot's Hollow was far enough away to be beyond his reach.

"Lady Sibba is about the only one that can get a word out of Weyland these days. Other than me, of course. I've spent many a cold day in winter asleep near the forge. He shooed me away at first too, but I persisted."

That didn't surprise Alison. If there was one thing cats were, it was persistent.

Alison and Willow passed around the well and through the plaza as the church bells chimed one o'clock in the afternoon. They passed the schoolhouse–Alison glimpsed Lady Sibba's long golden curls trailing down her back through an open window. As they made it back to the corner to turn onto Orchard Lane, there was a blood-curdling shriek.

Alison turned to Willow, who was already bounding off in the direction of the noise. A crowd was gathering in a small alley between two sets of stone buildings. Alison edged her way through the crowd, standing on her tiptoes to peer over the shoulder of a dwarf.

The dirt of the alley was darkening as a pool of red seeped into the earth.

Blood.

Chapter Seven

THE WHITE COTTAGE

No, not blood. Ink.

"It was a thief. A thief in Herot's Hollow!" cried a tiny figure that flitted about on white wings. A fairy, a proper Seelie Court fairy. Alison had never laid eyes on one before. Her fascination was almost enough for her to forget the scene before her.

The fairy's tiny hands were gripping a shard of glass from a broken bottle. There were several other fragments on the ground, and two long strokes where fingers had swept through the stained dirt, perhaps retrieving something else that had been dropped. The strokes were made unmistakably by the hand of a Fulling, or perhaps the slide of an Eighthling, though no footprints continued beyond.

Alison felt a brush of fur at her ankles. "We should go," the cat said quietly.

Alison and Willow slipped back through the crowd without notice. Only once they were around the corner and back onto Orchard Lane did Willow speak again.

"They're going to suspect you," said Willow. She had hopped back onto the wall. "New in town the night before a robbery."

"That's absurd. I have an alibi–I was with you."

"It won't matter to the pair of idiots–I mean, to the good detective constables of Fossholm. They'll be here on the morrow, I should think. Don't be surprised when they go poking around your things. At least you're innocent. It should be okay."

Alison wasn't sure which to be more alarmed by–the implication that her innocence might not be enough to help her, or that this wasn't the cat's first run-in with the law.

"Here, give that hatchet a try," said Willow as she approached a hanging vine.

Alison donned the large leather gloves and retrieved the hatchet from its pouch in her satchel. She had to swing the hatchet over her head to reach, but she managed to chop the vine after a couple of attempts. As the section she had cut fell, it crumpled into ash. By the time it reached the ground, it was nothing but dust.

"That doesn't seem…ordinary," said Alison.

"There's nothing ordinary about this stuff. You were lucky. Once it reaches the ground again, it takes root. There are sections Gwenla must slice through four or five times before it turns to ash."

Alison saw the cat's point when she reached the gate of her cottage once more. Though the vine had only twined around the gate in a couple of small sections, it took many hits with the hatchet to free it. When she had opened the gate at last, she dropped the hatchet in surprise.

The vine had covered the land as far as she could see. It grew in dense thickets up to Alison's shoulders, reaching up and down and touching the ground in hundreds of places. It would take weeks to clear it all at this rate.

"Before you ask, it doesn't burn. Aras tried it. He used to come in here and cut it back, but he's only a fairy, after all. It's a lot of land to care for in addition to his own pastures. So now he just keeps it trimmed at the hedge."

"He's a fairy too? Any relation to the one whose ink was stolen?" The one who was likely to think Alison was responsible for the theft.

"Aras is Mezec's father, yes. Hmm." The cat's thoughtful sound came out something like a purr. "Maybe we can get ahead of all of that."

Alison was exhausted. Cutting a path to reach the cottage, a cottage she still couldn't even see, might not even be possible today. And even if she did reach it, she had no idea if it was even inhabitable, she had nothing to eat, and she was about to be falsely accused of a crime committed against her neighbor's son.

She was beginning to consider if it made sense to go back to the inn and to wait for the postal carriage to return. She could go back to Arcas Dyrne and pretend none of this had ever happened. Rinka would be disappointed, and Mr. Rosales would probably pass her over for the promotion if he didn't fire her, but at least she would be safe in her own bed.

"I hope you haven't been listening to this one. She's nothing but trouble," came a voice behind Alison.

The stout dwarf could be none other than Gwenla, Willow's companion and Alison's neighbor. She had wisps of white hair and a big gap-toothed smile. Her overalls were covered in dark dirt stains, and in her right hand was a machete with a deadly-looking blade. Willow purred and kneaded the ground as Gwenla approached. When the dwarf reached out her left hand for Alison to shake, the cat twined between their legs, bumping its head against their knees.

"That won't do at all," said Gwenla, gesturing to Alison's newly-purchased hatchet.

Willow protested. "She's clearly never held a tool before. I didn't want her to take her arm off."

"Watch how it's done, girl." Gwenla reached through the gate and made several quick swipes with her blade. The vine came off in satisfying chunks that gave a faint hissing noise as they disintegrated. She followed the path, cutting a way through with a strength and precision Alison wouldn't have imagined possible at her advanced age.

"Now you try." Gwenla handed Alison the blade by its handle. It looked menacing in Alison's small hand. Cautiously, Alison took a swipe at a vine near shoulder level.

"No, no," said Gwenla. "Aim near the ground. You don't want to leave any near the roots. Try it again, this time with feeling."

Alison took a deep breath and swung down hard before she could think too much about it.

"Wonderful!" said Gwenla. Alison caught her giving a wry look to the cat, who was bathing her paw and pretending not to notice.

"How far back is the cottage?" Alison asked.

"Far enough that I'm going to need to fetch my other machete. You hold onto that one–you're going to need it. Did Willow ask you about the meeting yet?"

"She mentioned it." Alison looked back to where Willow had been only moments earlier, but she was gone. Off to catch her dinner, undoubtedly.

"You simply must come. The town will listen this time–it's almost made it onto the common. It's going to eat all of Wilderise at this rate."

The dwarf had walked away as she was speaking, forcing Alison to follow. Gwenla led her back into the street away from town and to her gate on the other side as she asked about Alison's relation to Frances and her plans for the cottage.

"I'm here to figure that out," said Alison. "I have little in the way of knowledge of home maintenance. I've been in the city all my life."

"Ahh, like my Lady Willana," the dwarf said wistfully.

Alison didn't know what to say. Willow had told her about Lady Willana's passing. She hoped it wouldn't be rude to ask about her late love, but Alison often wished that people still talked about her father, so she gave it a go. "Lady Willana was a city elf?"

The dwarf turned from her gate to face Alison. She was smiling. "Oh, yes. I'm sure it comes as a surprise when you see the garden she made, but she lived for hundreds of years in the great towered buildings as they grew up from nothing. It's hard for the elves to be separated from the earth though. Well, it's hard for some of them. Lady Willana had a longing for the good and the green when she reached the end of her life, and so she spent her last decades here in my company. And it was good, and was it ever green." A single tear had formed at the corner of the dwarf's gray eye. Alison reached for her hand and gave it a squeeze, which the dwarf returned.

"Come and see the garden. I don't have the gift for it that she did, but I've done my best. If I could just keep that blasted vine away for more than a day."

Beyond Gwenla's gate was a strikingly beautiful sight. Though it was just now the end of winter, the garden was alive with color. There were dark hollies with bright red berries; huge bushes with flowers in shades of white and pink, petals neatly arranged in perfect little rows; sleepy cups of flowers nodding in heads of pink-tinged green; and scattered throughout, tiny purple flowers with bright yellow filaments in the center.

"Smell this one," said Gwenla, leading her to a bush with small clusters of white flowers that looked unremarkable compared to some of the others.

"Oh my," said Alison. It was the most appealing scent she'd ever smelled, jasmine and honey with a hint of spice.

"It was Lady Willana's favorite. Winter daphne. She's a fickle one, but worth the work."

Gwenla led Alison into her own cottage–a structure of stone and thatch like all the others but covered in window boxes and hanging planters that had just been worked. A fire crackled in the hearth, and a pot boiled on the stove. "The stew will be ready after we're done working. I've got some dried meat in the larder you can take, and some winter lettuce I can harvest for you. I'm sure Brytak will be by–he delivers the milk and eggs for the village, and he can help you until you get your own pastures cleared. Assuming you stay, of course." The dwarf winked, and Alison was grateful for the welcome.

The dwarf led her through the home to a shed at the back where she stored the tools. It was a wide assortment–machetes and axes in all shapes and sizes, hoes and rakes and a variety of spades. "Don't worry, Frances had all of that back there somewhere. It might have a little rust, but it's nothing we can't fix."

Alison liked the "we." It felt less hopeless having Gwenla around, and she wondered if the dwarf would be terribly offended if she asked her to stay until she had the hang of things.

Gwenla tried a couple of her machetes, feeling the weight in her hand, and then handed Alison a slightly smaller one. "This one should be a better weight for you. No, no, put that away." Alison had taken out a silver from her pocket. "I know that's how city folks work, but that's not how we do things around here. I can help you and so I will. And you can help me as well, by coming to the meeting."

"Of course," said Alison.

The dwarf nodded and led Alison back through the lovely garden–a robin came to perch on the bare red branch of a strange group of sticks as they passed–and back into Alison's gate. They had only been gone minutes, but Alison could swear the vine had crept along where she had just cut it.

"Let's stick to the path for today. We're losing the sunlight, and we need to clear a big enough gap around the cottage that you can get back out tomorrow."

The cutting was easier work with Gwenla's help and company, but it was tiring nonetheless. The path to the cottage felt like it stretched on for miles, and by the time it was in sight, Alison was drenched with sweat.

She had expected the cottage to be made of the same stone and thatch as all the other buildings in Herot's Hollow, and she was half right. The roof was indeed thatched with a graying straw, but the cottage itself was a white plaster. The vine had nearly swallowed it whole, but without a place to root, it was easy to remove it in large sections.

Once the cottage was fully revealed, Alison was quite taken with it. It was small and bare now, but it had a certain charm to it. The slightly asymmetrical windows that framed the off-kilter door frame. The moss that clung to the little section of thatched awning over the door. The little wooden fence, rotten though it was, that surrounded it. It was no elvish building of green and gold or geometric highrise in the stylish part of town, but it had a simple beauty that was undeniable.

She turned to thank Gwenla for her help, but the dwarf was already off down the path to fetch the stew. While she waited, she struggled with the door, finally wrenching it open with about all the force her arms had left after an afternoon of chopping vine.

The inside needed a bit of work, to say the least. The dust seemed to be an inch thick in places, and the cobwebs stretched from floor to vaulted ceiling.

"Oh dear," said Gwenla when she returned with a pot. "Well, one room at a time, I guess. Let's start with the kitchen."

Gwenla led Alison through the hall to the back of the home. She sat the pot on the wooden floor and headed through the back door. "You sweep, I'll fetch the water," she said without turning back.

Alison picked up the broom and worked from the ceiling down. She was forced to take the broom outside on several occasions to beat the webs and spider eggs out of it in order to continue. Gwenla had cleared the wood stove and lit it, setting the pot of water to boil. Then she rummaged in the cupboards for the bowls and silverware, which she dumped into the basin with the hot water. "Got to be some soap in here somewhere…" she muttered as she rifled through the cupboards.

Alison felt overwhelmed. She didn't know how to do any of the things Gwenla had just done–to fetch water from a well, to light a wood stove, to cook a stew. She reminded herself that it was temporary. She would be leaving next week, and Gwenla seemed only too happy to help her in the meantime.

Gwenla served the stew–it was earthy and filling, which Alison was grateful for after a long day–and bid her goodnight. "There's a good stream down in the woods for bathing, though I don't know if there's enough light left to-night. Call on me anytime, and don't forget the meeting Friday night!"

Gwenla waved off Alison's thanks and hurried back down the path. Alone again, Alison evaluated her physical state.

She was filthy.

She was covered head to toe in dust, ash, and cobwebs. She had rinsed her hands in the dish basin before dinner, but she had missed the dirt beneath her fingernails. The stream Gwenla had mentioned–the Winterburn Stream, she recalled from the deed–seemed like just the thing.

Alison set off for the woods, but she quickly realized the problem–the vine hadn't been cut back beyond the well. Lucky for her, the vine was thinner here, and she was able to make quick work of it before the sun had dipped below the treetops.

The light filtered through the bare branches of oaks and elms, while the wind rustled through the needles of the pines and firs like a whisper. The stream wasn't far from the forest's edge. She heard the trickle of water falling onto rock before she saw it.

It was larger than she had imagined, almost as wide as the river that flowed through Herot's Hollow. There was a nicely placed boulder along the bank that was perfect for storing her clothes, though truthfully they needed washing as well. She glanced around the woods–despite the lack of deciduous growth, the evergreens provided adequate cover–and stripped down to her bare skin.

The air was getting cooler now with the sun fading in the sky, but Alison's skin still burned from her exertion, and her belly was warm with Gwenla's stew. She dipped a toe into the slow water–it was incredibly cold, but it felt just perfect to her. The comforting chill that Nolwynn had described. She made a mental note to send the korrigan an invitation.

She walked carefully over the slick stones of the riverbed into the middle of the stream. There, the water came up to her waist, and she slowly lowered herself in until the water reached the tip of her braid. She released it and lowered her body the rest of the way until only her face was above the surface. The cold water flowed through her long dark hair, gathering it over her chest as she faced downstream. She washed the dirt and grime off of her skin and out from under her nails, scrubbing hard. As she contemplated walking back to shore and cleaning her clothes as well, she heard the snap of a branch.

A dark figure stood on the bank near the rock where she had left her clothes.

"What in the name of the Gods do you think you're doing?"

Chapter Eight

BOUNDARIES

Alison froze.

The stranger stepped forward into a patch of light. Though she couldn't make out his features from a distance, she could see he was human. He was fully dressed in a riding cloak and old-fashioned breeches, and as Alison's eyes lingered on his unusually fine clothes, she remembered she wasn't wearing any.

"Oh!" she squeaked, crossing her arms over her chest.

The stranger had the same realization at the same moment. He quickly turned around to preserve her modesty. "I'll ask you again," he said, his voice deep and stern. "What do you think you are doing?'

Though the strange man coming upon her naked in the woods should have registered as a threat, Alison couldn't help but feel annoyed rather than fearful. This was her land, after all. "I'm panning for gold. What does it look like I'm doing?"

"Trespassing," he said. "You are trespassing in my stream."

"Your stream? 'To and including the Winterburn Stream.' This is my stream." Memorizing the deed had finally paid off.

"You see that oak tree?" Without turning, the man pointed his arm from beneath his cloak upstream about twenty paces from the boulder where Alison had left her clothes.

"Yes."

"That's where your land ends. This is my stream, and you're trespassing."

"Oh," she said. She wasn't sure she believed him, but even if he was right, she hadn't intended any harm. Surely they could address their property dispute at a more opportune moment.

Whatever heat she had retained from her exertion had gone. Her teeth began to chatter.

"Come out of there at once," he said. "The water is like ice."

"My clothes are over there," said Alison. "If you wouldn't mind."

She had expected him to turn further so that she could dress in peace, but instead he glanced at the clothes on the rock. "That's all you brought? Are you mad?"

"What's wrong with my clothes?" Alison had taken the careful steps back to the bank. The wind was frigid on her skin. She needed him to look away so she could dress, and quickly.

"They're filthy, and far too light for this weather. I can hear the south in your voice. This land is not to be underestimated."

Alison had had enough of this. The stranger was rude and condescending, and if he thought he was helping, he had a funny way of doing so. "It's all I brought, so it will have to do for now. My cottage is nearby, and a good fire still burns in the stove. Now please, leave at once so I may be dressed before I freeze to death. I promise I won't go past the oak again."

The stranger did move, but rather than turning away, he took off his cloak. He held it out behind him so that Alison could take it without losing her privacy.

"Take it," he said when Alison did not.

The cloak was a dark gray, almost black, and looked to be made of fine wool. It would undoubtedly offer better protection than Alison's filthy garments; it even had a hood to contain her wet hair. She didn't want to owe the stranger anything, but she also couldn't handle the thought of pulling her dirty clothes back onto her clean skin.

She took the cloak, her hand brushing the bare skin of his wrist as he pulled back his arm.

He held his hand to his chest as if he had been stung. "You're freezing cold. Go home at once and sit beside the fire." Though he was still being an officious nuisance, his voice was tinged with concern.

Alison wrapped the cloak tightly around her and then bent over the boulder to retrieve her garments. She walked in front of him, intending to tell him what she thought about being bossed around.

The sun had gone now. In the twilight, she could see his dark eyes widen as he beheld her. And as she beheld him, her eyes mirrored the gesture. He was far more handsome than she had expected, with chiseled features that were perfectly proportioned for his face and a jaw that was strong and firmly set. His jet-black hair was neatly arranged, if a bit overgrown, and his clothes were even finer than they had appeared from a distance and well-kept, with perfectly polished buttons. For a moment, she forgot she'd been angry at all.

He held his hand up then thought better of it, pulling it back to his chest. And then he changed his mind again and reached for the hood of the cloak, pulling it over her wet hair and around her face.

Alison felt her pulse quicken as she gave him a half smile. "I'll return it on the morrow," she said.

There was something in the air between them, something more he wished to say, but to her disappointment, he withdrew. "No need," he said as he walked away from her in haste.

Reluctantly, she followed the path of her own footsteps back through the woods as the moon began to rise.

❧☙

The cottage was dark by the time she had returned. The only light was the pale glow of the moon through the windows;

the fire in the kitchen wood stove had burnt down to em-
bers.

Alison threw in another log to rouse the fire and then
slumped into a kitchen chair, exhausted. The stranger's
cloak was still wrapped around her. It smelled pleasantly of
fresh fir and the smoky scent of a campfire, and there was a
deep and earthy hint of sweat that Alison was embarrassed
to admit she liked the best of all.

The stranger was infuriating–bossy and obstinate and
impolite–and yet he had shown her concern and kindness
in lending the cloak. She wondered who he could be. No
one she had met so far had mentioned a dark and handsome
human man living next door, and he certainly wasn't the
fairy shepherd.

There was a scratching sound at the door. At first, Alison
hoped it was the stranger, coming for his cloak. But the
sound was low to the ground, and Alison quickly realized it
was a cat.

"Willow!" She hadn't expected the cat to return to her.
She hoped that Gwenla wasn't missing her.

Willow remained at Alison's side, sniffing the stranger's
cloak. "Wherever did you get this?" she asked. There was a
hint of suspicion in her voice.

"I was hoping you could tell me, actually. There was a
stranger in the woods when I went to bathe. He said I'd
crossed into his part of the Winterburn Stream. I'm going
to have to check the deed because I believe an oak is the
eastern bound, not the western. But regardless, he gave me
this cloak because my clothes were quite dirty. Do you know
him?"

The cat purred and trilled. "I can't believe it. No one has seen Mr. Ainsley in years. Gwenla will be so pleased. Are you going to return the cloak? Could you ask him to come to the meeting?"

"Mr. Ainsley," Alison repeated. She hadn't heard the rest.

Willow purred more loudly. "I know that tone. You too, huh? Gwenla calls him Keir. She doesn't care for the human convention of calling people by their surnames. I wouldn't get your hopes up, though. You'll have to get the full story from Gwenla, but the way I've heard it, he doesn't talk to anybody. If you happen to be the exception, make sure you mention the meeting. I know Gwenla would be grateful."

"I will," promised Alison. She yawned loudly, and Willow echoed the gesture.

"It doesn't look like you and Gwenla finished cleaning. Have you checked the bedroom yet?"

Alison was certain what she would find there. Spiders and more spiders. "I think I'll sleep in here tonight. It's nice by the fire with my hair still so wet."

"On the floor? How catlike of you. Do you mind if I join you?"

"Not at all," said Alison. She retrieved a clean set of underclothes and a nightgown from her trunk–Gwenla must have brought it up when she wasn't paying attention–and then she wrapped herself in Mr. Ainsley's cloak.

Willow curled up onto her chest and began to softly snore. Once, when Alice awoke in the night, she could swear she saw another set of glowing eyes in the room. But the warmth from the fire and the cloak and the cat was too alluring of a sensation, and soon she was back into a dreamless sleep.

❦

Alison woke with the dawn. Or rather, with the roosters that woke with the dawn.

"Good Gods, how many could there possibly be?" she asked no one. Willow must have found a different way out; it was so like a cat to beg to be let in and out even when there was another path available.

Alison's left arm was slow to wake, and her hips ached from a night on the floor. The first order of business for the day would be to clean the bedroom and assess its condition.

Or perhaps the second order of business. The first order would be returning the cloak to its owner. Alison told herself it was important to do this so that she could invite Mr. Ainsley to the meeting; it was just two days away now. It was for this reason that she would go see Mr. Ainsley and definitely no other.

Alison dressed quickly, throwing on one of her last remaining clean garments, a dress in a lovely blue that matched her eyes. Not that there was any reason to draw attention to them in particular. But before she could brush the dust from the cloak, there was a knock at her door.

It was not Mr. Ainsley.

It was the young orc she had seen at the inn her first night in town. He was the picture of a farm boy in an oversized straw hat and suspenders; the only thing missing was the pitchfork. There was a cart behind him with large metal jugs, baskets full of food, and sacks of grain as big as Alison.

"Ms. Lennox," he said. "Name is Brytak. Pa runs the farm down by the river and the mill there. We do our deliveries in town, but Pa said you wouldn't have nothing to eat. We've got cabbages, carrots, lettuce, turnips, radishes, spinach, onions, broccoli, sprouts, leeks, potatoes, and peas right now. Oh and squash. And then we also deliver milk and eggs every morning, and we have butter, lard, oil, and flour too. This box is for you. Free today. A silver for a box after that. You tell me what you want."

As Brytak spoke, he filled a glass bottle with fresh milk from a metal jug and added it to a box with a bit of everything in the list. Alison didn't know what to do with all of it. She hadn't cooked a meal for herself in a long time, and the last time that she did, she followed a recipe she had cut from the morning paper.

"Let me get back to you in a couple of days with what I'll need," she said.

"Don't take too long," said the orc. He smiled and a hint of rose touched his gray cheeks. "I'd hate to have to make an excuse to come up here to see you."

Alison tilted her head. Was he flirting with her?

He removed his cap and brushed his hand through his dark hair, which had a nice wave to it. The gesture also highlighted the muscles in his arms.

Oh, yes. He was flirting with her.

Alison couldn't help but laugh. "Kid, I could be your mother." Maybe not quite true, but near enough.

"You could, but you aren't." Brytak wasn't the slightest bit embarrassed, but he also made no move towards her.

"Get out of here," said Alison, freeing one arm from the box to shoo him with a smile.

Brytak held up his hands. "Hey, it's not often we get a new girl in town. The only other eligible bachelorette is my sister. Can't blame a guy for trying."

That was fair. And at least he'd been nice about it.

When Brytak was on his way, Alison turned back to the cloak. It was surprisingly clean for having spent the night on the floor–Gwenla had somehow found the time to wipe the kitchen floors in addition to everything else she had done for Alison. Alison needed to find a way to repay her. The least she could do would be to get Mr. Ainsley to come to the meeting.

The path from the cottage to the street seemed narrower than what she and Gwenla had cleared the day before. And Alison was sure the vine had put down new roots as well. No wonder Gwenla was so concerned about it–if it grew this quickly, Alison would have to tend to it nearly every day. And how on earth could she sell a tenant on the place?

Adorable cottage steps from town but with the quiet of the woods. Plenty of land. Minor overgrowth removal required. Immunity to poison a plus.

Not that she was certain that the vine was poisonous, but there weren't many good things in the world that Alison could think of that dripped dark fluids from their thorns. And she wasn't sure, "Well, I didn't stab myself with the vine to see if it might be poisonous," would hold up as a defense in court were it to come to that.

Alison had brought the machete Gwenla had lent her and the gloves she bought from Mr. Gilroy to clear the walls on her property. And it was a good thing, too; the road turned downhill not far past Alison's gate, and the vine had spread beyond the walls and into the street in several places.

Mr. Ainsley's gate was at the end of the road, and it was almost completely obscured. It struck Alison that no one, not even Mr. Ainsley, had been down here for a long time.

Alison cut back a large section from the gate, but the growth beyond was just as bad as Alison's had been the day before. She wanted to see Mr. Ainsley–for Gwenla's sake, she reminded herself–but she didn't think she had the strength in her arms to cut her way through.

Plus, who knew? Maybe Mr. Ainsley liked the vine and would be deeply offended if she removed it.

So Alison turned back to her cottage; there was another path to try. She carried the cloak back up her path, cutting back a bit more vine as she went, and then continued back towards the woods.

In the light of day, Alison could see what she had missed the night before. The hedge Alison had taken as the eastern border of the property appeared to be, in fact, a hedge maze, though it was greatly overgrown and still covered in the vine. The path she followed led to the west, and the first set of trees she passed was quite clearly an orchard, though the twining vine camouflaged it well. Entering the woods, it was a short walk back to the boulder where she'd left her clothes. Where she had met Mr. Ainsley.

She followed the path along the stream. The land sloped downhill, and the water rushed white in places where it fell a short distance. Then the path left the woods once more and wound back uphill, but here, the vine didn't seem to grow. At the top of the hill, there were several great boulders in the long, brown grass. No, not boulders, but rather stones, the kind hewn from the ground by ancients using some long-forgotten method and arranged in a circle. There were seven stones in all, but only five of them remained standing. Alison could see down to her cottage from the vista, and just beyond the stone circle to the south was the hedge that marked the border of her property with Mr. Ainsley's.

Everywhere except for the area surrounding the stone circle and the path she had cut through the middle of her land was covered in the vine. Beyond covered, it was buried in it. But there was one more path cut into it, a path that led from the stone circle to a large stone structure with a thatched roof. Mr. Ainsley's house.

Alison followed the path, practically running down the hill. There was smoke from one of the chimneys–he was definitely home.

The vine had been cleared around the house, leaving some of the land workable for a garden and a small chicken coop. A rooster, one of the ones Alison had heard that morning, undoubtedly, crowed when she walked by.

Alison walked around the house to the front door. Then she knocked, once.

No response. Not a single sound at all.

Alison knocked again, a little louder this time.

She could hear movement within. She backed up and looked into the window in time to see the swish of a curtain.

"I know you're in there," she called. "I brought your cloak."

The man really was rude. He was clearly inside, and she wasn't unexpected. She told him she would return the cloak on the morrow, and it was the morrow. Would it kill him to have five minutes of idle conversation with her?

Alison knocked again. "This is silly. I'm not going anywhere until you answer."

She could hear him moving towards the door. When she was certain he was on the other side, she began to knock continuously.

"Go away," he called. His voice was muffled by the door, but it was definitely him.

Alison smiled. She was getting somewhere.

Chapter Nine

THE ODD COUPLE

The door cracked open. It was only a couple of inches, but Alison could see one of his brown eyes and the corner of his mouth. Progress.

"What do you want?"

"I told you I'd bring the cloak–"

"And I told you not to bother. How did you even get here? You didn't cut a path from the road, did you?" He pushed the door open a little more and stuck his head out to check.

Alison couldn't help but smile when she saw his face. In the daylight, she could see dark shadows under his eyes and a tinge of gray around his temples. Rather than dulling his good looks, it had the effect of making him appear scholarly and distinguished. And there was a dusting of stubble on his jaw, which only accentuated the sharp line of it more. He was infuriatingly handsome; there was no denying that.

"I followed the path from the stream. By the way, I'm fairly certain you're mistaken about the part I was bathing in when you interrupted me. It must be east of the standing stones, and they lie just north of the boundary hedge, so it must be my part. I can show you, if you like."

He pulled his head back inside and shut the door again.

"Hey!" Alison shouted. "I, for one, don't mind if you want to keep using it. Just so long as I can use it as well."

She heard his footsteps retreating. He was slipping away.

She banged on the door. "At least take your cloak. It's the last time I accept a favor from you if this is how you're going to be."

The footsteps returned, and the door cracked once more. This time, his hand appeared through it.

"Not a chance," said Alison, pulling the cloak out of his reach. "Look, I get the message loud and clear. You don't want company. But I have a favor to ask of you–yes, I know what I just said–and I'm not going to ask it to the door."

Slowly, the door opened just wide enough to fit his broad shoulders. Alison couldn't make out much beyond him, not that she truly wanted to look at anything else.

She hated him for being so appealing to look at. It made it very hard to stay angry with him, even though he was being an absolute twat.

"Thank you," she said. "Now, before you say no, I just want you to take a look around at your land."

He rolled his eyes, but when Alison refused to continue, he leaned forward a little to look beyond her. "What about it?"

"The vine, of course. You can't even get to your front gate. Not that I guess you want to, though I really can't see why because everyone in town is really lovely and helpful, and it's pretty silly to keep yourself locked away back here for–"

"Don't talk about things you don't understand." There was a warning in his tone.

Alison sighed. "Fine. Well, the vine is out of control, I'm sure you can agree to that. It's ruining Gwenla's beautiful garden. And the thorns are rather nasty, and pretty soon it will be in the village with the children…" His blank expression told her that none of her arguments were getting anywhere with him.

She shifted the cloak in her arms. "Look, here's the thing. I need the vine gone. I can't rent out the property with it there, and Gwenla thinks the only way we're going to get rid of this thing is if we get the town on our side. There's a meeting on Friday. That's two nights from now, in case you aren't keeping track out here on your own. And it would mean a lot to me if you'd come. Please."

He looked at Alison for a long moment, studying her face as if she was a puzzle to solve rather than a person. He sighed. "No."

Then he reached for the cloak, but not fast enough.

"No?" asked Alison. She took a step backwards, knowing he wouldn't follow. He wasn't getting off that easy. "Fine. You said I didn't have to bother bringing the cloak back, so I'm sure you won't mind if I hold on to it a bit longer. If you change your mind, you know where to find me."

She spun on her heels and raced towards the path to the standing stones, half expecting him to chase after her.

He didn't.

◦⊙⊙⊙◦

Back in the cottage, Alison channeled her fury into cleaning. She worked from the top down, clearing the cobwebs from the ceiling, opening the windows to let in some fresh air, then clearing the dust and removing the protective cloth covers from the furnishings and assessing their condition.

Most of the home and the furnishings appeared to be in good repair. There was a broken pane of glass in one of the sitting-room windows, a missing screen in the larder where Willow must have been coming and going, a couple of loose floorboards with a small tree growing between them, and most unfortunately, mildew stains on the bed linens. The mattress itself seemed in fine condition and appeared to be stuffed mostly with feathers, which were Alison's preference. But the linens would require replacing, since the dust cloths were far too filthy to sleep on, and that meant a trip into town.

Alison stopped suddenly just beyond the cottage's front door. The vine, which she had trimmed back just a couple of hours earlier when she was trying to find a path to Mr. Ainsley's house, had regrown nearly to the cottage walls. Its tendrils unwound before her very eyes, stretching before her so quickly that the growth was perceptible.

"Unbelievable!" Alison wielded the machete and slashed wildly, hacking every bit of vine she could see with a mad abandon. She took no care to ensure her cuts were near the root as Gwenla had instructed her, and in her fury, she had even failed to don the leather gloves. By the time she had reached her gate, the sleeve of her dress was torn in two places. The dark venom of the vine soaked into the fabric, turning blue to an unsettling deep plum black. The black of a night gone starless.

By the time Alison had made it to Lydiach's Woven Goods, a shop she'd noticed during her walk with Willow, the stain had spread up the sleeve an improbable distance. Great, another expense. She was going to have to have the sleeves replaced.

Alison could hear the squeaking of a fairy as she pushed open the shop door.

"Why on Earth would I steal from my own brother?"

Lydiach stood on the counter, tiny arms crossed. She was much like a miniature human, except for her white wings and green hair, and her face bore a remarkably human look of utter contempt for those that stood before her.

Leaning against the counter and scratching away at a notepad was the youngest elf that Alison had ever seen. He looked as fresh-faced as a teenage human, all swagger and arrogance and wild-dreaming. Standing beside him and yawning was a plump dwarf with a crooked nose and a long white beard. Both of them wore the black uniforms and badged hats of the King's Constabulary.

"Gentlemen, I can't say it's been a pleasure, but I have a customer, and surely the king's finest wouldn't stand in the way of the work of an honest businesswoman. Have a nice—watch out!"

As the elf dipped his pen in his inkwell, he overturned it, spilling its dark contents onto the counter and a dress sized for a Quarterling that hung from it.

"Terrific! Just incredible. You asked if the pigments that were stolen from my brother's shop could be used to dye clothes, and now you're going to find out firsthand why they aren't. Look at the way the blue of the ink and the green of the dress combine." Lydiach lifted the stained dress, dripping ink onto the floor. The elf leaned closer for a better look. The dwarf didn't budge.

"See how it's not a clear and beautiful teal. It's muddied. Dull."

"Of course," said the elf. He could clearly see something Alison couldn't because the dress looked fine to her. "I'm very sorry to have wasted your time." He shook the remaining ink from his notepad onto the counter. Then, realizing his mistake under the fairy's icy glare, he wiped up the mess with his handkerchief.

The dwarf grunted and shuffled past Alison to the door.

As the elf hurried to catch up with him, he caught a glimpse of Alison's stained sleeve. "Excuse me, Miss?"

Alison thought of giving a false name, but that would be prolonging the inevitable. "Ms. Lennox," she said.

The dwarf, who had almost made it out of the shop, turned with a surprising quickness.

"Ms. Alison Lennox?" he asked. His voice was low and gruff.

"The same," Alison said.

"Not in my shop," said Lydiach. "Ms. Lennox has only just come to town. I won't have her accosted in my place of business."

The elf opened his mouth to protest, but the dwarf held up a single fat finger. "We'll be outside when you're finished," he said to Alison.

Just what Alison needed. More time away from the work of repairing the cottage to deal with false suspicions.

Once the constables were gone, the fairy flitted over to Alison. "I hope I haven't put my faith in you prematurely. Gwenla is quite taken with you, and my father has been meaning to stop by to thank you for keeping the vine clear. I can't see you as a thief. Lydiach," said the fairy, holding out her tiny hand. Alison extended her index finger, and Lydiach wrapped her hand around it, giving it a surprisingly forceful shake.

"Alison Lennox. And no, I didn't take anything from the apothecary. This stain is from the vine. Do you know anything that can take care of it?"

Lydiach flew backwards away from Alison. "Are you hurt? Did it get you?"

"No, not that I can tell. My dress got the worst of it. Do you know what the vine does?"

"I don't, and I wouldn't want to find out. Do you mind?" The fairy flew into a back room and returned carrying a pair of scissors as large as she was tall.

"Sure, go ahead."

Alison marveled as the fairy deftly maneuvered the proportionally enormous scissors to cut the stained fabric from her sleeves. She then tossed the scraps into the fireplace, where the fabric burned around the stain, but the stain itself didn't catch.

"Interesting. There could actually be some value in that," said Lydiach as she sewed a new cuff onto Alison's sleeves with such quickness in motion that Alison could barely perceive it.

Alison appraised the changes in a looking glass near the counter. The fairy's work was fine, and the shorter sleeves would be more comfortable with the coming warm weather anyway.

"Anything else I can do for you?"

"A set of bed linens, if you have them."

The fairy offered Alison the choice of a variety of fabrics: linen, flannel, silk, or cotton in crisp percale or fine sateen. Alison chose the most affordable cotton option; it was only a temporary arrangement, after all. She thanked the fairy for her help and begrudgingly made her way outside to the waiting constables.

"Ms. Lennox. We were hoping to have a word," began the elf.

Alison had not stopped walking after she exited the shop. If she had to entertain this farce, the least they could do is go along with her to the rest of her errands.

"About the robbery, I presume. Very well. Keep up," she called over her shoulder. The elf caught up to her almost immediately. The dwarf trudged along at his own pace.

"I'm Lord Wexenas, Detective Constable of King Derkomai's northern division," the elf said with a bow, "and this here is DCI Tirrin. Wait, how did you know what we were going to ask you about?"

"Well, you're certainly not here to help with the vine. I was there in the alley yesterday just after it happened. I heard the shriek and ran to see what was the matter. At first, I thought it was blood that had been spilt. But then I saw the fragments of the jar and realized it was ink. And then the fairy proprietor started yelling about a thief, and so I deduced it must have been a robbery."

Alison tapped her temple in a sarcastic gesture, but Lord Wexenas seemed impressed.

"That's just how we've heard the tale. Although…" He scratched his neck underneath his golden braid. "Maybe you fled the scene of the crime and then returned to conceal your involvement."

"That doesn't seem like the wisest move considering the thief should have ink on their hands," said Alison. She looked back at the pair long enough to see the dwarf shoot a knowing look at the elf.

The elf gulped hard. "That's just what DCI Tirrin said. How did you know that?"

"Forgive the young upstart here. I've told him he's barking up the wrong tree," said the dwarf.

"I'm twenty years your senior!" said the elf.

"Not on the force, you're not," said the dwarf. "Can you finish with your questions so we can let her be on her way?"

They had reached Alison's destination: the mill, where Alison could order some floorboards and a cover for the broken window until she could have a replacement installed.

Alison chose to be forthcoming to prevent wasting any further time. "I saw the swipes in the dirt as if a Fulling had retrieved something they dropped. Your robber should be easy enough to spot; stains like that won't come out of skin for days." Alison spoke from experience; she'd dropped an inkwell or two in her time. She handed the elf her bed linens and held up her own hands to let him inspect them. "The stains on my dress earlier were from the vine. What else? Oh, before I heard the scream yesterday, I was with the blacksmith Mr. Weyland Gilroy and Willow the cat."

"Mr. Gilroy didn't mention you," said the dwarf, raising one bushy eyebrow.

"Mr. Gilroy barely spoke to me at all. Willow did the dealing for me. You can come by and see the purchase I made if you don't believe me."

"We may do just that," said the elf. "I have just one more question. We heard that on your first night in town, you were spotted writing in a book. Is that a common pastime of yours?"

Alison could see the connection; a writer would have cause to be an ink thief. There was nothing else for it. She reached in her satchel and handed the elf her journal. "I do write, but as you can see, only in black ink."

The elf couldn't resist the temptation. "Lonesomeness and longing hidden, Winter's kiss and song forbidden–"

Alison snatched the journal back. "Maybe not that one."

The dwarf cracked a rare smile. Alison couldn't meet either of their gazes as she shoved the journal back towards the elf, turned to a less mortifying page.

"The Korrigan's Courage."

Deep in the woods, in darkness Stygian,
Down where the moon refuses to shine,
She pulls back her hood, her eyes obsidian,
And calls him forth, through song divine.

The poem continued for three more verses, but the elf seemed satisfied after reading just the one out loud. "It's, umm. Well, it's not the most terrible poetry I've ever read," he said.

Alison had heard worse. "Thanks. Well, the point was I don't use other inks. Just black."

"So it seems," said the elf. "Well, thank you for your time. We may follow up about the trip to the blacksmith, just to make sure there are no stones left to turn."

"I'd appreciate it if you kept quiet about the ink-stained hands until we've had a chance to find them," said the dwarf.

"Understood," said Alison. The elf tipped his hat, and the dwarf nudged his slightly, which Alison figured was the best she would get from the grumpy old man, and they were on their way.

Chapter Ten

THE RELUCTANT PATIENT

The next day, in the sleepy haze of early morning, Alison mistook the water dripping on her forehead for the coolness of a breeze through the window. But when she turned onto her side and the water slid down her neck, she woke with a start.

It was dark in the bedroom, but Alison didn't need to see to know what had happened. The roof was leaking, and badly. The rain poured in a steady stream right onto the bed and in several other places. Alison stumbled down the stairs into the kitchen where the stove light cast a faint glow. She fumbled in the cupboards for a match and candlestick, and then she searched for buckets, cups, and containers of any size or shape that could hold water.

It took her the better part of an hour to find all the leaks and arrange the containers in such a way that she could leave them unattended until dawn. But she found herself unable to return to sleep, and instead she took advantage of the water's incursion to scrub the floors and walls she hadn't yet gotten around to cleaning.

The rain ceased just as dawn was breaking. Alison made her way outside the cottage to assess the damage.

At first, Alison couldn't see any glaring flaws in the structure of the thatch roof. But as she walked the perimeter of the cottage, she witnessed the culprit in action. A wren landed on the corner, grasping a single piece of straw in its talons and flying off towards the ornamental hedge.

"Ms. Lennox?" a voice called.

Brytak was at Alison's gate with his cart. He hacked at the vine with an ax and made his way up the hill. "I wasn't expecting to see you up so early. I have your delivery here."

"Thanks for bringing the lumber. You don't carry thatch for the roof by any chance, do you?" asked Alison.

"I'm afraid not. You'll be wanting the thatcher, Mr. Craig. He lives in Fossholm. If you send him a bird today, he might be here by Monday."

"Monday? I can't wait that long." The skies had not yet cleared, and dark clouds loomed in the distance.

"If you don't mind me saying, that house has been empty since I was just a boy. I don't think a few more days are going to matter."

Maybe not for the condition of the home, but it certainly mattered for Alison's schedule. "Thanks anyway," she said. "Say, if you're going into town, do you mind sending that bird for me? I've got a lot to do around here. A silver for the trouble."

Brytak was more than happy to run errands for her, especially with such a generous tip involved. Alison was burning through her coin faster than she would have liked, but she had only a week left of her stay in Herot's Hollow, and she'd never get everything done without some help.

Alison carried the lumber out back to a shed she'd found near the hedge maze. The vine was cooperating today, the slowdown in its growth enabling her to focus on other tasks. In the shed, she had found the late Ms. Lincoln's tools, as well as an old iron key that fit no lock she could find. She spent the morning measuring and cutting the lumber with a rusty saw, replacing the warped floorboards and tacking a thin sheet of wood over the broken windowpane and missing screen.

"Sorry, Willow," she muttered once the panel was in place. The cat would have to make do with asking to be let in and out. And Alison would have to learn to live with the annoyance.

Having never done home repair work before, Alison was surprised by how easy it was. Sure, the boards were a little crooked, and there were some gaps around the window frames, and yes, she had managed to hit her thumb with the hammer a few dozen more times than she would have preferred, but it was good enough. She was so pleased with herself, she started getting ideas about the roof.

In the back of the cottage near the woods, Alison had been gathering sticks and twigs into a pile. The act of cutting back the vine meant cutting down some of the normal vegetation that dared to spring up around it and removing the dead wood that had died because of it. Alison couldn't help but notice how much the bundle of sticks resembled the thatch on the roof.

The roof came down so low to the ground that Alison could reach it on a small stepladder she'd found in the shed. The process seemed simple: take a bundle of sticks and hammer it into the gaps where the birds had taken the straw. And if that didn't work, there was also a tarpaulin on the shed's roof that would surely do better over the bedroom. At the least, Alison could sleep dry.

Alison didn't feel nervous on the ladder or even on the roof. She had lived all her life in high-rises–on lower floors, sure, but even the lowest floor she had lived on had been higher than the highest chimney in her cottage. She focused on the worst areas in the corners first, and like the floor repair, she was surprised by how easy the task was.

She had just approached the area over the bedroom when the wren returned. Alison waved a stick at it, which seemed to annoy it more than anything. It flew right at her head, a little brown blur flapping around her and diving for the roof.

"King of the birds, indeed!" Alison yelled. In her haste to be free of the bird's interference, she did not realize she had lost grip of the ladder.

The last thing Alison saw was the wren flying away carrying one of her sticks as the rain began to fall.

❧❧❧

There was movement somewhere in the room, but Alison could see nothing.

Her eyes were closed, she realized. They didn't seem to want to open. It took all of her effort to convince them to open a crack.

The light that entered was blinding, and the world she beheld was awash in a blurry glow.

It was too much for her. She closed her eyes again and drifted back to sleep.

☙✷❧

The second time Alison woke, the room was much darker. The air smelled of antiseptic and citrus, and as Alison's vision cleared, she realized she must have still been dreaming.

Mr. Ainsley hovered over her, inches from her face. He reached a large hand to her head, brushing something in her hair.

It was bad enough that she found it hard to stop thinking about the man. But now to be dreaming of him too? She wasn't having it.

"I want to wake up right now. I refuse to do this. No. No more dreams," said Alison, but the few words that came out were muddled. "Swrong wimme?" She shook her head and tried to snap herself awake.

"Stop that. You're injured," said a voice.

She wasn't waking up, and that was really very annoying. She tried to sit up. If she could fall out of this–bed? She was in a bed in her dreams? That was odd. But if she could make herself fall out of the bed, that would wake her up for sure.

"What are you doing? No, stop that. Ms. Lennox. Lay down at once!"

Mr. Ainsley grasped her by her shoulders and pushed her back down into the bed. There was a part of her that liked that particular action very much. She started giggling uncontrollably, rocking back and forth a little in the bed.

"Ms. Lennox, you've fallen from some height and suffered a serious head injury. If you refuse to lie still, I'll have to restrain you."

"Liketosee youtry," said Alison.

Mr. Ainsley looked bereft. In order to tie Alison to the bed, he'd have to let her go. And once he did, she was falling herself awake.

"Ms. Lennox," he said softly. "What would you like to do?"

"Tofall."

"To fall?"

"To wake. Up." It took some effort, but the words were beginning to match her thoughts better.

Mr. Ainsley sighed. "You are awake, I'm afraid. Can you follow my finger? With just your eyes, not your head."

He released Alison and sat up on the bed beside her. Then he held up his right index finger, waving it back and forth in front of Alison's face.

"Good," he said. "Do you know who the king is?"

"Derkomai. King Derkomai." The words were coming more quickly now, and the fog felt like it was lifting. And yet she still did not wake, which was making her angry.

"And do you know who I am?"

"Mr. Ainsley," she said. "Keir." The last part slipped out without conscious thought. When she said it, she thought she noticed a little shiver go through him.

"Good. And do you remember what happened to you?"

That was foggier. "I. Hmm. I seem to remember a roof. I was on the roof. Fixing the roof." Images were flooding back in now. "A bird. It was a bloody wren. It stole my roof. My thatch."

Alison was surprised at the rage that she felt. Her heart was pounding. She felt the heat rise through her chest, and the sudden feeling frightened her. "I'm angry. Extremely angry. I could hit something. I don't understand."

Mr. Ainsley patted her hand once, hesitated, and then shook his head and patted it again. "It happens sometimes in head injuries. The feelings can be sudden and intense. It should pass with time."

"Are you a doctor?" Alison asked. He seemed to know a lot about injuries, though the room she was in didn't look like a hospital.

It looked like a bedroom, a small bedroom in a stone house. Mr. Ainsley's house, she imagined. She really was awake then; this was nowhere she had ever been before. There was a heavy tan blanket on the bed and matching curtains around the sole window. The light coming in was warm and golden, the fading light before sunset. A candlestick with one half-burnt candle sat on the table beside her, along with a tray holding various bottles, tools, and a roll of gauze.

Upon seeing the gauze, Alison reached for her head. There was a bandage there wrapped all the way around the crown. When she pulled her hand back, there was a drop of blood on her finger.

"Don't mess with that," said Mr. Ainsley. "It needs changing. And no, I'm not a doctor."

"Is it bad? My head?"

"The abrasion is small and will heal quickly. The bump will take longer. The part I'm most worried about is your brain. I'll need to monitor you to see how bad it is."

Her brain was bad? Alison didn't like the sound of that at all. She liked it so little that she began to cry.

"I don't know why I'm crying," she said. "I'm not sad."

"It's all right. It will pass." Mr. Ainsley handed her his handkerchief. When she held it to her nose, she could smell the same scent of the cloak he had lent her. It calmed her.

"For someone who isn't a doctor, you seem to know a lot."

Mr. Ainsley frowned. He looked pained as he said, "I was a doctor once."

"You can stop being a doctor?" Alison asked.

"I guess not," he said, gesturing to the tools on the bedside table and to Alison. "Let me change that bandage. Then you need to rest." He stood and began working with the tools in the tray, cutting a fresh bandage and applying some sort of ointment and tape.

"How did I get here?" Alison asked. "Did you find me?" It had suddenly occurred to her that she had no memory of how she had arrived.

"No," he said as he gently removed the old bandage from Alison's hair. "Gwenla did. Then the orc boy carried you."

"The orc boy? Oh, you mean Brytak."

"If you say so."

Mr. Ainsley wrapped a new bandage around Alison's head. She tried not to twitch when his fingers brushed against her face, tried not to breathe too hard when he leaned over her to reach around to her back. She couldn't tell if her head was spinning from the injury or something else entirely.

"Get some rest. I'll bring you some broth in a few hours."

"Are you going to leave me here alone?" Alison felt suddenly frightened. She reached for Mr. Ainsley, gripping his arm. His eyes widened in alarm, and underneath her grasp, she felt his pulse quicken.

Then a change came over his face, a calming look of recognition. "I'll be just downstairs. I'll check in on you often. Hold on, I have an idea." He strode from the room quickly, leaving the door open. After a long moment, he returned holding a small silver bell.

"I'll place this here on the nightstand. If you need me, give it a ring."

Alison nodded. The fear had begun to subside, and in its place was a feeling of loneliness and melancholy. The last time she had been hurt, after she'd fallen as a child, it was her father who had stayed with her while she healed. And when he had gotten sick, it was Alison who stayed by his bedside in the hospital. Sometimes, even years later, she missed him so terribly it felt like the walls were collapsing around her, the roof was gone, and the stars were tumbling down to the earth. Everything was falling and broken with nothing there to hold it up.

She knew the sensation well, but she was struck by how near and present it felt now. Maybe this is what her mind was, stripped of whatever kept it going from day to day. Maybe this is all that anyone was deep down. The sum total of their traumas and desires, held back by the thinnest veneer of politeness. The fleeting veil of "How are you?" and, "Nice weather we've been having," between human and animal need, the protective shell over the gooey center of raw feeling.

Whatever it was that she was missing, she hoped it would come back soon.

Chapter Eleven

FROM "IS" TO "WAS"

Mr. Ainsley gently shook her awake after what felt like only moments. Alison felt her knee strike something as she rose to sit against the pillows he was propping up for her. It was a tray with a steaming cup of broth.

The broth was salty and had a surprising amount of heat. A garden-grown chili, Alison imagined.

"It's good for the constitution," said Mr. Ainsley. He gave Alison half a smile when she stuck out her burning tongue.

"I think you're trying to kill me," said Alison.

"On the contrary."

"Why are you helping me?" she asked. The thought had formed in her mind earlier, but she couldn't quite grasp it. Now, as her senses returned to her, she was remembering the cold reception he had given her previously and wondering what had changed.

"You were brought here because I'm the only one in the village with medical knowledge. Well, apart from the vet, I suppose, though I don't know how much good she would have done you. You wouldn't wake, and they were worried you wouldn't make it to the doctor in Fossholm. Of course, it really makes no difference where you were taken. We have few remedies for a head injury other than time and vigilance. There are some remedies mentioned among those that still practice the old magic, but they are rare these days."

It was the most Alison had ever heard him say at once. He had a pleasing voice with a low and soothing tone, and Alison found she'd like to hear more of it. "How am I doing? How long until you know if I'm going to be okay?"

"You were in and out for quite a while, and when you last woke, the first signs weren't good. But you seem to be rapidly improving. You have the advantage of age on your side. I wouldn't say you're out of the woods yet, but lasting damage is getting less likely by the hour. Tomorrow, we can see how well your balance is. And your coordination, as well."

"Tomorrow?" Alison hadn't realized he planned for her to stay the night. She had none of her things here, and though Mr. Ainsley was growing on her, she didn't know how she felt about staying with him alone in his home overnight. And then she thought of another issue. "But I'll be able to go to Gwenla's meeting tomorrow night, yes?"

"Of course not. A couple hours ago, you could barely talk. You need care and monitoring for a week, at least."

"A week?" Alison felt the blood rise to her cheeks. She was livid again. "I'm leaving in a week. I have to be in a carriage to Sudport in a week, or I won't make it back in time for work."

"Then it's a good thing you fell today. In a week, you should be well enough to travel, barring any incident between now and then."

He wasn't understanding her. "I can't stay in bed for a week. I came here to fix up the cottage. That's not going to happen with me in bed."

Mr. Ainsley's face had gone cold. "The injury has made you irrational. The worst symptoms often don't appear until several hours have passed. You need to stay here, and you will." He turned from her towards the door.

"I don't want to stay here." Maybe it was something in the heightened emotions talking, but Alison didn't want to be here if he was going to be like this. "I want to go back home. I'm feeling fine now. And I will not–*will not*–miss Gwenla's meeting after everything she has done for me." Alison leaned forward in the bed to stand. She realized two things suddenly: first, that she wasn't wearing her own clothes, and second, that she needed the toilet very badly.

"Get back in bed at once." Mr. Ainsley lifted her bare legs back into the bed before she could protest.

"Where are my clothes? I have to get up," said Alison, swinging her legs over to the other side.

"No, you don't," said Mr. Ainsley, but when he circled the bed to place her back in it, she swung her legs over to the first side again and made for the door as fast as she could move.

"See? I'm fine."

Mr. Ainsley was on her heels. She wouldn't be able to outrun him in her state, or to overpower him in any state, and so she turned to reason with him. "I'm not leaving. Not right now. I just need…I need to…"

"Oh," he said. "Of course. Hold on." He reached under the bed and produced a large pot with blue floral glazing.

Alison froze, her eyes wide, incredulous. "Absolutely not."

"Do they not have chamber pots in the city anymore?"

Alison could not fathom the concept of anyone, at any time, doing their business right in their bedroom. "No! We have toilets. Have you heard of them? A wonderful invention, truly. Oh, how I miss them. Surely you have an outhouse. I'll just find that."

"You shouldn't even be out of bed. Come now, I was a doctor. I've seen worse things than the contents of a chamber pot."

The word "slosh" came into Alison's mind as she imagined him carrying the full pot down the stairs. No, it would not do. Alison had little to her name, but she would not be robbed of her dignity. "I can make it. Then I'll go back to bed, and we can revisit the rest in the morning. Deal?" She needed to convince him quickly. She wasn't sure she could last much longer.

"No deal. Please come back here before I have to come get you myself. It's for your own safety, Ms. Lennox. I'm not trying to be unkind."

"And I'm not trying to be unreasonable, but I am a lady. You are a gentleman. I'd prefer to keep it that way. There are some mysteries that should remain mysterious, don't you agree? Now, please. If we dally much longer, the discussion will be moot."

Mr. Ainsley sighed. "You are exasperating. If I let you go, I'll be standing just outside."

"No! Keir, please." There was that name again. Alison didn't understand where it was coming from, this bold urge to use the given name of someone with whom she was barely acquainted. It was shockingly rude of her. And yet the way it felt on her tongue, the faintest tap of her soft palate falling into a light and breathy sigh, was entirely too pleasing. And the way he responded–the shock, the frisson– was almost addictive.

He sighed again. He reached for the bell on the nightstand. "Take this at least. And you'll need this, as well," he said, handing her the candlestick. "I'm waiting at the door of the house, and that's final."

Alison agreed. She headed into the hall and descended the stairs. The flickering light of the candle bounced around, casting strange shadows on the ground. Alison didn't feel dizzy, but it was hard to see the wooden steps, and they were quite uneven. Once, she almost lost her footing, but Mr. Ainsley, who was so close behind her she could hear his breathing, caught her by the elbow. This caused her to swing the candlestick, nearly taking out his eye. He grumbled something about ridiculous notions of modesty and terrible decision making, but Alison had a need too urgent to care.

She took no time to look around the kitchen once she reached the landing. She gestured to the door with the candle, to which Mr. Ainsley assented.

"It's cold out there," he said.

"Don't care," said Alison. She was out the door into the darkness, following the path as quickly as her shoeless feet would take her towards the outhouse.

"That's good because you still have my cloak," he called after her.

Alison smiled as she reached the outhouse door. She shoved the candle and the bell inside and finally took a seat.

If there was any better feeling than relieving oneself after a long wait, Alison didn't know it. Only after she was finished did she realize she was outside in a tiny dark room in nothing but what appeared to be a large tunic of Mr. Ainsley's. No trousers. No shoes. She felt utterly absurd.

As she stood to leave, the bell, which she had forgotten was beside her, tumbled forward to the ground, ringing as it fell.

"Ms. Lennox!"

"No, I'm okay!" She could hear him running through the yard. "Don't come in here!"

She couldn't find the latch. She settled for a wooden crossbeam of the door, holding onto it and pulling it toward her with all her strength.

He was just outside, pulling on the handle.

"Are you alright? Have you fallen? Ms. Lennox. Alison!"

Alison let go of the door at the shock of her own name. It flew open, blowing out the candle in the gust.

Mr. Ainsley reached for her in the darkness. He found her arm and then her hand, pulling her out into the cold. He squinted at her, trying to make her out in the dim light of the crescent moon.

"I'm alright," she said. "I just dropped the bell." Her teeth chattered on the last word.

"You're freezing," he said. "Let's get you back inside."

Before Alison knew what was happening, he had lifted her from the ground into his arms. She pressed her head against his chest. It was hurting again, and that was the only reason she was allowing him to carry her, she told herself. Never mind the soothing smell of fir and woodsmoke. Never mind the beat of his heart, which raced as he carried her through the night back inside.

⁂

Whatever appreciation Alison had mustered for Mr. Ainsley had all but evaporated by the morning. He had insisted on waking her several times in the night to evaluate her condition. By the third waking, she contemplated faking some kind of episode to get rid of him at least long enough for him to summon a carriage to the nearest hospital. By the fifth, she was ready to knock him out with the candlestick. Then she could wake him up repeatedly while he attempted to rest to see how he liked it.

Other than the exhaustion, Alison felt much better when she woke for good. The ache lingered in her head, but it mostly seemed centered on the impact. There was an impressive bump forming there that she hoped would not linger. The haze and fog of emotion that had consumed her the night before were held at bay, though she could still sense the rough edges of feeling just beyond reach as if they could return at any opportune moment.

Following a hastily served breakfast porridge, Mr. Ainsley's absence was conspicuous. He seemed to grow more discontented the better she became, and he spent less and less time by her bedside as the night wore on. In the light of the morning, Alison felt well enough to stand and peer through the window of the bedroom, and there she found him in the garden.

He was almost unrecognizable in a pair of well-worn overalls and a cap with a narrow brim, rake in hand. Alison supposed that she should have known he must spend a lot of time tending his garden; his hermitage would only be possible if he managed self-sufficiency, and judging by the rows of healthy crops he managed, he had achieved it. But it was still somewhat of a surprise for her to watch him work. There was a stiffness in his movement and an awkwardness with his tools that suggested a higher level of breeding than the typical farmhand. But there was also a strength in his arms that suggested years of hard labor. Her curiosity overwhelmed her. She had to find a way to learn more about the man.

Alison took the opportunity to poke around his home on her way to greet him. The bedroom she stayed in was sparsely decorated with only the requisite pastoral paintings in addition to the plain furnishings. The drawers, which she opened without hesitation, were empty save for remedies and implements of medical import. The wood-paneled hall-way was similarly unadorned, and she found the other door on the other side of the stairs to be locked. His bedroom, Alison suspected. He must have anticipated her curiosity, for surely he didn't leave the room regularly locked with no one coming to visit.

The trip down the stairs was easier in the daylight and with the dizzy feeling having subsided. There were several trunks and baskets under the landing with dry goods and spare serving-ware that looked to have rarely seen use. To the right was a small sitting room with a couch in a sturdy brown fabric, a great stone fireplace with a mantle that matched the exposed timbers that lined the ceiling, and a pair of wooden chairs covered in dust. To either side of the fireplace were a writing desk and bookshelf. Alison scanned through the titles: mostly medical tomes, a handful of adventure novels and serials that were generally preferred by younger men, and a book on the old magic of the fey folk. Given what Mr. Ainsley had said about magic remedies, Alison wondered if they held a particular interest for him. Perhaps, like Alison, he had been tempted to see if any of the old magic flowed through his own veins.

The writing desk had drawers as well, but this is where Alison finally found herself unsure. It would feel like a violation to have her own journal and letters read, and as much as she wanted to know more of her caretaker, she couldn't bring herself to intrude upon him in that way. She did pause to take note of the inks—all in black, no colors to be seen. And of course, she had seen much of his hands this past day and noted no stain upon his tanned skin. Though he may not have been the thief, Alison wondered how he came in possession of any ink at all without venturing into town.

There must have been a number of things the man would have needed that he could not produce for himself. How could it be that no one had spoken to him in years? Did he have a secret benefactor? The answer was almost certainly within the contents of the writing desk. It was tempting. But Alison managed to pull herself from the room, past the front door where he had stood two days prior when she had attempted to return his cloak, and into the kitchen she had rushed through the night before. This room was nearly identical to the kitchen in her own cottage, though it was far better stocked, especially within the attached larder. There was just a single chair at the kitchen table; the others had been claimed for storage. From one of those, she found a pair of trousers and a cord which she looped around them to hold them up. They were far too long for her, so she rolled the legs until she could walk comfortably.

Alison looked out into the garden once more from the window in the back door. Mr. Ainsley was kneeling on the ground, a folded paper packet in his hand. Alison watched as he carefully poked a small hole into the dark earth then tilted the packet, producing a small seed and dropping it into the hole. Then he carefully replaced the dirt and pressed it down gently with his fingers. He repeated this motion several times before standing and moving to the next row. The movements were slow and deliberate, almost meditative. Finally, when the last row had been planted, he filled a watering can at his well. Then he returned and slowly passed it over each seed, being careful not to overly disturb the soil.

There was a comfort in watching him work. She felt a sense of communion, both with him and with something older and greater than either of them. The mastery of the land and the life that came forth from it. It was a sense both familiar and unfamiliar to her. Like a long-forgotten memory brought back to the surface.

She pushed open the door. Though the breeze still held the morning's chill, the sun was bright in the sky and warm on her skin. The powerful scent of freshly disturbed earth filled the air with the pleasant sourness of new growth.

That was funny. Alison had never found it pleasant before.

Mr. Ainsley had taken to the shade of a chestnut tree as wide around as the postal carriage that brought her to Herot's Hollow. Though the leaves were still tiny, the wide old branches cast shadows of their own. He leaned against the twisting trunk, wiping the sweat from his brow with a handkerchief and sipping water from a mug.

"A fine and sunny morning to work outside," said Alison. He startled and stood up straight as she approached.

"What are you doing out of bed?"

"I feel much improved, and I thought the fresh air would do me some good."

He paused for a moment to consider this. "Perhaps, but you should not be on your feet." He herded her to a bench on the other side of the chestnut and fully within its shade. "You can stay there for an hour. No more." Then he walked away.

Not so fast. "What are you planting?" asked Alison.

"Early spring crops."

"I could have guessed that. Which crops exactly?"

His lips had formed into a thin line. She watched as he tried to come up with what to say to end the conversation as quickly as possible. "Peas, carrots, parsnip, leeks, sprouts, potatoes."

Alison scrunched up her nose. "I hate sprouts."

"What a childish thing to say."

"How impossibly rude you can be. Sprouts are vile. Mushy, bitter, and disgusting."

"I've found that the fault often lies with the cook in such cases. Though I imagine you have had little produce that hasn't been kept for far too long and traveled much too far to have any of its original flavor left."

Alison did not mention that the fault in the cooking was not her own, if it existed at all. She didn't need to provide him further fuel for his fire of derision. On the count of the quality of the produce she was accustomed to, he was correct. She had noticed a far greater intensity in flavors in the foods prepared here in the country. There was but a single instance in her life from which she could recall a similar experience.

"I did have fresh produce once," she said. "My father got the idea that we would grow a herb garden in our kitchen window. He brought home a little tray of seedlings: basil, parsley, mint, and this awful little herb that tasted of soap. Oh, coriander it was called. Foul stuff. The rest grew well, if a little tall, and my mother was so pleased she decided to plant the seed of a tomato. It was the small kind, a little round one, and so my mother reasoned the plant would be small as well. She was wrong, of course. Within weeks, it had stretched into a monstrosity bigger than I am. It took over the entire kitchen, climbing through our cupboards and putting out more branches every day. I can't imagine we had enough light for it with our small window on the fifth floor, but it didn't seem to mind. It produced dozens of the little tomatoes before the season was over, so many we couldn't give them away. My mother hated it, even though it had been her idea. She threatened to cut it down a hundred times, but my father said it would be a pity not to let it do what nature intended, and so she never did. That was what he was like. He would've loved to have seen all of this. There were few things he didn't love, to be honest." Alison's voice choked a little on the final words. She turned from him so he wouldn't see the mist in her eyes.

He cleared his throat. Though she did not look at him, she could hear his breathing had gotten heavy. "I can't–"

He hurried away in half a run towards the house, where he slammed the door behind him.

Alison was perplexed. Though she seldom spoke of her father to others, the typical reaction to date had been an awkwardness of conversation that followed, or perhaps a perfunctory attempt to provide comfort. She could not recall one instance in which someone had been so overcome to have fled the discussion entirely.

She took her time returning to the cottage. The only thing she could reason was that Mr. Ainsley had experienced some dreadful loss of his own to which her story had served as a cruel reminder. She would have chided herself for her thoughtlessness, but she had no reason to have known it would cause him offense. Still, amends would need to be made. He had done a great and selfless thing in providing her care, annoying as he was about it.

Alison could not find him within the house. He must have retired to the bedroom. She knocked gently on the door.

"Mr. Ainsley?"

He did not answer. Alison held her ear to the door, searching for sounds within but finding nothing. She tried knocking again, but still gently.

"Are you in there? I'm very sorry if I caused some offense. It was not my intention."

There were still no signs of movement. Alison was unsure if perhaps he had gone through the house and out the front again. She glanced down the stairs to the front door, but it was still latched from within.

Alison stared at the brass knob, willing it to open. The heightened feelings were creeping in again. Rather than a simple regret, she was feeling a sense of despair. She slumped to the floor, her back against the door.

"I don't know why I told you that story. I don't talk about my father often, but truth be told, I would like to. I think sometimes that the hardest part about losing him was the way it changed all of my fond memories. There are so many moments full of joy and laughter from the time we had together that became tinged with sadness overnight. But sometimes, when I share them, I can forget the sadness for a moment. When I talk to someone who doesn't know that he's gone, I can pretend that I'm using the past tense because it happened long ago, not because everything about him is past tense.

"That first week was the hardest. When I went with my mother to the funeral home, I kept saying, 'My dad is.' 'My dad is fond of white roses.' 'My dad prefers his gray suit to the black one.' 'My dad likes to watch the sunset over the River Eabrun.' The first time I said, 'My dad was,' I cried for an hour. The change from 'is' to 'was,' from sweet to bittersweet."

She sighed, feeling the tightness in her chest. "It's been eight years now. I'm not the person I was back then, and yet in some way, I'll always be her. I will always be the girl beside the hospital bed, holding his hand through his last gasping breath. That's a part of me now, and even when it hurts, I don't regret it. I know I'm lucky to have experienced that kind of pain at all. To have had a love worth the pain of losing. If I upset you through my words and my feelings, truly I am sorry. But if you have known the same kind of love and pain, then perhaps you are lucky as well, even if it doesn't feel that way sometimes."

Close behind the door, perhaps just on the other side, she heard a kind of sigh. She pressed her palm on the smooth wood, imagining his face just there. She longed to comfort him, to know what pain and what secret he was holding close to his heart.

But she knew he would not let her. And soon, she would be gone again, back to her own life in the city, although it felt very far away now. There were things she must do before then, but she found that even though she could have left and returned to her own cottage to resume her work without his notice, she could not bring herself to leave him this way. Instead, she returned downstairs to the kitchen to help him wash up. As she scrubbed the pots and plates in the washbasin, she remembered the tomato vine twining the cupboards in her childhood apartment and smiled.

Chapter Twelve

PARTINGS

Mr. Ainsley found Alison in the kitchen an hour or so later. She was not an accomplished cook, but she had found the loaf of bread he had baked in the morning and a knob of salted butter in the larder. With the butter, she had found a dark jam, possibly blackberry, and a crumbly cheese with blue veins that tasted as strong as it smelled. She had placed a copper kettle on the stove where it had just begun to whistle, and she had filled two mugs with a spoonful each of tea leaves she'd found in a canister on the counter.

Mr. Ainsley had changed from his work clothes into his typical formal attire, and from the flush of his cheeks, he had recently refreshed himself with the cold water in the bedroom's washbasin. He met Alison's gaze for half a moment before lowering it to the table and the single chair. Wordlessly, he removed a set of prongs for tending the fire from one of the other chairs and placed the chair across from his at the table.

"Where did you find that jam?" he asked. Alison took that to mean the discussion from earlier was over. Perhaps she had not been forgiven, but he had moved past whatever had come over him, nonetheless.

"In the larder unopened. I hope you don't mind. The opened one had grown something fuzzy, so I dumped it outside with the garbage."

"The garbage?" He stood again and came up beside her, looking out the window. "Where exactly did you put it?"

Alison pointed to a pile of earth and scraps she had found near a shed. "Just there."

"Good. That's the compost pile."

"Wait, it can't be," muttered Alison, still looking outside. The vine, which had been at least a dozen feet away from the shed just minutes ago, had twined itself over it and into the compost pile.

Alison was out the door. She yanked up an ax from a stump used for cutting firewood and rushed to the shed, Mr. Ainsley close at her heels.

She spun to face him, ax in hand. It must have looked somewhat threatening because he took a step backward.

"What is this thing? How does it grow so quickly at times and so little at others? Do you know anything about it?"

"I don't," he said, though he still didn't meet her gaze. "It's been here for years. Probably dropped by a traveler or a pilgrim on their way to the outer shrines. It's a nuisance, yes, but I've seen no evidence yet that it causes harm."

"It's not natural. Nothing natural grows in this way." Alison hacked at the sections that were taking root near the compost pile.

Mr. Ainsley just watched.

"Please. Come with me to the meeting tonight. We've got to find a way to stop this thing," said Alison through gritted teeth in between huffs of exertion.

Mr. Ainsley looked at the ground near her feet. "So that you can put your cottage up for rent?"

"Well, yes. Of course, that's part of it. Even if I could rent it out to some poor unsuspecting fool, I wouldn't. I don't know if that stuff is poison, but it's nothing good. It stained my dress a most hideous color and refused to catch on fire."

He raised an eyebrow at that but didn't reply.

"It's not just about me and what I plan to do." To be honest, what exactly that was had been growing murkier in Alison's mind. If she solved the issue of the vine, she would be free to rent the cottage. But it was getting harder for her to picture someone else within it. Harder to picture returning to the city and never coming back here. That was a thought that would bear examination at a later date. For now, the only thing that mattered was being rid of the vine.

"The vine must go. Not just for me, but for Gwenla and Aras and Brytak and his family. For all the town. If it grows like this here, it must have overtaken my cottage again, and if it had just reached the walls of the common, I'm sure it's within it now. It's a matter of when, not if, that someone will be harmed. If not by some kind of poison, at least by the damage it's doing to the crops and the pastures."

"And what do you think the town is going to do about it you and Gwenla and the rest can't achieve alone?"

Alison had given this some thought. "If everyone were to cut it back at once, we could clear it all. Sure, someone might miss a root here or there, but those could be taken care of easily on a second pass. If we all just worked together for a weekend, we'd be rid of the problem for good."

"So Gwenla didn't tell you then. They tried that two years ago. And again last year. They stomped all through my land without my permission for days. It came back worse than ever."

Alison dropped the ax. Why hadn't Gwenla told her they tried removing it before? And what did she hope to achieve this time if the previous ventures had failed?

"Well then. Okay, no, she didn't tell me. But I'm sure she has some other idea then. Or perhaps that's the point of the meeting. To solicit one. If two heads are better than one, two dozen heads must be better still."

"You said the vine is unnatural. But perhaps it's the only thing that's natural. Perhaps it's the land reclaiming itself."

"You think this is a thing of nature?" Alison held up a small section that was visibly creeping back towards the shed, taking care to avoid the thorns. "It is hideous. The color is dark and wrong—look at the way it swallows the light. Nothing in nature grows like this, without rhyme or reason. Although…"

It wasn't quite true that it grew without reason. It avoided the woods, although it didn't mind other areas shaded from the light. And it avoided the stone circle.

"Be careful with that," said Mr. Ainsley, coming closer but keeping his distance from the free section of the vine.

"Why?" asked Alison. "I thought it was natural."

"Nature can be cruel. Nature is a beautiful and wild thing. It cares not for good or evil, for light or darkness. It just is, and we are at its mercy."

"At its mercy? Or a part of it as well?" Alison crept her fingers along the vine's length, edging closer to the nearest thorn.

"Stop being foolish. You know my meaning." Mr. Ainsley's body had grown stiff, his hand clenching into a fist at his side.

"If there's nothing to fear from this vine, then surely it wouldn't matter if I were to touch one of these thorns. This one, right here." She lifted her index finger from the deep purple section, passing fractions of an inch over an oozing black spike.

Mr. Ainsley inhaled sharply. "That's enough, Alison! You've made your point."

Alison felt goosebumps climb up her neck at the sound of her name. If he realized what feeling it elicited in her, he surely would not have done it. Because it gave her quite an incentive to continue misbehaving.

"Very well," she said, gently lowering the vine to the ground. "So we're agreed that the vine must go. Will you not come to the meeting? I don't have an answer for it, and by the sounds of it neither does Gwenla, but at least she's trying something."

He sighed. "I can't."

"Can't or won't?" asked Alison.

"Both," he said. "I wouldn't be welcome there. You don't understand."

"Because you won't explain it to me. Which is fine. It's your secret to keep," she said over his protests. "But you're wrong about not being welcome. I'm sure of that. Willow would never have asked me to ask you if you weren't welcome."

He laughed somewhat bitterly. "You're taking the word of a cat over mine."

"Willow has kept nothing from me. Nor would she. I can't say the same for you."

"If that's how you feel, it sounds like you would be better off without me there as well."

"You know nothing of how I feel." Her cheeks were flushed with anger. His face registered surprise, and then he looked as though he had been stricken.

"I'm sorry," he said softly. "I can't go. And you don't have to either. Nothing will come of it. I know you seem on the mend, but if you were my patient, I would make you stay in bed for another full day at least. You don't have to leave."

There was something raw in his voice that made Alison hesitate. But she could not do it. "I made a promise to a friend who has shown me nothing but kindness. I am nothing without my word."

"Stay, at least, for the luncheon you've made?"

"Okay," she said, maybe a little too quickly.

Though she tried to enjoy the pitiful luncheon and what remained of her time in his company, there was something in the air between them now. The conversation remained polite and detached, as though slipping in any detail of importance would have somehow broken some unspoken promise.

After they had eaten, there was nothing left but to bid him adieu.

"I must thank you most profusely for your care. I am quite in your debt," she said, cringing at the formality that she couldn't quite shake now.

"You owe me nothing," he said, his face unreadable.

"I'll return with your clothes, at the least, after I've given them a wash." It was an expected courtesy, she told herself, not the promise to return that Alison found necessary to enable her to leave him.

"Goodbye," she said. She willed herself not to look back as she followed the path to the woods, clearing the vine as she went.

❧

When she returned to her cottage, she found Willow waiting outside. "I saw you leaving from up on the wall. I've been keeping an eye on you for Gwenla. She's been worried sick."

"Will you walk with me?" Alison asked. "I haven't much time before the meeting, and I need to bathe and change into my last set of clean clothes."

Willow accompanied Alison to the stream while Alison bathed. She sat on the shore, reaching a single paw into the cool waters in pursuit of a fish.

"Tell me of Mr. Ainsley. Gwenla hasn't even spotted him for months, and he shoos me away whenever he notices me watching. How was his temperament?"

"Better when I was unwell. Worse as I got better. He is obstinate and still quite rude at times. But I cannot fault the care he took with me."

"That's good. Gwenla worried about that the most, but she didn't know where else to turn. We almost brought you to Fossholm, but we weren't sure you'd make it there. I convinced her to try with Mr. Ainsley. He'd lent you the cloak, after all. We thought he might have a fondness for you that might allow him to overcome whatever blame he still carries."

"Blame for what exactly? He wouldn't say."

"I'm not surprised," said Willow. "Gwenla just told me what she knew of him yesterday, and only because of your predicament. From what I heard, there was a child that fell ill in the village several years ago. Keir did all he could, calling on them day and night. He wanted to take the child into his care in his own home, like he did for you, but the father would not allow it. When the child did not recover, the father blamed Ainsley. The mother was too consumed with her sorrow to protest. Neither Gwenla nor I were there to witness it firsthand, but there was a scene in town. The family ended up leaving Herot's Hollow for good, and Mr. Ainsley shut himself up in his house and has rarely been seen since. That was around the time the duke stopped coming by as well."

"The duke?"

"Lord Ainsley, Duke of Merelor. The owner of most of these lands. Keir's father."

Alison suddenly remembered where she had heard the name Ainsley–the deed. Her property had been deeded to her ancestor by a Mr. Ainsley long ago, perhaps a second son of an earlier duke.

But there was more to unravel in Willow's words. Mr. Ainsley had lost a child in his care. Caring for Alison must have triggered a number of terrible memories for the man. Alison felt guilty for defying him as she had done and making something that was already difficult worse. And her talk about the loss of her father would have done no better.

"Oh, dear. I've been quite a fool, Willow, and a heartless one at that. I was defiant and the cause of much vexation, I'm sure of it."

"I'm sure you didn't mean it. To be honest, we weren't sure you'd wake when we delivered you. You were so small and fragile in your sleeping state. When I saw you run out of the house last night, I almost thought something had possessed you. You are made of tougher stuff than you look. I'm sure Keir took no offense at the words and actions of someone recovering from such an ailment."

"I'm afraid he did. I'm certain of it." Alison sighed. "There's nothing to be done right now. I'll make him a sincere apology when I return his clothes. And his cloak."

"I must make a confession as well. I've been using the cloak as a bed as it is so very soft on my paws. Gwenla let me into your cottage when you didn't return last night. You see, you've shut out my path inside, which is fine for me. But Dinah was quite upset."

"Dinah? Oh, the cat that belonged to Frances. I've never seen her."

"She's shy. Perhaps you could leave her a little room to come in and out through one of the windows. I understand why you'd prefer to keep the larder closed."

"Of course," said Alison. She had finished bathing and was pulling on her last clean dress. "And don't worry about the cloak. I'll give it a good brushing before I return it."

"If you're sure you must return it," said Willow, trotting along after Alison as she returned to the cottage.

Alison smiled at the cat. "I must. Come, we mustn't be late for the meeting."

Willow dashed off ahead of her, leading her into town.

Chapter Thirteen

THE TOWN MEETING

A pixie lit the streetlamps as Alison and Willow made their way up the high street. They found Gwenla within the town hall setting up the chairs.

"Oh, thank goodness you're alright!" Gwenla pulled Alison into a big hug. "Willow kept me updated on your progress. You must come by and tell me everything tomorrow."

"Of course I will. Tell me what I can do to help."

"Can you bring in the Eighthling chairs for me? They're outside in the model village."

Alison walked past the rows of Fulling chairs Gwenla had just finished setting up and out the other side of the room. There, spanning the length of the town hall, was a perfect replica of the village at one eighth the size, complete with a stream flowing through the middle and a functional mill. The buildings reached up to Alison's waist, and she had to take care to avoid stepping on the Eighthlings as she walked around the outside to the replica town hall.

She retrieved four stacks of chairs roughly the size of her hand and tucked them against her side, carrying them back to the larger town hall.

"Just in the front, dear," said Gwenla. "Willow, will you go make sure everyone knows we're starting at seven?"

"Yes, ma'am," said Willow.

Alison helped Gwenla set out the tea and biscuits. Then she made a sign-in sheet and placed it on a table by the entrance.

"Oh, I don't think we need that," said Gwenla. "I know who everyone is."

"It's not really for us. I had an idea about the thief. I'm not leaving a pen out. Let's see if some of our neighbors supply their own."

"I'd say that I wouldn't expect the thief to be so foolish, but they did rob a store during daylight after all. And it's more than the constables have done so far."

As they spoke, the villagers trickled in. There were many Alison recognized: the schoolteacher Lady Sibba, the blacksmith Mr. Gilroy, and the innkeeper Mr. Rainey. Brytak had come with his parents, who he enthusiastically introduced to Alison, and the fairy brother and sister Mezec the apothecary and Lydiach the tailor introduced Alison to their father, her neighbor Aras who herded sheep. There were also a dozen or more faces unfamiliar to Alison. It seemed the entire town had shown up. Everyone except for Mr. Ainsley, Alison noted. She hadn't expected him to show, and yet she was still disappointed when he didn't.

The last to arrive were constables Tirrin and Lord Wexenas, undoubtedly hoping the meeting would provide a new lead in their case. Or perhaps merely to enjoy the free refreshments, of which they took more than their fair share.

"Thank you, everyone, for coming." Gwenla had taken her place at the podium. She gestured to Alison to join her in the chair to the right. Willow hopped into Alison's lap once she had taken her seat.

"I called this meeting to discuss the situation with the vine. Most of you have been involved in our previous efforts to eradicate it. Those efforts failed. We're here to share knowledge and discuss new ideas to solve the problem for once and for all."

There was a "here, here" from the crowd, but no one stood to speak. Gwenla continued.

"As for me, I've developed a routine of slashing that keeps the worst of the growth at bay. I've tried pulling it up by the roots, but they refuse to pull in one piece, and any tiny segment will grow a new section. They also don't turn to ash like the main stretches. And while they can be cut into pieces, those pieces must be stored because they will not burn, and I've yet to devise a suitable container that they don't ultimately escape. They've broken glass jars and wooden boxes, and Weyland here helped me seal them in a box made of iron which I thought would surely do the trick, but before the month was out, the box had cracked open, and on they grew."

There were some murmurs and gasps throughout the crowd. Even Alison was surprised. What kind of horrible thing could split its way through iron? If this was truly what the vine was capable of, Alison couldn't help but think maybe it was time to abandon the town. Maybe the entire continent.

But there was one man who was unimpressed. The Halfling innkeeper Mr. Rainey raised his hand and slowly stood up. "I get that it grows like crazy. But why is that such a problem? No one has been hurt as far as I know. We've got a real problem in this town that nobody's talking about. There's a thief in our midst!"

"Mr. Rainey, sit down," said Mezec, the fairy who had been robbed. "The constables are here for a reason. There haven't been any other robberies after mine. It seems that I was targeted. I'm sure they'll get to the bottom of it soon enough."

Detective Constable Lord Wexenas saw his moment and took it, striding forth to stand beside Alison in the front. "We've been following up on a number of leads. If anyone has any information to share with us, we'll be here after the meeting. And please come to us soon. We'd like to get out of this town before that vine eats you all." That elicited a couple of nervous giggles from the crowd. Lord Wexenas was pleased with himself. He gave an exaggerated bow and returned to stand against the back wall with Tirrin.

"Many thanks to our fine constables," said Gwenla, taking her meeting back. "Now, has anyone tried anything else to eliminate the vine? Or does anyone have any ideas they'd like to share?"

Silence again. Willow adjusted her position in Alison's lap as Alison fidgeted with the clasp on her satchel.

Finally, the fairy shepherd Aras flew up from his seat at the front until he was level with Gwenla's head. Alison could see the family resemblance between Mezec, Lydiach, and Aras–all of them had the same green hair in varying shades and large elvish ears. Aras wore a tiny set of farm clothes that were so like Mr. Ainsley's, it was as if Mr. Ainsley had purchased a matching set for a doll and gifted it to the fairy.

"I've tried quite a few things myself. I tried burning it to no avail. Then I hitched a plow to my horses and tried turning the dirt over. It keeps it back for a time, but if any roots survive, it returns, and often far worse than before. I've wondered sometimes if the vine doesn't have a mind of its own. I've noticed that it responds to my more drastic measures with violent regrowth, sometimes popping up somewhere else entirely. I spend most of my days keeping it out of my sheep pasture. The only way I've been able to keep some land free for their next rotation is with Gwenla's help. It's more work when the vine is as big around as you are."

"Thank you, Aras," said Gwenla. "I've noticed the response from the vine as well. And for those of you who joined us on our last great cutting, you'll recall how the vine had been barely growing for weeks when we decided to tackle it, and how once we'd begun, it regrew with such force that I thought we'd have to abandon the town."

"What happened then?" asked Alison. "How did you get it back under control?"

"We didn't. We kept cutting back a perimeter, and within a few days, it seemed to return to its normal growth. We didn't dare try such a drastic removal again," said Aras.

"I wrote to our lord the Duke of Merelor at the king's court after that incident," said Gwenla. "He responded with his concern and suggested a few remedies that unfortunately we had already tried. I sent a few more requests for further aid, but I never received a response."

"You should tell that useless son of his to get off his arse and take care of his birthright," said the innkeeper. There were some nods and murmurs of approval.

Alison realized he was talking about Mr. Ainsley. She wasn't sure what he meant by his birthright; she supposed Mr. Ainsley's father must have owned much of the property in Herot's Hollow, and that Mr. Ainsley must be in line to inherit it.

"Keir is not our lord. I believe we should try his father again, unless anyone has a better suggestion?" asked Gwenla.

Lady Sibba rose to speak. "Perhaps the scholars at the University might offer some assistance?"

"That's a good thought, my lady. Would you be willing to help us with a letter?" asked Gwenla.

"I would be delighted. They may require some time to deliberate on the best course of action. I shouldn't think it would be more than a year or so before we have a response."

"Leave it to an elf to offer a solution that none of us may live to see," muttered Willow so that only Alison could hear her. Or so she had thought. A couple of fairies giggled, and Lady Sibba gave the cat–and Alison–a stern look.

"What of the king?" asked a Quarterling Alison didn't recognize. The small woman didn't look like the hobgoblins who had carried her cases at the inn or the korrigan who she'd met on the ferry. She wore a shimmering gray gown and had long copper hair which reached to the floor. A selkie, another rare type of fey folk. Although maybe they were less rare than she thought.

"The king will offer us nothing," spat Mr. Gilroy. The blacksmith, who had been imprisoned and enslaved by King Derkomai, unsurprisingly had little good to say of their ruler.

"I don't have an idea to share, or anything that I've tried personally, but I do have some information that might be interesting," said Lydiach. "When Ms. Lennox visited my shop the other day, her dress had been torn on one of the thorns. The sap soaked into the garment, and when I threw it into the fire, the cloth did not burn. There may be some use for the vine after all. Perhaps we should seek to control it rather than destroy it. If someone were able to assist me with taking a sample, I'd be so grateful. I'd try myself, but the thorns are as big as my head."

"I'm not sure we should try to take samples. Alison, were you harmed by the vine at all? I wonder if that has anything to do with your fall," said Gwenla.

"I don't believe I was. There was no mark upon my skin," said Alison.

"Gwenla, I've told you the nonsense about the poison is just that. If the vine does have some use as Lydiach says, the scholars would love to hear it. They may expedite our request. I'll help Lydiach with the sample. I can send it with the letter," said Lady Sibba.

"Now, I don't think that's a good idea. What if you were to injure yourself?" asked Gwenla.

"The hands of an elf are a finer tool than the hands of a dwarf," said Lady Sibba coolly.

"I don't need educating on elvish hands, and you know it," said Gwenla. Her ears reddened, and she stood up as tall as her elderly posture allowed.

Alison could see that this was going nowhere. She stood to take the podium. "Thank you for your offer of help, Lady Sibba. In the meantime while we await the University's response, what else can we do? Does anyone have any ideas for immediate solutions?"

A Halfling with glasses and tightly coiled hair raised his hand meekly. "Yes, please stand and speak," said Alison.

He addressed Alison directly, looking only at her. "Hello, Ms. Lennox. I am the town historian and archivist, Mr. Duncan Corbett. I believe the issue with all of our solutions is that we aren't getting to the 'root' of the problem, if you'll allow it. Where did the vine come from? It seems important to know its origin if we're to find a permanent solution."

Many people began speaking over each other.

"Hold on, Mr. Corbett. We've just established that there could be value in the vine–"

"Value or not, the vine is a threat, and we must find a way to rid ourselves of it before–"

"Before it tarnishes the appearance of the village? Outside of its threat to the farmlands, I really don't see–"

"Enough!" shouted Alison. She rubbed the knot on her head. Shouting had set off the headache once more. Maybe Mr. Ainsley had been right about staying in bed a while longer. "We are discussing all ideas. We've heard from those that want to study the vine. Now let's hear ideas on getting rid of it. No one is jumping up to do anything right at this moment. There's no harm in hearing everyone out."

Gwenla nodded and grimaced, her face an apology for getting caught up in the fray.

"Thank you," whispered Mr. Corbett. "Now, I've read many books on the flora and fauna of Wilderise and Loegria. And even some on the lands further south and east. And I've seen nothing matching the description of this vine in any book on nature. I posit that this is because the vine is not natural. It is supernatural. It is of the old magic. And the solution will lie with the old magic too. Has anyone encountered the spriggan lately?"

The old magic. Mr. Ainsley had a book on the subject. Alison would not bring it up in this forum, however. She would have to ask Mr. Ainsley about it directly when she returned his clothes.

"No, and I hope your plan don't involve him. He's not too fond of townsfolk," said Brytak. "The smithy is close to the forest, and I'm certain he's to blame for the sudden gust of wind that nearly takes my dear sister Strelka off her feet and over the ledge when she brings the cart down from the mountain. The dwarves in the mine say the spriggan fights with the knockers that help them down there and leaves them bloodied. He's probably the one that stole the ink from Mezec. And I heard a tale of a changeling child–"

"Thank you, Brytak. Can someone tell me what a spriggan is? And does he bother travelers?" asked Alison.

"Alison, no. You can't go," said Gwenla. She had seen Alison's design. "It's much too dangerous. He's an old spirit of the woods. No one has seen him in ages–we don't dare approach him. He resents the village for clearing his forest. That's why he hurts us."

Alison could see the realization as it dawned on Gwenla. "Ah. A spirit of the woods with a grudge, and an unstoppable magical vine."

"I'm not suggesting that the spriggan has unleashed the vine, though I can't rule out the theory," said Mr. Corbett. "I've seen no such suggestion in the works I've studied, but many were lost in the fire last century. But if someone were to understand the vine's magic, then it has to be someone who remembers the old ways."

"I will seek out the spriggan," said Alison. "I'm not of this town, so perhaps he will be kinder to me."

"Your ancestors were here once, though. A distant memory for your people, but maybe not for the spriggan," said Gwenla. "We don't know how to seek him anyway."

"There is one who could help," said Willow. She hopped up onto the podium, and no one appeared alarmed by her speech. Gwenla, however, looked betrayed. "The Wildcat of the Woods. Though he can be foul-tempered, and perhaps it's unwise to trust his guidance. But if someone knows how to find the spriggan, it's him."

"Will you take me to him?" Alison asked.

"On the morrow," said Willow.

"Well, that's settled then," said Lady Sibba as she rose. "I'll collect the sample and send it to the scholars with my letter. Ms. Lennox will seek the wildcat and the spriggan. Gwenla will write to our lord once more. We have our course of action."

"Yes, well–" Gwenla started, but the crowd had applauded. Then they began to take their leave.

"The plan is sound, Gwenla. I'll be careful seeking the spriggan," said Alison.

"Let's discuss it more tomorrow. Both of you," she said with a glare at Willow. "Thank you for helping. It's a shame Mr. Ainsley couldn't make it. I'm looking forward to hearing of your time with him."

Alison felt the heat rise in her cheeks, though she didn't understand why. There had been no suggestion in Gwenla's query.

"Oh, what of your ploy with the sign-in sheet? Do we have a culprit?" asked Gwenla as they walked toward the exit together. The constables were busy chatting with the innkeeper and Brytak's father.

"Let's see," said Alison. "Hmm. It looks like there's one name in green ink: Mr. Weyland Gilroy. But it can't be him. I was with him when the robbery occurred."

"Well, it was a fine idea anyway," said Gwenla. "Come, let's head back. I'm exhausted."

Alison was too. She and Gwenla followed Willow down the lamplit path to Orchard Lane. When Alison reached her gate, she felt compelled to continue down to the gate at the end of the road. But she turned back inside; she told herself she would see Mr. Ainsley tomorrow, and that would be enough. She almost believed it.

Chapter Fourteen

THE WILDCAT OF THE WOODS

A weight pressed against Alison's chest. It went from a general feeling of heaviness to the clear sensation of two points pressing just below Alison's collarbones as she rubbed the sleep from her eyes.

"Food."

Alison tried to sit, but the weight held her down.

"Food," it said again. Alison reached for the matches at the bedside. The movement caused the mass to shift and then to jump to the ground.

It was a cat, of course, but it wasn't Willow. Alison fumbled with the matches in the dark, finally lighting the candle on the nightstand.

The cat was larger than Willow but leaner, and while it had some of Willow's tabby markings on its face, most of its body was the color of crème brûlée; its ears, legs, and tail the same color as the dark patches that formed where the sugar turned to caramel. Its eyes were as blue as Alison's and almost as large, the largest eyes Alison had ever seen on a cat.

"Dinah," she whispered. The cat purred and brushed up against the bed in response.

"Food." Dinah lifted a paw and pulled it towards her face.

Alison yawned. "It's too early, girl. The sun isn't up yet. I don't know if I have anything you could eat, anyway."

Dinah hopped back onto the bed and stomped her way onto Alison's lap.

"Food."

Alison realized this must have been what Willow meant when she said she had been teaching Dinah to speak. "Is 'food' all you can say?"

Dinah repeated the gesture to her face. "Food."

"I'll ask Gwenla if she has anything in a couple of hours." Alison tried to turn to blow out the candle, but Dinah didn't budge.

"Food," she said, but a little more desperately.

Alison groaned. "Why don't you go to the stream and catch a fish? Or look around the cupboards downstairs for a mouse. Or even better yet, there's a wren that needs to be taught a lesson somewhere near the hedge maze."

Dinah stomped up Alison's lap to her belly.

"Ow," said Alison, trying to avoid the cat's claws without pushing her off entirely.

Dinah purred loudly. She tucked her head under Alison's arm, forcing it into a pet.

"If you're smart enough to do that, you ought to be able to feed yourself."

Dinah turned her big blue eyes up at Alison. "Food?"

There was no avoiding it. Alison sighed loudly, rolling from the soft comfort of her bed in resignation. She carefully avoided the pails and cups she had spread around the room to catch the rain, following Dinah down the stairs into the kitchen.

"Can you eat cheese?" she asked the cat. Brytak had brought a hard yellow cheese in a cloth with one of his deliveries.

Dinah gave no verbal response. She had reverted to the more feral meows that Alison was accustomed to.

Alison tripped her way to the larder with the cat circling her legs all the while. "How about some eggs? Would you eat some eggs if I fried them?"

Dinah meowed excitedly.

Alison lit the stove, groggily preparing Dinah a finer breakfast in the middle of the night than she normally made for herself on a lazy Saturday morning. When it was ready, Alison placed it onto a small dish in front of Dinah.

Dinah gave it a hesitant sniff, and then a tiny lick. And then she ate a dainty bite, and finally she gave such a huge chomp that it looked like she had unhinged her jaw like a snake.

"Glad you like it. I'm going back to bed," Alison said. She dragged her exhausted body up the first few stairs, glancing back to the cat.

Dinah had stopped eating, leaving half of the meal untouched.

"Really?" said Alison. After all of that, this was all the cat was going to eat?

Dinah purred. She ran past Alison and up the stairs, back onto the bed.

Alison wedged herself next to her, one leg off the bed and most of her body uncovered as the cat pressed the linens down.

"Great," said Alison. "At least one of us will sleep well."

Dinah was gone by the time Alison woke again to the knock at her door. Alison was cold and cramped from the unnatural position she had assumed during her second sleep. And worse yet, more rain had fallen overnight. The first task of the day, after answering the door, would be emptying the containers before they overflowed.

Her morning visitor was Gwenla. The dwarf looked at Alison's unkempt state with concern. "Are you unwell? Should I see if Keir will come by?"

Alison briefly considered whether or not to feign an illness just to see him, but she didn't want to worry him unduly. "No, I'm quite alright. I received a visit from Dinah in the night. She insisted upon a five-course breakfast, and I had no choice but to oblige."

Gwenla laughed merrily. "Oh, that Dinah! She is a troublesome girl, but I'm glad to hear that she's come 'round. Willow will be so pleased to know you're caring for her."

"Perhaps Willow can ask her to await the dawn before demanding her breakfast tomorrow."

"I wouldn't count on it."

Gwenla swept through the cottage, taking care of Alison's neglected chores with the same haste as on the day they had met. She even helped with the clothes washing, a task Alison hadn't done by hand in quite some time. All the while they spoke, first of her fall and Mr. Ainsley.

"By the time I found you, you were drenched to the bone. Brytak was out in the street; I got him to bring his cart up so we could move you without jostling you too much. When Willow suggested Keir, I thought we were making a mistake."

"Why is that?"

"It's not that I don't think him capable as a physician. But after what happened with little Jack, I thought he wouldn't be able to handle it."

"Was that the boy he lost?" asked Alison.

"Yes," said Gwenla, looking up from the washboard into the distance. "It was such a shame. The child was no more than seven, a bright little boy. About the same age as Keir's brother was when he died, and the boy had a bit of Danny in him too. The same wild courage and mischief."

Alison paused from attaching the clothespins to a dress. "Keir–I mean, Mr. Ainsley–lost a brother?"

Gwenla's eyes were misty when they met Alison's. "Oh, that was a tragedy too. Keir has had more than his share of them, I'm afraid."

"What happened?"

"To Danny? I heard the tale from their governess when she passed through town. The boys were playing near the falls. Fossholm–that's where the duke's manor is–it's down in the valley, and there's a spectacular waterfall just a bit before the lake."

Alison realized she had heard of the exact place from Nolwynn, the korrigan she had met on the ferry. She chose not to interrupt Gwenla, though. Her voice was quivering with emotion, and Alison didn't want to sidetrack her needlessly.

"Keir was older, ten maybe, but he was the more cautious of the two. When they'd come 'round Herot's Hollow, Keir would always be quietly reading under a tree while Danny was up at the top of it, throwing acorns down at passersby. The way Keir told it when he came back alone was that he had warned Danny not to go out too far in the river so near the falls, but Danny didn't listen. I don't doubt that was the case, but Lord Ainsley blamed Keir nonetheless. With their mother gone since both were very young, there was no one there to set him right."

Alison stood still, holding her breath. "That's horrible."

"Aye," said Gwenla. "And the little boy Jack was so like him. Keir had gone off to study medicine at the King's College, and when he came back, he took up the house down the street. Jack was the first baby he delivered."

Alison couldn't imagine why Mr. Ainsley would return here at all. "Why did he come back here if this place holds such terrible memories for him?"

Gwenla resumed running Mr. Ainsley's clothes over the washboard. "He has no choice. He will be the duke one day, no matter what his father thinks of him. I imagine his living here is part of whatever bargain they struck."

The curse of the fee tail again, only worse. Mr. Ainsley's life, privileged with wealth and comfort though it may have been, was set out before him from birth. Whatever circumstances had befallen him since mattered not a bit.

"And what happened to Jack? Willow mentioned a sleeping sickness."

"It came on slowly. At first, it was cute. Jack would nod off in the middle of running around or talking. It seemed like his playfulness was just catching up to him. But the sleep lasted longer and longer until he was out more than he was awake. That was when they took him to Keir. The man tried everything. He was down at the schoolhouse and the archives and the post office every day, reading and writing letters, trying to figure it out. He poked and prodded at the child, tried tonics and herbs and all sorts of remedies. I'd see him running down the street in the middle of the night, torch in hand, off to try some idea he had in his sleep."

"But nothing worked."

"No, it didn't. Finally, the child fell into a deep slumber and did not wake. At first, they managed to feed him and keep him clean. But eventually he could no longer eat or drink. Keir refused to leave his side. I brought him some things from his house during that time. I'm not sure he even saw me in the room, he was so mad with exhaustion and desperation. I heard later that he didn't want to leave Jack even after the undertaker had come for the boy. That was the final straw for the father, who had somehow convinced himself that Keir killed Jack."

Alison was disgusted. "Why on earth would he think that?"

"Don't be too hard on him. The man was consumed with grief too. I'm not saying what he did was right, and it certainly cost Keir a lot. But it was a terrible time for the entire town."

"What did the father do?"

"I wasn't there to see it, but I heard it from Mezec afterwards. At first, the father just yelled and cursed at Keir in the street. But eventually, he threw a punch. And then he drew a knife. Weyland–he was different then; this is before the king took him–had to hold the man until the constables arrived. Keir ran off, and he closed himself up in the house. I guess he thought we all blamed him for what had happened. I went by fairly often at first, but he refused me. I left him some things outside, and for a long time he refused them as well. But finally one day, he took my offering of ink and paper. I brought him a variety of things over the next few weeks, learning what he needed from what he took. I still bring a few things by every now and then."

Alison felt a wave of warmth in her chest for the lovely old dwarf. "So you're his secret benefactor. How incredibly kind of you."

Gwenla smiled gently. "Kind, I suppose, but there's a bit of a selfish reason behind it. I watched Keir grow up over all those years; we both did. Lady Willana had a soft spot for him. She used to teach him old songs and tell him tales of the old days. It brought her such joy. I know it would pain her terribly to see him this way. It's part of why I was so excited that you'd seen him and talked to him. And why I gave in and took you to him even though I wasn't sure he would help you."

"What did he do when you brought me there? Was he angry?"

"Not at all. He brought you inside by the fire, dried you off, and dressed you in the shirt off his back. I hadn't seen him that way…well, since Jack. He was frantic but focused. He called out orders for Brytak and me. We did our best to keep up, but he pushed us aside when we couldn't move fast enough for him. He was in his element, and though I was terribly worried for you, I felt I'd made the right choice in bringing you there. I stayed for a little while, out of the way. Once he'd finished bandaging you, he snapped back out of it. He turned cold and distant and asked me to leave."

"He was the same when I was there. It was like he only knew what to do with me when I was at my worst."

Gwenla had finished the washing and emptied the basin out in the yard, as far out as the vine would allow her. "Be gentle with him. It's been a long time since he's had any sort of regular company. Will you see him before you go to the Wildcat?"

"The Wildcat first, to give the clothes time to dry. Although that's if Willow shows up to take me."

The cat took her time. By the time she had arrived, half of the morning was gone, and Gwenla and Alison had caught up on all the chores.

"I wish I could come with you," said Gwenla as they were preparing to leave. "But the Wildcat holds a grudge, and he hasn't forgiven me for the last time."

"What happened last time?" asked Alison.

"She threatened to have him neutered," said Willow.

Willow led the way down the garden path and into the woods. There was a fog hanging low to the ground that obscured the view and wrapped the bare trunks of the trees in a clinging mist. Alison felt it cling to her skin as well when she passed through it.

Once they reached the stream, they turned to the east.

"Won't this take us through Aras's property?" asked Alison.

"Yes, but paths like this are free for anyone to roam. And it's quicker than going into town."

Willow trotted along confidently, stopping only occasionally to examine a particularly interesting bug. The woods grew denser the further they ventured, and the path was more poorly defined. Branches hung low and crossed into the path, forcing Alison to duck down to avoid getting scratched.

Before long, they reached a stepping-stone path across a shallow point of the stream. Willow pranced across, barely altering her gait. Alison was more cautious, carefully stepping with both feet on each stone. "How much further?" she asked when she reached the other side. It was cool in the forest's shade, and the impenetrable canopy beyond made her uneasy.

"We're nearly there," said Willow. "Watch your step."

A tree had fallen over the path; its trunk reaching higher than Alison's hips. Alison clambered over it, pulling her skirt nearly to her waist to clear the trunk. Willow jumped on top of it in a single bound. She sharpened her claws on the bark before jumping down on the other side.

"See that den up ahead?" she asked, pointing with her body at what Alison had seen as a pile of sticks.

Upon further inspection, Alison could see the handiwork in the burrow. The sticks were propped against the hollow of the roots of an enormous birch, forming a kind of hut in the tree's shade. A wisp of smoke trailed up through a gap in the structure and along a white trunk into the tiny green leaves that made up the canopy. Though the craftsmanship was not remarkable, there was a rustic appeal to it. And Alison had learned from recent experience that she could do no better.

"He's home," said Willow. She turned to face Alison, the tabby "M" of her brow furrowed and tense. "He can be temperamental. Just follow my lead, okay?"

Alison nodded. Willow bounded up the path and scratched on the door with Alison trailing behind.

"Who goes there?"

The voice from within was deeper than Alison had expected. There was a hint of a growl to it, a warning.

"It's Willow. And my human companion–"

"Not Gwenla." The Wildcat hissed.

"No, not Gwenla. She's a dwarf. This is Alison, a human, as I said."

Alison felt she ought to say something, but it seemed strange to talk to a house. "Hello, there," she called, trying to visualize the Wildcat's location within.

"Does she not know I can hear her?"

The Wildcat pushed through an opening in the sticks that seemed impossibly small for a creature his size. He was bigger than Willow, but only just. His fur was much like

Willow's tabby coat except longer, browner, and full of stripes in place of her spots. His tail, which he raised to allow Willow a sniff, was shorter and thicker than Willow's with a set of perfect black rings near the tip. Though he stood tall, puffing his fur out as intimidatingly as possible, Alison couldn't help but find him very darling.

She had quite an urge to scratch him behind his lovely ears, but she resisted. "Dear Wildcat," she said. "I come to you for help."

The Wildcat laughed. "Bold, isn't she?" he said to Willow. He paced around her, sniffing her fur and paying Alison absolutely no mind.

"She is a good friend to us. Dinah is quite taken with her," said Willow.

"Dinah is a simpering fool. Beautiful, but foolish," said the Wildcat. "And you are as well, if you're out here helping this one. Though she does have beautiful eyes. Quite like Dinah's, I'd say."

"Indeed," purred Willow. "She is a pretty thing, and kind. She seeks the spriggan. Not for her own gain, but to help the town."

"Then she is a bigger fool than Dinah. The spriggan will never help her."

"Why not?" asked Alison. She was beginning to feel quite foolish indeed, standing around in the woods watching two cats talk about her as if she wasn't there.

The Wildcat finally turned to face her. "Because of what your kind has done to our land. There were once a thousand wildcats and walruses and will-o'-the-wisps, bears and boars and beithir, cù-sìth and cat-sìth and spriggans too. Now the few of us that hold on have little left, and there are whispers of a great change coming from o'er the sea. The spriggan has no love for the village, and he'll have no love for you either. You'd be wisest not to seek him. The old magic flows through him still, and it has powers beyond your wildest imaginings."

"What do you know of the old magic?" asked Alison.

The Wildcat hopped up a path through the roots of the tree until he rested on a branch above Alison's head. "I know enough to not want to know more."

Alison sighed. "I'm not thrilled to find out more myself, but in case no one has mentioned it, we're overrun in the village by something that came from the old magic. A vine. And it was suggested that the spriggan might know something."

"You blame the spriggan? Foolish girl. Willow, I hope you have other company. This one isn't long for this world, and Gwenla is a miserable old witch."

Willow hissed and bared her teeth. "Watch what you say."

The Wildcat arched its back and bared its fangs as well. They were quite a big longer than Willow's and scarily sharp. And the Wildcat had the high ground. Alison didn't fear for herself, but she wouldn't be able to stand it if Willow was hurt.

"Yes, I'm foolish, but no, I don't plan to tell the spriggan someone suggested the vine was his doing. I just want to ask him if he knows anything of it. Not how to get rid of it, not how it came to be. Just a general question of knowledge. And if he takes great offense, I'll leave," said Alison. She had spent much of her walk with Willow considering how best to address the creature.

"If he lets you," said the Wildcat. "Fine, I can see that you are decided. To bring him forth, you must bind branches three: oak, fir, and chestnut. Bind them with a strip of willow bark and carry them through the woods to the north of here. Chant three times: 'I summon the spirit of the forest.' If he doesn't appear, you haven't gone far enough."

"I'm to summon the spirit of the forest with broken branches? Won't that make him angry?" asked Alison.

The Wildcat stretched and yawned, jumping down to rest at her feet. "You asked me how to find him, and I told you. If you have another way of bringing him forth, by all means."

"And if something were to go wrong? Do you know of anything to subdue the creature?" asked Alison.

"A fair question. I would suggest something of the old magic–the vine, if you can bring it along."

"It turns to ash when cut."

"Even better. Perhaps scattered in a circle, the ashes would bind him. I can't say for sure, but I certainly wouldn't let him see you try." He turned to face Willow. "The next time you come, I hope you'll come alone. Or perhaps bring that Dinah with you. If I must meet with fools, I might as well meet with pretty fools."

The Wildcat slipped back into the crack between the sticks without another word.

Willow trotted back the way they came, pausing to rub against Alison's legs once they were out of earshot.

"He was in a fine mood today. Come, let's hurry back. I'm sure Gwenla can help us with the branches."

"No need," said Alison. "I know just where to find them all."

A thrill ran through Alison as she considered the locations. The willow from the fence that circled her house. The oak by the stream where she'd first met Mr. Ainsley. The chestnut in his yard, where she had sat with him on a bench. And she had always smelled fir on his clothes, so she knew there must be one nearby. Her heart fluttered in her chest as she thought of seeing him again.

"Hurry," said Alison to Willow, racing along ahead of her for once. "There's no time to lose."

Chapter Fifteen

THE SPRIGGAN

Alison wielded her machete with wild abandon, removing the vine and scooping its ashes into a small pouch. Then she freed a strip of willow bark from her fence before whacking her machete once more at an off-shoot at the base of the oak by the stream. With the sun directly overhead, she had only a few hours left to see Mr. Ainsley and meet the spriggan before dark. In her haste, she almost set off for his house without the clothes she'd borrowed from him. She doubled back down the path to the cottage, yanking the tunic and pants from the clothesline without removing the pins.

She practically ran through the woods and past the stone circle, nearly catching her dress on the vine once she reached the path down to his front door. When she arrived at the cleared section of land that made up his yard, she finally slowed down. Her heart was in her throat, pounding from the exertion and the anticipation.

As she made slow and careful steps forward, she pictured herself knocking on the door. What would she say to him? She knew she mustn't mention what she learned of his past from Gwenla lest he retreat into himself once more. But what could she possibly say to convince him to stick around for a while? She was met with a dark thought: what if he didn't want that? What if he didn't wish to see her at all?

Her fears proved to be quite unfounded. Before she had reached the door, Mr. Ainsley threw it open, taking long strides to join her in the yard. His face was freshly shaven and his hair newly trimmed, and he wore a fine gray waistcoat over a white shirt, the sleeves rolled up to the elbows. The lighter colors made a nice contrast with his tan skin and dark hair. Alison felt a flush rise into her cheeks when he greeted her with a surprisingly bright smile.

"Ms. Lennox," he said, bowing his head slightly. "How kind of you to return my clothes so promptly. Freshly laundered, as well. And you've also brought me…some sticks?"

"Oh no, those aren't for you. Although now I'm feeling quite regretful that I didn't think to bring you a gift to say thank you for caring for me," said Alison. She hadn't been expecting the warm reception, and frankly, it put her a bit off her guard. She wondered if perhaps she had misremembered him.

He closed the distance between them and took the clothes from her hands while she fumbled with the branch and the strip of bark. He smelled delightfully of his usual fir and woodsmoke, along with the hint of something citrusy and vaguely medicinal, a shaving balm, perhaps.

"You've cut your hair," she said lamely. Her usual easy manners just weren't coming to her.

"I have," he said. "The days are getting warmer now, and it's nice to feel the breeze on my neck."

"It suits you," she mumbled. "Not that your hair wasn't fine before. It was."

His face registered surprise and then a hint of a smile followed by the briefest look of longing before settling once more on pleasantly neutral. He was a man of many thoughts, and Alison wished she knew exactly what they were. "Would you like to come in for tea?" he asked.

Alison could see then what this was; the manners of someone raised to become the duke had returned to him at last. "I would love to, but I'm in something of a hurry. Actually, I could use your help. Would you mind if I cut a small branch from your chestnut? And do you know where I might find a fir tree?"

Mr. Ainsley frowned, his demeanor shifting. "What need do you have for all of that?" he asked.

"If you had been at the meeting last night, you might have already known," she said lightly, trying to make it sound like a tease rather than an admonition. "There are a few plans in motion to deal with the vine, but my part of it is to see the spriggan. I've been to the Wildcat of the Woods just now, and he told me how to–"

"Are you mad?" He said each word slowly, enunciating them as if each were a separate sentence. The light and joy had drained completely from his face. Alison felt an immediate regret for ruining the moment.

"No, I don't think I am. Mr. Corbett–he's the Halfling that keeps the town archives–believes the vine is of the old magic, and I tend to agree. The spriggan is of the old magic as well. To be honest, I didn't quite get a sense of what the spriggan is like other than that he has a tense relationship with the villagers, but I take it he's some kind of forest spirit, and there's a logic in asking a wood spirit about a vine, don't you think?"

As she spoke, Mr. Ainsley paced back and forth, his eyes on the ground. He stopped in front of her suddenly, punctuating his words with the movement of his hand. "No, I don't think there's a logic in risking your life over nothing. This has gone too far. I've a mind to see Gwenla and insist she stops this nonsense."

"Don't talk about Gwenla that way. She was against seeing the spriggan as well. But the other solutions could take ages, and we have to try something. I'm not from this village. There's a chance the spriggan won't be threatened by me."

"A chance. You want to risk everything on a chance? Do you even know what a spriggan is?"

Well, he had her there. "I assume it's like a talking tree or something?"

"A talking tree with the power to bring down the forest on top of you."

"So I was half right," she said. She couldn't help but smile a little.

"I can't believe you aren't taking this seriously. I know you think we're needlessly superstitious out here, but there are things here that you don't understand. Dangerous things."

"Like the vine?" This time, she had him. "Look, I am going whether you help me or not. I'm sure I can find another chestnut tree, and I suspect there's quite a bit of fir around here considering the way you always smell of it…" She trailed off. She hadn't meant to say that part out loud.

Mr. Ainsley swallowed and stared at the ground in front of her. "I won't let you do this," he said, but he couldn't meet her gaze.

"How are you going to stop me? Will you tie me to the bed as you threatened the other night?"

He opened his mouth as if to speak and then closed it again. Alison felt the heat climb the back of her neck. "I'll be on my way then," she said, turning back towards the path.

"Wait," he said, grabbing her arm. "Fine. If you insist on risking your life this way, so be it. But I'm coming with you."

If he had expected her to protest, he was sorely mistaken.

❧❀❧

With the bundle of oak, chestnut, and fir tied in willow in hand, they set off through the woods the way Alison had come in the morning. When they passed the spot of the stream where they met, Mr. Ainsley shuddered. Alison hoped the memory wasn't unpleasant for him, but she was too afraid to ask.

Truthfully, she was too afraid to say much of anything. Her fear was not of the creature they sought out; she suspected that if it was anything like the Wildcat, the threat was rather overblown. But she worried that if she said the wrong thing, he might leave her on her own. And the woods were much less pleasant without his company.

When they reached the fallen tree, Alison stopped. "The Wildcat lives just up there. He said to head to the north from here. And we're to say, 'I summon the spirit of the forest.' Then the spriggan should appear. If it doesn't, we're to keep going and try again."

"That doesn't sound like any old magic I've heard of. I believe the Wildcat has played you for the fool."

Alison was tempted to ask more about Mr. Ainsley's experience with the old magic. But she resisted the urge. Instead, she led him over the log and up the path where it turned to the north. "If he has, then no harm done. Perhaps Mr. Corbett can help me research other methods."

"Why are you so determined to do this? Shouldn't you be working on the cottage?"

Indeed she was. "There's little to be done until the thatcher comes on Monday," she said, justifying her actions to herself as much as him. "And the worst of the problems is the vine, so this seemed like a worthwhile endeavor."

"And if the spriggan has a solution for the vine problem, and the thatcher fixes the roof, what then?"

It was a good question. The answer was that then she would be free to do as she had planned all along. She would visit the real estate agent Lady Selelas had recommended and would craft an ad for the local newspaper, and then she'd be off back to Arcas Dyrne. Back to number-crunching and dear Rinka and the squalid little apartment they shared. It was what she wanted, after all. Wasn't it?

Alison found she couldn't say it out loud. There was something wrong with the words. "I don't know," she murmured.

The woods looked different here, wilder and more ragged. In place of the oaks and birches and hazels were great conifers–spruce, pine, and even more firs than in the copse on Mr. Ainsley's property. The land had been rising since the stream, but here it rose more sharply until Alison's shoes struggled to get a grip of the ground. Seeing her struggle, Mr. Ainsley offered her his arm. At first, she refused it, but on her second slip, she took it gratefully. "Do you suppose this is far enough north?"

"I doubt it would hurt to try. I doubt it would do anything at all," said Mr. Ainsley. His expression was smug.

Alison ignored him. She held out the bundle of branches in front of her, reaching her arms into a ray of light that passed through the canopy. She closed her eyes, listening to the sounds of the woods around her. The wind through the trees. The scratch of a squirrel climbing nearby. Birdsong and the flap of wings. She inhaled the strong scent of evergreen, a scent that was irrevocably tied in her mind to Keir. She took a deep breath and let it out slowly. "I summon the spirit of the forest."

She opened her eyes. There was nothing.

"As I said," said Mr. Ainsley. "Can we put this farce to bed?"

"Hold on," said Alison. "We're probably not far enough north."

Mr. Ainsley sighed. "It's a tough climb from here. And we don't want to be in the woods after dark."

"There must be hours of light left," said Alison.

From his waistcoat pocket, Mr. Ainsley pulled a small gold pocket watch on a chain. "A few," he admitted. "But I'm keeping track of how long the trek takes us. We turn back when I say we must, spriggan or no."

Alison could see from his stubborn expression that he didn't mean to continue until she agreed. "Fine," she said.

It was slow going up the hillside. The path was rarely trodden out this far from the town, and twice Mr. Ainsley had to stop her before she walked headlong into a spider's web. He took the lead, pausing every few minutes to allow Alison to try her summons again, and also to let her catch her breath.

"My flat is on the seventh floor. You'd think I'd be used to climbing," she said as she took a sip from his canteen. They sat together on a large stump, backs turned to each other.

"Are there no lifts in your building?" he asked. Alison remembered that he had studied at the King's College and that he had likely spent some time in Arcas Dyrne while there.

"There are, but they're always going down. The building extends quite a bit underground. For the dwarves, you see."

"Of course," he said. "Gwenla's the only dwarf I've met that has a taste for surface-dwelling. And even she used to spend more time in the cellar than anywhere else."

Alison had never heard him speak of the past in such a way. "Back when Lady Willana was alive?" she asked cautiously.

Mr. Ainsley's breath caught in his throat. "Yes," he said. "Back then."

"I'm sorry," said Alison. She leaned back against him. "Gwenla said you were close."

"She had a good, long life." He shook the sadness from his shoulders, standing once more and evaluating their surroundings. "Wait here," he said. "I'll only be a moment."

Alison realized what he must have meant; the call of nature was inescapable on such a long journey. She felt it too. And so rather than doing as he asked, she slipped off into the woods in the other direction.

When she had finished, she returned to the path. He wasn't back yet, but that wasn't necessarily cause for alarm. She took a seat once more on the stump and waited.

Though she had no pocket watch of her own, she could tell when too much time had passed. She retrieved the bunch of branches and set out from the path in the direction he had traveled. "Mr. Ainsley?"

She stood still and listened. The same sounds as before—wind, scratching, and birdsong—nothing more.

She took a few more steps off the path, peering around the trunks of the trees and looking for the sign of footsteps among the undergrowth. "Mr. Ainsley? Are you there?"

This time, she heard the distinctive snapping of branches. The rhythmic sounds of footfall in the forest, heading away from her. "Mr. Ainsley, are you alright?"

She followed the sounds, but the steps were increasing, speeding into a jog. She couldn't see a sign of the man; the branches of the conifers reached out in sharp spikes that concealed much of the view. On more than one occasion, she felt the scratch of their bark against her skin and heard the rip of fabric as they pulled at her dress. She hurried nonetheless, gasping as the ground continued to climb.

She couldn't keep up. The snapping sound was near continuous and fading, growing more distant. She broke headlong into a run, holding her arms and the bundle of branches up to shield her face from the grasping limbs of the evergreens, her heart racing from the effort.

She did not see the cliff until she was over it. She felt her foot dangle into thin air, and then her other foot was slipping on straw and gravel, pulling her over the edge. She frantically reached with her arms, grasping onto a root and holding on with all of her might. The bundle of branches careened down the cliff face, smacking into loose boulders on its way to rest in the valley below.

Alison tried to pull herself up, but she lacked the strength. Her arms strained from the mere effort to hold on. Her head spun–if she could not think of something, she would die here. Or worse yet, the fall wouldn't kill her, only maim her terribly and she would die slowly at the bottom of the valley with the bundle.

And with Keir. She'd heard the footsteps; he must have come over the edge as well. But why had he been running? Had something been chasing him?

He had been right after all. Right about the danger, right about her foolishness. Her hands hurt terribly, from both the effort to grip onto the rough bark and from the scratches she had sustained in running through the forest. She could not hold on any longer. Her left hand faltered and slipped.

"Keir, I'm sorry," she said.

"Alison!" He was calling her, but not from the valley of sharp boulders below. From above, from the forest whence she came.

"Keir!" she cried out. "I'm down here. Hurry!"

"Alison? My Gods," he said. He was standing over the edge, his foot wedged among the roots. He leaned forward, grasped her reaching arm, and pulled. Alison felt a sharp pain in her shoulder, but she didn't care. She clambered up the cliff side, kicking upwards with all of her might. When she'd nearly made it up, he grasped her around the waist with his other arm and pulled her back to him with such force that he fell back into the woods, with Alison coming to rest on top of him.

He panted heavily and held her tightly to him. She could feel all of his strong body against her, the firm muscles of his legs, his abdomen, his chest. The warmth of his skin. And then the brush of his lips on her forehead–momentary, fleeting. Enticing. His arms wrapped around her and stroked her back, then he lifted his hands to her face as he sat them up.

He pulled her head against his chest one more. "I thought I lost you," he whispered.

Before she could reply, there was the snapping of branches again. "Keir–"

Something was moving around them, twining and pulling them apart. Something that looked like a vine, but not the one that enveloped the town. A brown vine that more closely resembled the upper branches of a tree than any kind of ivy or honeysuckle that Alison knew. It pushed Alison backwards and pinned her against the dry bark of a pine as it wrapped itself dangerously around Keir, binding his hands and feet and wrapping around his mouth as he struggled.

The spriggan.

Chapter Sixteen

THE TIES THAT BIND

The spriggan was more tree than man. Though he had the form and size of a human, his skin was made of twisting bark, and his limbs stretched and grew into the restraints that bound Alison and Keir.

The spriggan had taken far more care with Keir's bindings than Alison's. Hers held her to the pine only at the ankles and across the chest, freeing her to move her arms.

There was no time to calm her heart or steel her nerves. She plunged her hand into her dress pocket for the satchel of the vine's ash, taking advantage of the spriggan's focus on Keir. She pulled on the string as carefully as her shaking hands could manage then reached inside with her thumb and index finger, withdrawing just a pinch and dropping it beside her. The ties loosened further.

The spriggan had closed in on Keir, tightening the branches around him like a vise. Keir struggled and thrashed to little effect. The spriggan pulled him upright by the restraints. He wove more and more branches around Keir until the man was nearly indistinguishable from the monster.

Alison never took her eyes off the pair as she slipped from underneath the last of the bindings that held her. She moved quickly, relying on the twisting branches for cover, as she made a circle around the grove of trees. The small pouch of ash wouldn't cover much ground; she had just one shot at binding the creature.

As she reached the halfway point, Keir gasped. The spriggan tightened the restraints on his chest and throat, choking the air from his lungs. Alison broke into a run. A branch flew out towards her, missing her cheek by inches. Another pulled at her ankles. She stumbled, nearly losing her footing, but she managed to stay upright by sheer force of will.

Her pulse pounded in her ears. Her instinctual urge was to run away, to leave the woods and never return. But a single look at Keir–bound, helpless–sent her in rather than out. She cut off the last quarter of the circle, making a straight line for the tree where she had been held.

It wasn't so much a circle as it was a polygon, but the sizzling sound and flash of light told Alison that the binding had worked. The spriggan's branches released Keir in a whirl of winding wood, sending him forcefully out from the ash circle and careening into the base of a cedar.

"Keir!" cried Alison as she ran to him. He was covered in scratches and deep red marks where the branches had ensnared him, and his head lulled forward in a way that brought Alison's stomach into her throat.

"He lives. Though why you desire that, I do not know," said the spriggan. Its voice creaked, the sound of the bending of treetops in a strong breeze. Its long limbs were fully rewound, and it stood cross-armed in the center of the ash circle, resigned.

A different version of Alison might have found the impossible creature fascinating. But this Alison cared about only one thing: the unconscious man slumped to the ground before her. "Keir, please," she whispered. She gently shook him by the shoulders, but he did not wake.

"I can feel him still in this world. The old magic that flows through him binds him to it. Free me from this circle, and I can put an end to that."

"No!" Alison jumped to her feet and stood between the spriggan and Keir, hands shaking at her side. "You will not hurt him."

"Are you sure you don't want me to?"

"I've never been more certain of anything," she said. Her eyes flashed dangerously. If it was unwise to defy a creature such as this one, she did not care. She would not let anything harm Keir.

The spriggan seemed to shrug its wooden shoulders.

Seething with anger, Alison had missed what the spriggan said of the old magic. As her pulse began to slow with the realization that the binding would keep the spriggan from harming them, she grew more curious. "What do you mean 'the old magic flows through him'? Why are you trying to kill us?"

"Not you. Him. Only him."

Alison scoffed. The spriggan was surely what had led them to the cliff. "I nearly died just now."

"That wasn't my intention. But sometimes these things happen." He shifted from foot to foot as if they were uncomfortable without their roots in the ground.

"Why are you trying to kill him then?"

"He is marked by the old magic. Consumed by it. It's a force he can neither control nor understand. It would be a kindness, to him and to this world, to release him from it."

At first, Alison didn't catch his meaning. But then it came to her. "The vine?" she asked. "He's responsible for it?" She looked at Keir's sleeping form, peaceful and pitiful on the ground. Surely it couldn't be true.

"Yes," said the spriggan plainly. Its face, or rather its strange wooden approximation of a face, was unreadable.

Alison felt many things–anger, disbelief, regret–but the most poignant of them was betrayal. How could he have let her come out here if he knew the truth about the vine all along? Why didn't he tell her?

"How did it happen?" she asked the spriggan. "Did he summon it?"

"He did, but he does not know it. It was born of a magic he called on, but it twisted itself in his pain to something beyond his reckoning or recognition."

"The child," Alison realized. "It was from the child he tried to save." He hadn't lied to her then; he didn't even know himself what he had done.

"I'm surprised you can't sense it. I feel a shadow of the old magic in you as well."

"What does that mean? Am I connected to the vine as well?" Had she been scratched by it after all?

"No, at least not as far as I can tell. I can't read you the way I can read him. You are a whisper whereas he is a full-throated shout." He kicked at a patch of dirt. "Will you release me? Do you see now why he must perish?"

"Is there no other way to be free of the vine?" asked Alison. "What does it matter to you what happens to the vine anyway? Aren't you of the old magic too?"

"I am born of it. He has attempted to bend it to his will, but it refused him. The old magic is neither good nor bad. It simply is. There is something he needs within the magic he has brought into the world, but what impact that magic will have on the world is beyond his control."

Alison recalled Keir saying something similar about nature. She longed for him to wake so that he could hear this too, but she worried what he would do once he realized he was to blame.

"Why do you want to stop it?" she asked.

"I am a guardian of these woods, and I wield the old magic as their champion. I extinguish that which threatens them. In this case, the threat comes from him."

"There must be another way. A way to stop the magic without taking his life with it."

The spriggan stood still for a long moment, so long that he blended into the trees around him. Alison could almost forget that he was capable of moving at all. She checked on Keir–sleeping, but beginning to stir–as she waited. Finally, after a long silence, the spriggan spoke. "There may be. But it will be for him to decide, and I can feel in his heart he isn't ready. I can't feel your heart, but I feel in your words you care for him. I understand that. I care for these woods in the same way. I long to see them restored to what they once were. I long to see the stones stand again and the village at peace with the forest. Yet I cannot make it so. I do what I must."

Alison searched the spriggan's words for an answer. There was something there, she just knew it. "The stones," she mused. "Do you mean the stone circle? It's on my property. Well, the border between mine and his."

The spriggan swiped a woody arm in a dismissive gesture. "The stones belong to the land, not any one person. They have fallen now; the people have forgotten the old ways. They do not honor the land. They take from it what they like and offer nothing in return."

"I don't know the old ways. I'm not from here. But I do know the village, and the people there are good and kind. I was sent here by them to see if you could help us get rid of the vine. If I got them to raise the stones again, would it help?"

"It may. But it may not. Either way, they cannot raise them without my help, and they will not let me near the village."

"I'll talk to them. I can get them to understand. Come to the stones tomorrow at midday. I'm certain we can raise the stones."

"And if it doesn't work?"

She took some time to think of her answer. She knew the vine could not persist, but she also knew in her heart that she could not let Keir go. "I'll take him from this place.

We can go high into the mountains away from anyone or anything that could be harmed. I'll care for us there. I promise I won't let harm come to these woods. Will you promise not to harm him if I release you? Nor the village nor the villagers?"

"I have no desire to harm anything that does not threaten the woods. You have a deal," said the spriggan. He reached out a woody hand. Alison kicked away some of the ash from her binding circle, offering her own hand to shake.

"Ah, the bark has broken your soft skin," he said. "Here." He squeezed a milky yellowish sap from a knot on his arm into the palm of Alison's hand. It smelled strongly of pine. "A thin layer on the wounds will help."

Keir groaned on the forest floor. Alison knelt over him and saw to his abrasions before her own, gently rubbing the sap on his legs, his arms, his torso. She took a deep breath and held it as she touched the soft skin of his neck, felt the stubble that had formed there and on his chin. She hesitated before touching his soft lips, remembering the kiss on her forehead. As she touched them with her fingertips, he let out a soft sigh that Alison felt echo deep within her. Finally, she turned to the delicate skin of his eyelids, taking care to avoid tangling his long lashes. He looked beautiful and fragile in the dappled light of the sun through the trees. She longed to hold him, to care for him. To take away his pain.

She knew then that she would not tell him what the spriggan had told her. She could not bear to see his guilt, to watch him retreat into himself once more. Not when there was another way.

When she looked back into the circle, the spriggan had gone. She hoped the creature would keep his word. And she hoped that restoring the standing stones would be enough. It had to be enough.

"Alison?" Keir groaned, his brown eyes fluttering open.

"I'm here," she said.

Chapter Seventeen

THE PLAN

Keir struggled to sit up, still dazed and trying to make sense of what had happened to them. Alison watched as the memory came back to him. The panic took hold, forcing him to his feet in search of the spriggan.

"It's okay," she said, taking his hand. "It's gone."

"Where did it go? What's this?" He scraped at the drying sap with his free hand, removing it from his cheeks in flakes.

Underneath, the skin was pink but perfectly smooth. Not a scratch on it.

"That's incredible," said Alison. "The spriggan regretted hurting us, so he gave us some of his sap. I had no idea it would work so well or so quickly."

"You covered our open wounds in sap?" He looked at her skeptically but did not let go of her hand.

"I did. I believe the villagers have gotten the wrong idea about the spriggan. He doesn't wish them harm. He's just defending the forest."

"And you know this because you talked to him? How? The last thing I remember, he was trying to kill us both. You were bound just as I was."

"Not quite as well," said Alison. "And I had a secret weapon with me. Some of the vine's ash. It was the Wildcat's suggestion. I should have brought some for you as well; I'm sorry I didn't think of it."

Keir kicked at the broken remains of the ash circle, pulling Alison along with him. "You bound him. Lady Willana taught me about binding. Smart to use the ash rather than salt."

He looked at the light hitting the forest floor; it was tinged with gold and pink and coming in almost sideways. He pulled his pocket watch chain, the watch itself having been displaced in the fray. The watch dangled in front of him, hitting his thigh. As he pulled it into his hand, he let go of Alison. She felt the lack almost immediately.

"We must leave at once. I doubt we'll make it back before dark. Have you found the trail?"

Alison had not even looked for it. "I'm afraid not."

"Come," he said, taking her hand once more. A thrill pulsed through her. "We won't err by heading downhill. If the sun is just there, then this way is southwest. And southwest is home."

Keir was exactly on target. In just a few short minutes, they were on the path again. He held onto her as he led her through the woods in the dying light, warning her of obstacles and holding back branches.

"Was the spriggan not angry to be bound?"

"No, not really. He didn't seem angry at all."

Keir turned back to look at her. "He tried to murder us moments before, and when you stopped him, he didn't seem angry? Is that not odd to you?"

She couldn't explain to him the spriggan's motivations, not without revealing the truth about the vine. "I know it will be hard to understand, but I felt I could trust him."

He laughed darkly. "Did you?"

Alison stopped in her tracks and withdrew her hand. "I did. And I got us both out of there alive and well, don't forget."

He looked at her as if she had slapped him. "I'm sorry," he said. "I'm just trying to wrap my head around this. I thought I was dead–I thought we both were–and I awoke to find you had befriended our killer."

"He was only trying to kill us because he believed we were a threat to the forest," she said. It was at least half true. "Once I told him we were looking for a solution to the vine, he realized we were on the same side. He was once a friend to the village."

"And what of the vine? Did the spriggan know anything about it? How to get rid of it?" Keir asked, pulling Alison along once more.

"He did," said Alison, choosing her next words carefully. "It is indeed of the old magic." And he did know how to get rid of it, but there were some of the spriggan's ideas that

Alison had liked more than others. "He wasn't sure, but he thought re-erecting the standing stones might help."

"The stone circle on my property?"

"On our property–properties," she corrected. "It lies on the property line. He's coming by tomorrow to help raise them. Though I suspect we'll need most of the village as well. He's strong, but he's only made of wood, after all. Those stones must weigh hundreds of pounds."

"Thousands," said Keir. "So you're asking the villagers to be comfortable with the thing they believe has terrorized them for generations showing up and demanding help? To expend incredible effort to restore something that no longer holds any meaning or significance for them on the whim that it might help get rid of the vine, maybe?"

"Yes," said Alison.

"And you have a plan to convince them?"

"No."

✤

The sun's rays had faded by the time they reached the fork to the Wildcat's home. An owl hooted somewhere nearby, and in the dimming light, Alison could see a pair of white eyes flash in the distance. Keir tugged at Alison's arm, pulling her down the path faster. She didn't know why he seemed to fear the woods at night, and there was little reason to ask; she had no problem with getting out of there as quickly as possible, and maybe there were some things she was better off not knowing.

"This way," Keir said once they had crossed the stream. There was another path there, but Alison was certain it wasn't the way they had come.

"Where are we going?" she asked.

"Into the common."

Night had completely fallen by the time they left the woods. The waxing crescent moon cast little light, but Alison's eyes adjusted just in time to see the vine before Keir tripped over it.

"Look out!" she cried.

Keir sprung backward, blocking Alison with his body. "What is it? Where?"

"The vine," she said. "It's in the common." She reached to her side and realized Gwenla's machete was gone, lost down the cliff side.

Keir knelt to the ground for a closer look. "It's not the vine. It's a vine, yes, but it's just wisteria. Beautiful, but about as much of a nuisance as the magic vine. Lady Willana warned Lady Sibba, but she didn't listen."

Alison nodded, relieved. She was glad the vine hadn't reached the common after all, but she did not regret warning Keir. The feeling of his body pressed against her, protecting her, had stirred something deep within her she did not want to unstir. When he stood back up, he wordlessly took her hand once more, but she did not move forward when he did.

"Keir," she said.

He turned back to face her. He was so lovely in the moonlight. His dark hair had become a tangled mess during the earlier action, and she could not resist the urge to reach up and smooth it behind his ears. And then there was the dried sap that still clung to his skin, and she found she could not resist the urge to peel it off and bare the raw skin beneath. He froze under her touch, transfixed. He didn't even dare to breathe.

"Thank you for saving my life," she whispered. She raised her blue eyes to stare into his directly, baring the gratitude and desire she felt for him.

"Thank you for saving mine," he replied. Gravity pulled him towards her, pulled on his head and shoulders until his face was so close to hers she had to close her eyes. So close she could feel the exhale of his breath on her cheek.

And then she felt the breeze of his withdrawal.

She opened her eyes to see that he had turned away from her, her hand still in his.

He cleared his throat. "We should be getting back," he said.

"If we must," said Alison.

He flinched. Was it regret or something else?

Alison was too afraid to ask. She let him lead her into the high street, past the schoolhouse and the line of shops. Mist rose from the river and rested among the lamps, bathing the town in a hazy glow. From over the bridge, there came a great roar of laughter.

"Come on," said Alison. She pulled Keir away from the turn toward Orchard Lane and toward the bridge instead. "Everyone in town must be at the inn. Let's tell them about the spriggan."

Keir did not move.

"Come on," she said again, gently. "They're waiting to hear about the plan to stop the vine. You don't have to say anything. I'll speak for us."

"I can't," he said. He withdrew his hand.

In his eyes, she saw the fear of a wild rabbit caught in the field. He was seconds from bolting. She had to say something to convince him there was no danger there for him.

"Gwenla told me what happened with the little boy. Keir, it wasn't your fault. They don't blame you. What that man said and did, he didn't speak for all of them–"

She reached for him, and he pulled away, dodging her grasp. "Stop!" he said. His tone was fearful but not final. Alison could feel that he wanted to believe her, wanted to trust her words, but that it had been so long that he couldn't. The boy and what happened to him and how the town reacted had become a part of him, and it would not be easily undone.

"You don't have to talk to anyone. I'll help you. I'll be right beside you. They are more worried about the vine–and maybe the robber; remind me to fill you in on that one–than anything else. Trust me. I wouldn't lie to you." As she said it, she felt a pang of guilt. She had lied to him earlier about what the spriggan had told her, but only to spare him pain.

She reached for him again.

And again, he withdrew, more forcefully this time. "I can't! You don't understand. You don't know me. You have no idea what I've done. Leave me alone, Alison."

His last words cut like a knife. She stood dumbfounded as he turned and ran off down Orchard Lane and out of sight.

Alison crossed the bridge alone. He was wrong; she did know what he had done. She knew about the old magic, but she could not admit as much without admitting what she knew of his relationship to the vine. And even knowing the consequences of his actions, the failure to save the boy and the terrible situation with the vine that followed, did not change her mind about him. He had tried to do what he thought was right. She could not fault him for trying. In his position, she would have done the same thing.

She wanted to go to him and tell him she didn't blame him. To tell him how much she cared for him. How it felt like she had been asleep for these past eight years since her father died, but how being here in this town, being with him, felt like waking up. Like coming up to the surface after nearly drowning.

But she didn't. The spriggan had told her Keir's heart wasn't ready, and she could see that it was true.

And so she entered the inn alone.

Chapter Eighteen

THE STONE CIRCLE

The first to greet her when she arrived at the inn was Gwenla.

"Alison! Thank the Gods you're alright. I worried all day. Did you find the spriggan?"

Gwenla's voice had carried over the din of the revelers and Mr. Smalls's music, bringing with it a hush over the crowd. They turned to Alison, waiting to hear her good word.

Alison shared the same version of the story she had told Keir, omitting the parts about how the spriggan had nearly killed them and Keir's connection to the vine. When she explained that the spriggan wanted their help to raise the standing stones again, the village greeted the proposition with a healthy dose of skepticism.

"Absolutely not," said Gwenla.

"Not a chance," said Mr. Gilroy.

"No way," said Mr. Rainey.

"He's trying to kill us," said Willow.

The only early supporter was Mr. Corbett, the archivist who had suggested reaching out the spriggan in the first place. He was seated at the low table Alison had taken on her first night in town, and the bard had wrapped his arm around him affectionately.

He hiccoughed before he spoke. "It would be ever such a treat to see how the stones are to be raised."

"Thank you, Mr. Corbett. Is there any risk in your mind to raising the stones? Anything from any of your readings that suggests that this plan could result in harm?" asked Alison.

"No, miss. Quite the contrary." Mr. Corbett rose, stumbling a bit. "The elves say they're like a lens. A magic lens." He made a circle with his hands and held it up proudly. "A good lens. To do…stuff. That was good." He swayed where he stood. Mr. Smalls helped him back into his seat.

"Er. Well. Thank you, Mr. Corbett. In order for this to work, we need everyone to help," said Alison, glancing meaningfully at Gwenla, whose good nature and persistence had rallied the troops before.

But it was Mr. Rainey who responded from behind the bar. "Everyone? Including the younger Mr. Ainsley?"

Alison was surprised. She hadn't spoken to the innkeeper directly since her arrival. How was it that he knew of her association with Mr. Ainsley?

"It's a small town," whispered Gwenla. "People talk."

"Right. Well, I can't say for certain. But I'll ask him to come, yes." And then, because of what Keir had said earlier, she added, "He would be welcome, right?"

"Of course," said Gwenla. Others seemed less certain.

"There's a sense that he and his father have abandoned Herot's Hollow," said Lady Sibba. The schoolteacher eyed Gwenla cautiously before she spoke. "Gwenla says it's not about us, but it's a little hard to accept when the first person he talks to in years is an outsider. No offense intended."

"None taken," said Alison. She sighed, trying to think of how to address the topic of Keir, whom she had grown to care for quite a bit in such a short time, to the entire town that thought he hated them. "Keir–I mean, Mr. Ainsley–is complicated. I think he blames himself for what happened years ago with the child." She looked to Gwenla, who nodded. "And he thinks you all blame him as well and despise him as he despises himself."

"Oh, that's quite sad," said Lady Sibba. "If the town has treated him coolly, it's because he withdrew from us."

"And he withdrew because we treated him coolly. I've tried to explain all of this to him, but he never heard it from me. It's been different with Alison here. He listens to her," said Gwenla.

Alison grimaced. "I'm not actually sure if that's true…"

"It's true," said Gwenla.

"If he does come tomorrow, I think the best thing for everyone is to sort of pretend it never happened," said Alison.

"I agree," said Gwenla. "And have patience with him. There's a lot he can do for us. He'll be the lord of this land someday. It's time we let bygones be bygones."

"Here, here!" yelled Mr. Corbett, toppling his small chair backwards in his excitement.

Alison couldn't help but laugh. "Does that mean you'll all come?" she asked.

"We'll be there," said Lady Sibba, casting a glance at a sullen Mr. Rainey that made him blush.

⊱✦⊰

In the morning, Alison prepared for the town and the spriggan's arrival by clearing the vine in a wide path from the street to the stone circle. Gwenla and Willow were busy in the kitchen with the refreshments: tea, scones, sandwiches, and lemonade made from a tree kept indoors. There had been no sign of Mr. Ainsley yet, so when she finished clearing the area around the stone circle, Alison walked down the path to his house.

She saw his shadow leave the kitchen window as she approached. She knocked on the back door, but he didn't answer.

She had expected this. "I know you can hear me. Look, everyone is coming today to raise the stone circle. You are welcome to come as well. I'm certain you're welcome because the topic came up last night. If people are upset with you, it's because they think you abandoned them. Nothing else. It would mean a lot to them if you would come."

She paused. "It would mean a lot to me if you would come."

She returned up the path. By the time she was back to the stone circle, the villagers were arriving. Brytak was talking to a female orc that could only be his sister Strelka, the blacksmith's apprentice. The pair stood in front of a great cart full of logs of various sizes, ropes, and several shovels and picks.

"Weyland got a bit excited after you left. Nothing to do with Lady Sibba's enthusiasm for the plan, of course," said Brytak with a wink. "Mr. Corbett vanished and came back with a newspaper article speculating about some kind of A-frame structure and a series of ropes being used by the first settlers. We spent all morning planning it out. Hey, Weyland! Come show Alison the plan."

Mr. Gilroy, who was taking measurements of some kind near the downed stones, reluctantly joined them.

"First, we dig underneath. Then we wedge in the first logs like so." Mr. Gilroy held up a rock the size of his enormous hand and a pair of twigs that had been clearly used for this demonstration a few times already. "Then we take two big logs and make the 'A.' A strap goes 'round the stone. Then the ropes go to the strap and through the peak of the 'A' like so." The blacksmith took another pair of twigs and crossed them right near the top, forming a little wedge in which the rope could be threaded. "Two ropes, maybe three to keep it stable. Then we lift a little, wedge in more logs. Then a few big pulls. It's going to take everyone we've got, but it will lift."

Mr. Gilroy didn't seem happy, exactly, but he seemed more comfortable than Alison had ever seen him. Strelka nodded along enthusiastically as he spoke. "There are a few other ideas if this method doesn't work, but it seems like we ought to do it the old-fashioned way if we can, don't you think?"

"I quite agree," said Alison. She was taken aback by the unexpected enthusiasm and the ingenuity of the townspeople in coming up with such a solid plan on little notice. "What of the spriggan? Is there a job for him to do?"

Strelka laughed. "I hope he's strong. I can pull my weight, but we need someone to pick up the slack for my brother here." She flexed the broad gray muscles of her upper arms and then wrapped them around Brytak's head, rubbing it until he howled.

As she wrestled with her brother, Alison saw a hint of red staining the gray skin beneath her gloves. Could it be that Strelka was the thief?

It would explain why Alison was just meeting her now. She must have been lying low since the robbery, and on the day itself, she was indeed missing from Mr. Gilroy's forge at the time in question.

But why would she have done it? What did Strelka stand to gain from robbing the apothecary? Alison knew what she was supposed to do: tell the constables what she had learned immediately. Old Tirrin and Lord Wexenas seemed harmless enough, but Alison didn't want to see Brytak's sister imprisoned. Not until she truly understood what had happened, at least.

She resolved to spend the day near Strelka, observing her and trying to figure out what her motive was. Unless Keir decided to show, that was. Alison walked through the crowd, searching through faces familiar and unfamiliar, but there was no sign of him yet. Or the spriggan, for that matter.

When the sun had reached its highest point overhead, everyone gathered within the circle. They stood waiting until Alison realized she was the one who needed to speak.

"Thank you all for coming," Alison began, but as she spoke, a rustling sound came from the woods to the north of the stone circle. "I believe our guest of honor is about to arrive."

A murmur went through the crowd at the sight of the spriggan. He moved slowly down the path, his limbs and joints creaking as he went. Out in the sunlight, Alison could see the intricacy of the strips of bark that made up his skin and how they attached to his form like muscles. There was a bit of moss where his hair would have grown were he human, and resting on his shoulder was a tiny woodpecker with a red crown.

"Hello!" She waved to him and crossed through the crowd to greet him.

He did not stop to speak to her. Instead, he crossed directly to the cart and began lifting the logs Mr. Gilroy and company had gathered there.

"Oh," said Alison, realizing they may have inadvertently caused him offense. "Umm. We're sorry for felling the trees. It seemed to be how the ancients managed it. We'll plant new ones–"

The spriggan had lifted the two largest logs together into the "A" shape Mr. Gilroy and Brytak had mentioned. He held out a hand, which extended into the long branches he had used to trap Alison and Keir. The branches twined around the "A" at the top, holding it in place. The spriggan then lifted an ax with his other hand and chopped the tied branches free.

"Incredible!" said Mr. Corbett. "That wasn't in the newspaper."

"Time to dig," said Mr. Gilroy. He passed out shovels to the strongest in the crowd–Strelka, Brytak, their parents, Lady Sibba, and finally to Keir.

Alison hadn't seen him arrive. He must have snuck up when everyone was distracted by the spriggan. She wanted to run to him and wrap her arms around him; she was so proud of him for coming. But she didn't want to embarrass him, so instead she waited until he'd been assigned a spot to dig by Mr. Gilroy to come up beside him.

"I'm glad you're here," she whispered.

He grunted in response. He was in his farm clothes: suspenders and a white shirt with the sleeves rolled up. Alison admired his arms through the thin fabric as he worked, watched the sweat form into tiny droplets on his brow. It was the most glorious sight. She had to remind herself not to stare.

Reluctantly, she left his side and walked around to talk to Strelka. "We haven't formally met yet," she said. "I'm Alison Lennox."

Strelka flung her long red ponytail over her shoulder and wiped the sweat from her face. "I've heard. You're all Brytak has talked about all week. We need to send that boy out to a good orcish stronghold. Show him a woman with a bit of meat on her bones." She flexed her own arm playfully. The channel she was digging under the fallen stone was the deepest by far. "No offense," Strelka added. "You seem lovely, but he hasn't had many options out here."

"He's a good lad," said Alison. "I can't imagine there are many options for you either. Do you have someone in an orcish stronghold yourself?" The question was more personal than Alison would have liked, but writing to a distant suitor would be a reason for Strelka to have taken the inks.

Strelka laughed. "That's not my style. I'm more of a matchmaker myself."

"Any interesting matches I should know about?"

"I've heard you've made quite an impression on our future lord." Strelka dropped her voice low so Keir couldn't hear her on the other side of the stone. "You could do worse. What he lacks in manners, he makes up for in ludicrous, someday-to-be-inherited wealth. And rakish good looks, although he could stand a bit more meat on him too."

Alison blushed, but there was no use in denying it. It was a small town, after all. "Well, we'll see how it goes."

"So you're planning to stick around then?"

"We'll see how that goes, too," said Alison. The question had been weighing on her mind a lot lately, but she wouldn't have time to consider it today.

Alison made her way then over to Mr. Gilroy's cart where a group was working on the ropes.

"What a turnout!" said Gwenla. "Even the children are here. What do you think, Tim? Are you excited about the stones?"

Tim was a small dwarf child of maybe eight who had been tying his section of rope around a little human girl's hand before Gwenla interrupted him. "I don't see what the big deal is," he said. "It's just a pile of rocks."

Gwenla and Alison laughed. "He's got a point," said Alison.

"I saw a certain someone with the diggers," said Mr. Smalls. He shot a meaningful glance at Mr. Corbett. "Should I be learning the wedding march on the lute?"

Alison pulled at the collar of her dress. Was it hot out here?

Mr. Smalls and Mr. Corbett burst into laughter. "Like a deer caught in the road by a carriage!" said Mr. Smalls. "Don't worry, I'm just teasing. I've been here a few months now, and I'd never laid eyes on him until you came. And now that I have, I hope you'll stick around for a while. It would be a pity not to have him out and about to look at, you know?"

Mr. Corbett frowned.

"Now don't you go getting jealous, Duncan. He's already spoken for," said Mr. Smalls.

Alison left them to their task. She approached the sprig-gan, who was anchoring the A-frame near the stone.

"What do you think?" she asked him. "Will our plan work? Will it lift the stones?"

"Perhaps," he said. The creaking of his voice alerted the other villagers, who paused their tasks to listen. "It has been generations for my people as well since the stones were first raised. The story is told to saplings, but I never thought I'd see it firsthand."

"It's time for the first logs," said Mr. Gilroy. "Mr. Spriggan sir, if you wouldn't mind. Come right down this end."

The end of the stone that was in line with the rest of the circle had been fully excavated. A ramp was dug out beneath it, sloping up to where the other end of the stone still lay on the ground.

Keir and Brytak had taken either end of a narrow log and were wedging it under the gap between the exposed end and the ground. Once they had moved it as far as they could, Mr. Gilroy, Lady Sibba, and Strelka took their places around the stone. The spriggan took the spot at the end.

"Ready. One, two, three, lift!" yelled Mr. Gilroy.

As they lifted the stone a fraction of an inch, Keir and Brytak pushed on the log.

It was no good. The stone wouldn't lift high enough to move the log into place without crushing it.

"New plan," said Mr. Gilroy. "We'll use the ropes and the shear legs." When everyone looked at him confused, he added, "The 'A'."

The spriggan yanked the "A" out of the ground where he'd just finished setting it and took it to the other side. Then Mr. Corbett and Mr. Smalls looped the strap over the exposed end and handed the rope off to the spriggan, who pulled it through the wedge at the top of the "A."

"Line up back here, as far down the ropes as you can go. We need it to be even on each side. We pull together, and we don't stop until I say stop."

There were two ropes extending a couple dozen feet down the slope from the circle. Alison took her place near the front of the right-hand rope between a man she hadn't yet met and Lady Sibba.

"Alright get ready. Steady. Pull!"

And then immediately, "Stop! We're uneven. Too strong on the right by far. Mr. Spriggan, to the left."

The spriggan, who was at the very back, switched ropes.

"Ready. Steady. Pull! No, stop!"

This time, the left side was far stronger.

"Well, Mr. Spriggan. We're quite outdone. Could you take a rope in each hand?"

The spriggan extended his arms once more, standing perfectly between the ropes and taking one in each hand.

"Ready. Steady. Pull! Yes, that's it! Keep pulling!"

Alison watched as Keir and Brytak scrambled with first one log, wedging it as far down as it would go, and then another and another until there were six logs beneath the stone.

"Stop!" yelled Mr. Gilroy. "That's done it. Well, the first part at least."

The next task was to get the stone down into the ramp they had dug in order to flip it upright. The spriggan moved the A-frame out of the way as the strap was moved to the other side of the stone, which was now suspended a couple of inches from the ground by the log rollers. The ropes were extended into the stone circle, parallel to the ground. The pulling team reassembled on the other side.

"Ready. Steady. Pull!"

This pull was far easier than the first. The stone rolled along the logs and onto the ramp in mere moments.

"Stop! Stop!"

There was just enough room with the wooden rollers to yank the strap from beneath the stone.

"Alright. This is the big one."

They moved the strap back to the other side. The spriggan placed the A-frame back to its original position, which was now roughly in line with the angle of the stone.

Alison looked around the crowd. They were really going to do this. The stones had been raised here thousands of years ago, beyond the memory of even the elves. And today, they would rise again.

"It's going to take a few pulls. We'll hold between pulls. Don't pull, but don't let go."

Gwenla stood across from Alison at around the same spot on the other rope. "This is it!" she said. "We're going to stop the vine at last."

"This is an incredible thing that you've done," murmured Keir. Alison looked back–he had joined her rope directly behind her.

"That we've done," she said.

"Ready. Steady. Pull! Pull! Keep pulling!"

The stone lifted incredibly slowly. By the time it had raised a few inches, Alison's arms were burning, and her legs were buckling beneath her.

"Hold! No, don't let go. Hold!"

It was no good. The entire town plus the spriggan just couldn't hold on for that long. The stone dropped back into its position on the ramp.

"We need more people," said Mr. Gilroy.

The villagers looked exhausted. Mr. Corbett was shaking his short arms. Gwenla had taken a seat on the ground, wiping the sweat from her forehead. Even Strelka was stretching her stiff back.

When Alison bent her arm at the elbow, it made a horrifying creak. No, not her arm. It was the spriggan. He was growing before their eyes, not just stretching as it had done with his arms but growing like a tree, the trunk getting wider and wider as it grew taller. It was ten feet then twenty then thirty. It kept going and going until it was nearly as tall as the trees in the woods behind it.

"Well, I'll be," said Gwenla.

"It's beautiful," said Lady Sibba.

"Of course," said Mr. Corbett. "The spriggans are descended from giants."

"Shall we give it another go?" yelled Alison.

Everyone ceased their stretching and moaning and got back into position. The spriggan stretched his arms into branches once more, but this time each twining branch was the width of a young tree.

"Does he even need us?" asked Strelka, but no one moved. Alison couldn't speak for everyone, but she knew why she didn't budge—even if the spriggan could have moved the stones alone, in all this time, he hadn't. There was something special about bringing everyone together to raise them. She wanted to be a part of it. To be a part of something bigger than herself, something that would endure long after she had gone.

"Get ready everyone. Steady. Pull!"

The stone lifted slowly again, and Alison was afraid for a moment that even with the giant spriggan, the plan wouldn't work. But then she felt the pull from behind; the spriggan had joined the effort. The stone inched upwards, bit by bit, until finally it reached the vertical.

"Stop!" yelled Mr. Gilroy.

Alison dropped the rope as everyone began to cheer. There were hugs and high fives, handshakes and even a lift off the ground by Brytak.

"We've done it!" he said.

"Half of it!" said Alison.

There was still another stone to raise.

Chapter Nineteen

STOLEN

By the time they'd gotten the second stone upright, the sun was low in the sky. As the stone came into alignment, Alison expected…something. She wasn't sure exactly what, but she expected something to happen the way it had when she closed the ash circle and bound the spriggan. A flash of light, a buzz of energy. A lightning bolt down from the sky.

But the only obvious response was from the villagers. Though she knew they had to have been as exhausted as she was, their cheers didn't show it. Alison let herself get swept into the energy of the crowd, feeling the white-hot pulse of it and allowing it to carry her away for a shining moment of pure, unvarnished celebration.

The triumphant trance was broken by Gwenla whispering in her ear. "Look." She pointed to the spriggan.

He was shrinking back into his normal form, but as he shrunk, he was changing as well. Tiny shoots were extending from within the bark of his skin, and from those grew a variety of things: flowers of yellow and pink, long fuzzy catkins, seeds with wings of red, buds of cones in many shapes and sizes. The green moss of his hair turned a pale brown and tumbled down his back in cascading ringlets. All of the beauty of the forest in bloom in a single creature.

"I've never seen something so incredible," said Alison. She began to walk towards him, to admire the sight from up close and to thank him for the help he had given, but Gwenla placed a hand on her arm, holding her back.

She pointed up the path from the stone circle towards the woods. There, just at the forest's edge, stood a stag. Its fur was as white as the great horns of its antlers, and it bowed its head to the spriggan from a distance. Gwenla and Alison watched the spriggan as it made its way up the path to join it, and they kept watching until the pair had disappeared into the woods beyond.

As Alison turned from the woods to look down to her cottage, she couldn't believe her own eyes. The vine was still there, but it looked to be graying at the ends. And there was a different quality to its motion. Alison had grown accustomed to the slow stretch of the vine, so much so that her instinct to track it with her eyes had subsided. But the movement it made now registered differently–it was shrinking, she realized. She placed a hand on Gwenla's shoulder and pointed her to the sight.

"It actually worked," Alison said. She hoped the disbelief in her voice registered as a reasonable doubt about trusting the spriggan rather than her concealment of a critical piece of information: the connection between the vine and Keir that she had neglected to reveal. Perhaps the spriggan had been wrong, and the origin of the vine had been unimportant to its eventual resolution. She wanted to believe this, but a sense of unease tugged at the back of her mind as she watched the vine slowly retreat.

"It worked!" cried Gwenla. The dwarf pulled Alison into a hug, the kind of warm and loving hug that took her away from her nagging guilt and right back to the happiest memories of childhood. "Oh, I'm so glad that you came to us. I never thought I'd see this day." There were tears in the dwarf's eyes as she pulled away.

The laughter and merriment of the crowd beyond them had reached a natural lull. "To the inn!" cried Mr. Rainey, filling the silence. "First round is on the house!"

The villagers cheered with almost equal enthusiasm to their celebration at the standing of the stones.

"I'll meet you there," said Gwenla. "I need to see the vine leave Lady Willana's garden with my own eyes." She gave Alison's hand a grateful squeeze and set off down the path alone.

As the crowd followed behind, Alison noticed Keir stood in place. "Come on," she said, looping her arm through his elbow. "You're part of this too." He gave her an uneasy look, but he acquiesced.

Every seat was taken by the time Gwenla joined them a little while later. Alison had been pulled away from Keir to recount her meeting with the spriggan again to some villagers who hadn't heard the story the previous night, and then she was pulled into the singing of a bawdy schoolhouse song by Mr. Smalls.

"There once was a man from the Golden Wood,
And though his dear wife was both fair and good,
He found him a lass,
With a gigantic arse,
And he touched it as oft as he could!"

"You have a fine little voice, Ms. Lennox," said Mr. Smalls when they had finished. "Have you ever considered the bardic profession?"

"Ms. Lennox here is a poet," said Lord Wexenas. The constables had already been deep in their steins by the time the rest of the village had arrived. "Get her to read you the one about her hidden longing–"

"Ignore him. He's drunk," said Tirrin.

"Now, now, old chap. I'm nothing of the sort. Elves don't get drunk. We savor our drink. It does not control us."

The lapse of his hand as he raised the glass to his lips, missing by more than an inch, suggested Lord Wexenas was operating with a different sort of truth.

"Do you really write poetry? Would you share one with me?" asked Mr. Smalls, turning from the drunken elf back to Alison.

"I'm afraid I don't have my journal with me. Perhaps another time."

"Ah, so you're a poet then. I wondered why a human would ask an orc about their writing habits," said Strelka.

Alison could glimpse the red on Strelka's hand from beneath the glove once more, and it was in full view of the constables had they been looking. "Come," she said to the orc, leading her to a table where Keir was sitting alone. "Let me tell you of the book of orcish poetry I read just last week…"

"What did you really want to tell me?" whispered Strelka once they'd taken their seats. Keir may have been out of practice in social settings, but he took that as the cue it was to head to the bar for a refill.

"I can see the red on your hand, and if I can see it, others might as well."

Strelka's dark eyes flashed with recognition. "I appreciate your discretion. I'll take my leave before someone else catches on. Come see me at the forge tomorrow. I'll explain."

"I'll do that," said Alison.

As the orc made her exit, Mr. Corbett stood up at his usual table and tapped the rim of his wineglass. "Excuse me," he said quietly. There was no response from the crowd; the conversation, singing, and laughter continued just as before.

Mr. Smalls strummed a loud and dissonant chord on his lute. "Listen up!"

"Thank you," said Mr. Corbett. "We all know why we're here celebrating. We've done something extraordinary today, something that hasn't been done in thousands of years. And none of it would have happened without one woman's tireless mission to protect us all from that terrible vine. Somehow, we've made it through without one scratch among us. And so I say we raise our glasses–three cheers for Gwenla! Hip hip–"

"HOORAY!" Alison raised her glass and joined in the toast to her friend.

"Hip hip–"

"HOORAY!"

"Hip hip–"

"HOORAY!"

There was scattered applause as the conversation began to resume. "Hold on," said Gwenla. "Yes, I've been fighting the vines for years, but all of it had been in vain until Alison arrived. She braved the Wildcat and brought home the spriggan. Three cheers for Alison!"

Alison felt the heat rising into her face until she knew she was bright red. Gwenla walked over and threw her arm around Alison's shoulders. Then she raised her glass into the air. "Hip hip–"

"HOORAY!"

"Hip hip–"

"HOORAY!"

"Hip hip–"

"HOORAY!"

It was Alison's turn to pass on the toast, and she knew exactly who to thank. But when she looked around, Keir was nowhere to be seen.

"Excuse me," she said to Gwenla. She sat her glass down on the bar and pushed open the door into the cool night air.

His figure was retreating down the road towards the bridge. "Keir! Wait."

He stopped at her word. She joined him at a half jog that left her a little breathless after the exertion of the past couple of days.

"You're not going back already?" she asked.

As she joined him in the lamplight, she saw that his expression was dour. It was quite a surprise after the raucous delight of the past few hours.

"I'm tired," he said and began to walk away.

"Are you upset with me?" she asked. "That business with Mr. Smalls, the singing and all. You didn't mind that, did you?" She worried her interaction with the bard may have seemed a little cozy.

"No, not at all," said Keir. His response was genuine, but his tone was grim.

"You are upset with me though," she said with some certainty. "Would you walk with me and tell me why?"

Keir sighed. "I thought you would have known already. It seems you can read me like a book."

Alison knew what she wanted to be the matter with him. She hoped he shared her particular affliction: the miserable perturbation of unexpressed longing and deep desire. But she dared not express it–she couldn't bear it if she were wrong.

"I'm afraid I'm at a loss," she said.

She walked with him over the bridge, noting the way he avoided looking down into the river. The same river that led to the waterfall where his brother had perished. Alison had read that no man could ever step into the same river twice, for it wasn't the same river or the same man. It was true that this wasn't the same river. But perhaps this was the same man, or rather the boy who had been there that day within the man's body.

She led Keir to the right after they'd crossed the river, taking the way they had come the night before rather than the path directly home in order to prolong their walk.

"You've done what you set out to do," he said after a silence. "You stopped the vine, and now you're free to do as you had planned: to put the cottage up for rent."

There was a part left unspoken. It wasn't that Alison was going to let the property. It was that Alison was going.

Alison wasn't quite ready to face that reality yet herself. "Well, there's still much to do before then. The thatcher is to come tomorrow. And if the vine keeps receding, I'll have access to the rest of the property, and with that comes a great deal of work, I'm sure."

"But you're still leaving on Thursday?" There was a raw quality to Keir's voice.

"I–" Alison frowned. "Hmm."

She hadn't had a chance to properly sort through her feelings on the topic of leaving the village yet. She considered giving him a generic response and changing the subject, but after all they had been through together over the past few days, she owed him more than that.

"It's complicated. There's someone back home that needs me–no, not like that," she added when she saw the shock on his face. "She's my flatmate, Rinka. Her parents couldn't pay for her upkeep, and with no marriage prospect in sight, she had no choice but to seek out a job. But the only place that would hire her was on the opposite side of town, in the run-down neighborhood near the office I had worked at for years. I'd had some luck that day–one of my colleague's grandmother had died.

"Now, I know how that sounds, but you don't know what it's like finding a place in the city. The medical college had its own accommodations, I'm sure, but most of us are fighting over the scraps that the elves and dwarves haven't snatched up yet. I'd been commuting over an hour each day myself from my mother's latest flat, and on top of that, I'd been losing my mind living with her, so when I heard the grandmother had a flat in a building nearby, I ran over there to meet the landlord before he could put it on the market. The problem was that he was able to bring the rent back up to market price with the death of his tenant, and so while I would still save on all the listing fees, the cost per month would have been my entire salary. So I made up a poster: *Flatmate wanted. Good cooks preferred*, you know the drill. And I was hanging it on a lamppost across the street when an orc in a butcher's apron came running over, covered head to toe in blood. Her salary is even less than mine, but we make it work together, and she is a good cook."

Alison said all of this quickly, in part because she missed Rinka, and in part because it was easier to suppress her other thoughts when she was distracted with speech.

"So you see, I can't just leave her there. Even if I did want to stay, I can't leave her with no way to pay for her home. She'd be out on the street."

"That is a conundrum," admitted Keir. "Although, if you were to raise some kind of income from the property–say, by selling the fruits from the orchard at the market, or keeping a herd of sheep or cattle–you could send her enough money to help until she's able to find another flatmate."

Keir's face was carefully blank, but he couldn't conceal that he had already given some thought to Alison's prospects in the village.

"It's not the only issue," Alison said. They were treading closer to the heart of it, into uncertain ground that Alison hadn't allowed herself to yet fully cross. "You see, I'm a number-cruncher. That's someone who–it doesn't really matter. What matters is that it's a job in an office, 'A proper job,' my dad would say. Both of my parents worked in a manufactory; my mother still works there to this day, in the place where they met. I suspect you learned something of the working conditions in the manufactories while at the medical college?"

"The first bone I ever set was broken in a manufactory, and he was one of the lucky ones."

"Indeed. My parents wanted better for me, so they moved us to the district with the best school in the city, even though it meant they commuted hours each way and had to take opposite shifts in order for someone to be at home with me. They sent me to college. Not the King's College, but the School of Numbers at Arcas Dyrne–"

"That's a fine school," said Keir. "Although it's not cheap either, as I understand it."

"I received nearly a full scholarship. But still, my parents paid for my room and board and supported me until I had my degree. And I had met someone in school whose father needed a number-crunching apprentice, and so I walked into my first job just after graduation. My father was ever so proud. He often said that it was the greatest achievement of his life, having such a clever daughter with a real, proper job to be proud of."

"And you lost him not long after," said Keir. He had been listening on the other side of the door that day when she told him about her father.

"I did. And though there have been times when it's been tough, when the hours have been long and the money not that great and the boss a royal pain, I take comfort in knowing this is what he wanted for me. He was proud of me. Not everyone has that."

"No, they don't," said Keir. His hand, which had been resting at his side, clenched involuntarily.

Alison realized what she had said. "I'm sorry. I shouldn't have–"

"It's fine," he said. "I'm glad that you were able to have that. But that's the life he wanted for you. What about what you want?"

How could such a simple question have such a complex answer?

"I thought I knew," she said. There was a chill in the air. Alison tried to rub some warmth back into her arms as Keir reached for his cloak reflexively. But of course he wasn't wearing it; she had forgotten to return it to him.

"I thought I would work my way up at Andsaz Industries. And one day, I'd maybe become their first human executive. And if I was careful with my savings, I'd have enough to live in one of the fancy buildings downtown. Maybe I'd hire a staff to take care of the cooking and the cleaning. But I'd pay them well and treat them kindly and give them lots of time off and never make them feel bad for asking."

"You never pictured someone beside you?"

Keir held his face as innocently neutral as possible, but his eyes betrayed him: he was deeply invested in the answer to this particular question.

Alison felt the heat rise on her neck. "Honestly, not really. I thought it would have happened by now if it were ever going to happen. And after watching my father die…I didn't want to be the cause of so much pain. Not that I regretted a moment I had with him, and nor did my mother. Just that being alone seems–"

"So much less complicated." Keir paused before the turn down Orchard Lane.

"Exactly," said Alison. "Anyway, that was my plan, and it wasn't going as well or as quickly as I had hoped, but it was working. And I wasn't happy, exactly, but I was getting by, and that felt like enough. It was more than most had. But then I got the letter saying I had inherited this place. And at first, it seemed like a shortcut. I thought I could sell it and bypass some of the time it would take to get what I truly wanted. And then when I realized I couldn't sell, I thought I could at least bring in enough coin to hold on to what I had."

They had reached her gate. Rather than opening it and continuing up to the cottage, she stood in front of the wall in the light of a nearby streetlamp.

"I didn't expect to feel the way I do out here. I mean, look at it."

The night was clear and beautiful. The flicker of the lamplight caught on the shiny flint of the wall and the cobblestones of the street. In the distance, a nightingale sang. And the sky above was filled with stars, more stars than Alison had ever seen. So many that it made her dizzy. She grabbed Keir's hand to steady herself.

"Have you ever seen anything so amazing in your life?" she asked.

"I haven't," he said, but he wasn't looking at the sky. He was looking at her.

Alison looked back. She felt an overwhelming urge to hold on tighter, to fall into his embrace and to never let go. But this conversation had given her a chance to articulate something she'd been feeling for a while but couldn't put into words, and she didn't want it to end just yet. She released his hand with some difficulty.

"There is something magical about this place. I hardly knew anyone in Arcas Dyrne, and I lived there all my life. The city is always coming and going. You make a friend and then one day, you never see them again. Sometimes you don't even say goodbye. They're in your life, and then they're gone.

"But out here, these people are a community. And it isn't perfect because nothing made by people ever is, but they care for each other. They help each other without asking for anything in return. And I would love to be a part of that."

"But?" Keir couldn't meet her eye.

"But. I don't know if it would be enough for me to harvest fruit or raise a herd of cattle. I don't know anything about being a farmer, and from what little I do know, it's hard work. There is something satisfying in living off the land. Something deeply natural about making something with your own two hands, something enchanting about nurturing something and watching it grow. Maybe in time it would be enough.

"But I think there's a part of me that needs more. If I bought a little desk and set it in the sitting room, maybe I could work on my poetry. And maybe I could get good enough one day to put my poems together into a book. When I picture it, I'm happy in a way that I've never truly felt before. I'm so happy that it terrifies me."

In the image in her mind, she was not alone in the room. Keir was with her, bringing her a mug of hot tea while she worked. Willow was sleeping on the hearth, and a tiny version of Alison was running around and chasing Dinah's tail.

Alison kept the rest of the image to herself. She didn't want to scare Keir away.

She exhaled heavily. "But when I think of my father, what he wanted for me, it feels like giving up. He worked so hard to give me the life that I have. He sacrificed everything for it. It feels like an insult to his memory to throw it all away."

"Alison." Keir leaned towards her and took both of her hands in his. She trembled in his grasp. "Your father wanted you to be happy. From what you've told me of him, it's all he wanted. You can't imagine how lucky you are to have that. Your father set you on a path that he thought would give you happiness. That path made you who you are. It's not a betrayal to make a turn down a different road to find the joy you've been missing. It's exactly what he would have wanted."

Tears sprang to Alison's eyes. He was right, of course.

His voice was tender. "What do you want, Alison?"

The answer was hanging in the air between them.

It was a single word: *you.*

She was certain of it, more certain than she had ever been of anything. Whatever would become of her life, whichever path she chose, she knew she wanted him beside her. He saw her in a way that no one ever had. He knew her deep down in the only way that mattered. After just a few short days in his company, she could not imagine being without him. She didn't even want to try.

"I want you," she whispered.

He dropped her hands in shock. His body reeled, his face churning through a hundred emotions.

Had she misread him? Surely this was the answer he wanted. But maybe he, like her, had not dared to let himself hope for it.

He turned from her and began to hurry away. Her heart sank so far into her chest it made her feel sick.

And then he turned back.

He took her into his arms, one hand on the back of her head and the other on the small of her back. He pushed her back into the wall and kissed her, hard.

It felt like a 'lectric shock running through her, unknotting the tension in her muscles and relaxing her into him. She returned the kiss, pulling him in closer until she felt his entire body pressed against hers.

His lips were hungry, and his hands were even hungrier. She gasped as he moved to kiss her cheek, her jaw, her neck. The spot where her neck met her shoulder. She wanted him, all of him, so badly in that moment she could scarcely breathe.

And then it was over. He released her and took two huge steps backward. He ran a worried hand through his hair, just where her own hands had been moments before.

"I–I'm sorry," he said, and he broke into a run, away from her into the night.

Chapter Twenty

THE SECRET GARDEN

"Keir, wait!" she called after his retreating figure. Her heart was pounding in her ears. She could still feel the echo of his touch on her skin, could still smell the woodsmoke in his hair and taste him on her lips.

But he was gone. Though she couldn't see in the dim light of the streetlamps, she heard his gate slam shut.

It was her fault. She had pushed him too far too soon. She had tried to be careful, tried not to let herself get carried away. But she had blown it.

Dejectedly, she marched back up the path to the cottage. Dinah and Willow were waiting inside.

"Hello, Alison! Gwenla left these tins of fish if you wouldn't mind helping us–Oh, Alison. What's wrong?"

Alison slumped down onto the couch. She picked up a pillow and held it while she softly sobbed.

Willow rubbed against her legs and hopped up on the couch beside her. She nudged Alison's elbow, asking for a pet. Alison obliged her, and she had to admit that the sensation was as comforting for her as it was for the cat.

"I think I've gone and ruined it," said Alison through her sobs.

"Ruined what? The standing stones are up again. I went by after everyone had left. And the vine is nearly gone. Gwenla was so pleased when she got home and saw the garden."

"It's not that," said Alison. "It's Keir. I pushed him too far. I should have given him more time. The spriggan said he needed more time. And all I did was dredge up terrible memories and whine about my problems–Oh, he'll never forgive me. Why would he?"

Willow hopped onto the coffee table to face Alison. "That infuriating man. I've watched Gwenla fret about him for years. If something happened with him, I'm certain it's not your fault. Besides, he likes you more than I've seen him like anyone. I'm sure he'll come around."

"Do you think?" said Alison pitifully. Yes, she was letting herself be comforted by a cat, but she was glad not to be alone with her sorrow and humiliation.

"Of course I do. If he doesn't, he's dumber than an idiot. Now, I hate to have to ask, but Dinah here hasn't eaten all day…"

Alison wiped her tears with her handkerchief. "I'm sorry, Dinah. Let me help you with those."

Dinah pawed at the tin of her choice–mackerel–and Alison fetched a pair of bowls from the kitchen along with a saucer of water.

"Food," said Dinah.

"Yes, Dinah, it is. Isn't she clever?" said Willow.

"Quite," said Alison. She smiled.

❧

By the time morning broke, Alison was feeling better about the whole thing.

Yes, he was giving her mixed messages. But a mixed message was better than a "no." And yes, she probably should have resisted the urge to express her animal desires. But where was the fun in that? In the end, she had no regrets whatsoever about the events that led to that incredible kiss. Her only regret was that she may have prevented future kisses in her haste.

She resolved to take a step back and to let him come to her. There were still a few days left of her trip, regardless of her decision about what happened after, and while she didn't enjoy the thought of not spending every possible moment in his company, she thought a little distance would do him some good. Perhaps he'd come to miss her. Just as she already missed him, mere hours later.

Alison performed the morning's chores, grateful to start a day with any activity other than vine removal. She let out the cats, fetched the water, and lit the wood stove without ever missing the lost machete. She was just sitting down to enjoy her cup of tea and toast with a homemade strawberry jam gifted to her by Gwenla when she heard a crashing sound on the roof.

Alison ran outside, an unchewed bite of toast still in her mouth. When it came to home ownership, nothing good ever came from sudden unexpected noises. But this time was an exception: the thatcher had arrived and had apparently started working without addressing the lady of the house.

"'Lo, miss," he said. "I'm here about the roof."

That was plain to see considering he was on top of it. The thatcher was human and younger than Alison had expected, with broad shoulders and hair the color of the fresh straw piled in his cart.

"Good morning, Mr.?" Alison asked.

"Name's Craig. I'll get you fixed right up. Might make it before the end of the week, might be a little after. Long as the weather holds, that is."

The end of the week! "What is this going to cost exactly?"

"This here's a re-thatch job. Too much gone and rotted to repair." The thatcher cut what appeared to be perfectly fine thatch with his knife. It fell down the side of the roof into a messy pile on the ground next to Alison. "Job this size? Around fifty gold, thereabouts."

"Fifty gold?" Alison was in disbelief. Fifty gold was the entire inheritance after the solicitor had taken his due.

"Could do forty if you have it now." Even forty was more than she had left after leaving coin for Rinka to cover the rent and her travel expenses.

"Could you just fix the worst parts? How much would that be?"

"Could, but it wouldn't last. Can't guarantee it won't leak later neither." The thatcher stood still. Alison couldn't tell if he had already gotten started as a tactic to strong-arm her into paying or if this was just how it went around here.

"I'm afraid it will have to do. How much for the partial repair?"

"Five," he said. "I'll be done today."

Alison hated cutting corners, but she couldn't justify the expense to have the entire roof replaced. Not unless she was staying, which was far from certain.

"Say, miss?" the thatcher called after her. He was at the very top of the roof, quite near to the spot where Alison had fallen. "That's a nice garden you've got back there."

He pointed to the hedge maze. What did he mean about there being a garden?

Alison hadn't had the opportunity yet to explore the hedge maze; it had been far too covered in the vine, and carefully removing it while also solving the maze had seemed impossible. But now she was free to explore it at last, and that's exactly what she did.

The maze wasn't overgrown as badly as she had expected. The vine had suppressed much of the growth, but it had done little damage to the tough-as-nails yew hedges. A couple sections were turning brown, but Alison hoped the surrounding bushes would fill in and cover the gaps eventually. If not, she could always alter the maze to incorporate the missing sections.

The maze was small, and she quickly made it to the center. But she still had seen no sign of a garden. Rather than going back the way she came, she continued to the other side. She rounded a corner, and then she could see it through a hole made by some creature or another. There was indeed a garden hidden on the backside of the maze near to the woods. But how did one get in there?

Alison walked down the last remaining path, a path that should have run right on the garden's east side, but she was stopped in her tracks.

There was a section of the vine here. It was wilted and graying, but the thorns remained as sharp as ever. It trailed under the eastern side of the hedge and continued out into the field beyond.

Well, it was better than it had been, and surely it would all be gone soon enough. Alison retrieved the small hatchet she had purchased from Mr. Gilroy on her first day in Herot's Hollow from the house. It reminded her she needed to go see Strelka later to hear the reason for the robbery.

Alison hacked at the vine, being careful with the less effective tool. When it had turned to ash, she could see a keyhole among the yew branches.

A keyhole…but where had she seen a key?

"Of course!" said Alison. She had found the key among her cousin Frances's things the very same day that she'd gotten the hatchet. It had seemed strange to find a key with no lock, but now it made sense.

Alison returned to the house for the key, and on the way back, she stopped by the tool shed for a shovel, a spade, and a rusty watering can. She stacked the tools up outside of the garden door and turned the key in the lock. The lock creaked, and then the hinges of the door creaked even more as she pulled it open.

The sight inside was captivating. It was a small space, no bigger than the ground floor of the cottage, and yet it was full to the brim with plants of all kinds. There were quite a few that Alison recognized from Gwenla's garden, although they were much fuller than they had been there just a few days earlier. And there were far more plants that Alison had never seen before. (Or if she had, she hadn't noticed.) In the very center there was an old stone bench, covered up with moss and overhanging branches. Bees buzzed overhead, freshly awake for spring. And in a corner, a pair of blackbirds were tending to three tiny babies in a nest built from something that looked suspiciously like her roof.

Alison had no idea where to start. Well, she had one idea–there was a section of the vine in here as well. It seemed that nowhere, not even a garden that had been abandoned for years, was safe from its reach. She made quick work of it and then carried the tools inside, planning her next move.

"Alison? Are you here?"

Alison's heart skipped a beat. It was Keir. He had come to see her, and far sooner than she could have expected.

"Back here," she called. "Come through the maze."

"I'm in here. I'm stuck."

Alison laughed. "It's not a very big maze. Follow my voice."

It took him so long that Alison almost came to get him. But finally, he arrived. His face was flushed, and in his grasp was a bouquet–daffodils, likely picked from his own garden that very morning.

"For me?" she asked. She moved towards him, but he held up his other hand to stop her.

"Alison," he began, clearing his throat. "I'm afraid I must apologize for my most unfortunate behavior–"

"You have nothing to apologize for," said Alison.

That was not the response he was expecting. He was at a loss for what to say next. "Oh–I–"

"But thank you for the flowers." Alison took the bouquet from his hands and placed it in the watering can. "I haven't seen any daffodils in here yet, although I'm not sure I'd recognize them without the flower. In fact, truth be told, I can't tell a flower from a weed. Care to lend me a hand?"

Alison watched the wheels turn in his head. No, she wasn't angry with him. And yes, it's because he had read her correctly, and she did return his affections. And no, she hadn't even been put off by his dramatic exit; that part was less true, but she could see no value in berating him over something he clearly felt bad about.

Although now that she thought about it, was he apologizing for kissing her or leaving afterward? She'd cut him off before he'd had a chance to specify.

"Hold on, let's go back to that apology. Was it for kissing me within an inch of my life or leaving me abruptly once you'd gotten my hopes up?"

Keir coughed. There was a twitch in his left temple, and his cheeks were turning a darling shade of scarlet that quite matched one of the flowers she couldn't identify. "Both?" he said finally.

"That's a pity," said Alison. "I'd rather hoped it was the latter." She gave him a wink.

She was certain then that it was the latter. The look of longing he'd given her when she said the word "kissing" told her all she needed to know. Now she was just going to enjoy watching him squirm.

"So about these flowers…"

Keir cleared his throat once more. "Right." He passed by Alison–dangerously closely, close enough to feel the brush of his trousers on her knee–and knelt in front of her, regarding a small yellow flower on a long green stem. Alison struggled to focus on the plant rather than the man, the ripple of his firm muscle was ever so distracting through the pale blue fabric of his shirt.

"Surely you know this one," he said.

"It's a dandelion. The kind that turns into the little puffball that children play with. That's a weed," she said.

"Lady Willana said there are no weeds; only plants growing in the wrong place. The dandelion has been treated unkindly. It's an early source of nectar for the bees, and all parts of the plants are edible. My father–" He paused. Alison gently placed her hand on his shoulder. He turned back to her, finding strength in her eyes. "My father keeps an immaculate lawn at Weldan House. That's where I grew up. He will not suffer a dandelion to live on his watch."

"It can stay," said Alison. "It would be a pity for the bees to go hungry."

He nodded and smiled weakly.

"What about this one?" Alison asked. It was the lovely red flower that matched the blush of Keir's cheek.

"That's a camellia bush," he said. "A late variety, too. It's a distant relative of the plant that produces the tea that we drink."

Alison took him around the garden, asking him to tell her about every plant she could see. She delighted in the sharing of his knowledge and especially in hearing his stories. Though many of them were tinged with sadness, she was grateful to him for trusting her with them.

In the end, they removed only the most troublesome plants–poison hemlock ("See how the stem is smooth with purple spots. Wild carrots are hairy") and the blackberry brambles ("Delicious, but they'll take over this entire garden before too long, and the last thing we need around here is more thorns"). The others were pruned and trimmed; Keir found something he called "secateurs," a word she was pretty sure he had made up, and he wielded them like a madman.

"There's no way that's still alive," said Alison, surveying a sad stump with a handful of tiny green shoots that had been a great big bush of branches minutes earlier. "Are you sure you know what you're doing?"

"You have to do this to this type of rose to keep them compact," he said. "I have one like it in my garden. The flowers have an impossible number of pink petals and the most intoxicating fragrance. I can't wait to see what color this one is."

He looked at her expectantly. Testing to see if she had thought anymore about her future prospects, she guessed: would she be here to let him see the color of the rose?

"I'm sure it will be lovely," she said noncommittally.

The garden was looking much neater, if a lot emptier, than when she had found it. Keir assured her that this maintenance was necessary to bring the garden to its best. And she supposed she trusted him.

He rested on the stone bench, removing his gloves and wiping the sweat from his brow. He looked so peaceful and at home there. Alison didn't want this moment to end.

"Wait just a minute," she said. "I'll be right back."

She returned to the house, intending to bring him some of the leftover lemonade that Gwenla had left behind from yesterday's gathering. But she stopped on her return trip when she noticed the thatcher was not doing as she asked. Rather than repairing the worst of the damage, he appeared to be replacing all the straw as he had intended when he first arrived.

"Excuse me. May I ask what you're doing?" she yelled up to him. He was removing the thatch near the chimney in huge chunks, dumping it to the ground unceremoniously.

"Replacing the roof as ordered, ma'am."

Was this another part of his scheme to get more of her money?

"I didn't tell you to replace the roof."

"No, 'twasn't you. 'Twas the man of the house."

Alison stormed back to the garden, the lemonade sloshing from the glass and dripping down her hands.

"Why did you tell the thatcher to replace my roof? It's fifty gold I don't have." She shoved the lemonade into his hand.

He smiled smugly. "That was the price he gave you because he knew you didn't know better. He's doing it for twenty, and it's already been paid for."

She couldn't decide how to feel: livid because he'd overstepped his bounds, or grateful that the problem would be solved properly at no cost to her. She settled on both.

"I'm perfectly capable of handling my own affairs," she said.

"I know that. Consider it repayment," he said. He downed the entire glass of lemonade in one large gulp. Alison couldn't help but admire his strong jaw as he swallowed. It was not the first time she'd been infuriated by his handsomeness, and she was certain it would not be the last.

"Repayment for what?" she asked. If anyone was indebted, it was her. "You saved my life. Twice."

"Hmm," he said. He left the empty glass on the bench and stood to face her. "I guess that is true. Although you did save my life once as well."

"In which case the tally stands at two to one against. I'm afraid I'm still in your debt, and you can't expect me to accept the roof as well."

He reached a hand towards her, hesitant, but ultimately grasping a lock of her dark hair, which he tucked behind her ear. "In truth, you've saved my life twice as well."

Alison went still under his touch. "How so?"

"Whatever I was living before you arrived, it wasn't a life. It was half a life, at best."

"Well," she said. Her head was spinning. She was supposed to be the one making him squirm, not the other way around. "Then it's two to one and a half. I'm still on the bottom."

He smiled, a full, genuine smile that reached his brown eyes. His face was even more appealing when he was happy. "Ever a number-cruncher," he said.

He took her hand in his. His skin was rough and calloused by hard work, but he brushed her soft fingers gently.

"My darling Alison," he murmured.

Alison felt the hair on the back of her neck stand up on being called "darling." He looked into her eyes as if he were swimming in them. Drowning in them.

"I came here to apologize for taking leave of my senses. For letting the darkest desires of my heart overwhelm me. And yet it seems that when I'm in your presence, I simply can't help myself. I am drawn to you like a moth to a flame. I know my blackened soul is undeserving of your grace, but I cannot stop myself from reaching for it all the same. I want to be good for you. I want to be better for you. And I know, deep down, that the best and kindest thing for me to do for you would be to walk away. But I can't. I'm foolish, and I am weak. And so I'm asking you to stay. Stay with me. I cannot be without you."

He leaned forward and placed a delicate kiss on her cheekbone. "You make sense here. You bring this place to life. You called this town magical. And yet it is you who are magic."

He kissed her other cheek and held his face there, inches from hers. "And if you must go, then let me go with you. I would follow you anywhere. What do you say?"

It was everything she wanted.

"Yes," she said without hesitation. "To all of it, to all of you. Yes."

He planted his final kiss right on her lips. It was the opposite of the previous night's unbridled passion. It was restrained and tender, impossibly soft and shy. And yet it lit the same fire within her, burning brighter than ever through the denial, a tantalizing taste of more to come.

A promise.

Chapter Twenty-One

THE INK THIEF

Alison had no memory of how she pulled herself away from that moment. One minute she was in the garden, completely entranced, and the next, they were walking away from it together.

She must have said something to him, prompted him to accompany her into town. But if she had, she couldn't recall it. All she could think of was the sweetness of his breath on her lips, the long and lingering look in his eyes. She wasn't sure there was room in her mind for anything else. Her thoughts were full to the brim of him.

And so it came as something of a surprise to her when she found herself at the blacksmith's forge. But of course, there was a purpose to her visit; it was time to hear from Strelka why she'd committed that most heinous of crimes: the theft of art supplies.

"What's he doing here?" grunted Strelka, carrying something red hot with a pair of tongs and dropping it into a trough of water where it sizzled and boiled violently. Her forge gloves were black—wyvern hide—and reached up to her elbow.

"He's with me," said Alison. "He's not going to the constables, if that's what you're asking."

Keir gave Alison a look of confusion. Whatever automatic part of her mind had led her here hadn't bothered to fill him in on the reason for the visit, then.

"Good," said Strelka. "You've picked a good time to come; Weyland is up at the mines. This entire mess is his fault, and he knows it, but he would still be upset if he knew I was telling you."

"It was Mr. Gilroy's idea to steal the inks?" Whatever use did the blacksmith have for ink?

Strelka nodded. "It was meant to be a surprise. Remember I told you that I'm something of a matchmaker? Well, Weyland has a match in mind."

"Who?" asked Alison.

"None other than Lady Sibba herself."

"The schoolteacher?"

"The very same," said Strelka. "He's had a thing for her since before he was taken by the king. She wrote to him while he was imprisoned. They weren't love letters, if that's what you're thinking. Just the sort of affectionate letter you send a dear friend in trouble."

"So how does stealing the ink come into it?"

"I told him he needs to tell her how he feels before she finds someone else. You can tell she does have an affection for him. I don't know if it's love, but there's really only one way to find out."

Alison shot a meaningful glance at Keir, which didn't go unnoticed by Strelka.

"So did he confess his feelings?" asked Keir.

Strelka smiled as she hammered something dark and narrow. "Not yet. That's what the inks are for. Weyland learned to draw from one of the other prisoners during his enslavement. He was going to draw her a beautiful scene, and at the center, he would confess his love."

"But why not simply buy the inks? Surely Lady Sibba wouldn't want a love confession, no matter how beautiful, created with stolen goods," said Alison.

"Do you know who Lady Sibba's dearest friend is? Other than Weyland himself, of course."

Alison had no idea where she was going with this. She shook her head.

"Mezec," said Strelka.

"The apothecary?"

"Quite. It wasn't meant to be a robbery. Mezec usually closes up for lunch at that time, and he usually takes his lunch at the inn. I was to get the inks and leave the coin behind. And we would explain later, after the surprise had been delivered."

"But Mezec didn't leave."

"No, he did not. He came flitting down from the upper floor just as I'd stashed the first of the inks in my pocket, and so I panicked and ran. I dropped the red and the blue vials in my hurry. The red ink broke, but the blue remained intact, so I picked it up. But my hand was stained with red ink, and so I stayed out of sight for a few days. I thought the gloves would give me cover enough, but clearly some people are more observant than others." She gave Alison a wink.

"So why hasn't Mr. Gilroy written his love note yet? He could clear your name and put an end to this whole affair," said Alison.

"Because I don't rightly know what to say," said Mr. Gilroy. His entrance had been masked by the sound of Strelka's hammer.

"I can explain," said Strelka.

"No need," he said. "I got the gist of it. And Ms. Lennox here may be just who I need. I heard you write poetry."

Mr. Gilroy ducked his head down and opened a door into the enclosed part of the forge, which Alison realized was his house. He rummaged around with a stack of papers, pulling out three scrolls of parchment. He brought them back out into the open-air section and laid them on a table, using tongs and hammers to hold them open.

There were three lovely illustrations, each with a blank space in the center. The first was of the village, looking upriver from the bridge near the inn. The second was of the forest behind the common. And the third was of the schoolhouse and churchyard. All were exquisitely drawn in fine detail and with great care.

"They're incredible," said Alison. "How did you manage to create these with inks? I've never seen anything like it."

"You mix 'em up and add water. 'Course, I had to make do without the red, but I don't think it's too noticeable."

Alison felt that his explanation was quite an understatement; the skill required to create such a faithful reproduction in so many colors from so few was simply marvelous. But she wasn't surprised to find that the smith was a humble man.

"And you're hoping to fit a poem just there?" asked Alison, pointing to the blank space in the drawing of the village. "What do you want it to say?"

"That's the problem. I'm not much with words. Everything I've tried comes out all wrong."

"Well," said Alison, "First I'll need some ink and paper. And then you're going to tell me about Lady Sibba."

The enormous man blushed bright red. At least, Alison thought so. Truth be told, his skin was always a bit red.

"I can get you the ink, no trouble at all. But if I knew what to say about Lady Sibba, I'd write it myself."

"We're going to figure it out together. But first, the ink."

Mr. Gilroy returned with a fountain pen, an inkwell, and a used bit of parchment on which he'd scratched his own attempts.

My love is as hot as a ~~hammer~~ ax forge,
When I see you, my body does engorge

"Oh my," said Alison. She wanted to read the lines to Keir to hear his reaction, but she was not cruel. (She'd tell him later.) Instead, she asked, "What is it about Lady Sibba that you love?"

"Mostly, it's her face. Her face and her body. And her hair. Oh and the clothes she wears. And how they look on her body." Mr. Gilroy looked firmly at his drawings as he spoke, not once looking at Alison or any of the others in the eye.

"Yes, Lady Sibba is very beautiful. But there are many beautiful ladies in the world. Why her in particular? What of her mind? Her spirit? Her temperament?" asked Alison.

"She has all of those things. She is kind."

"Kind is good. What else?"

"She wrote to me when no one else did. She didn't forget me although I was a long way away. When I came back, and I didn't want to talk to anybody, she didn't get mad. She just sat there–right where you are–and talked to me. Didn't ask me any questions. Just waited until I could tell her a little."

His voice grew thick. "And when it turned out that I wasn't the same anymore, she didn't care. She never stopped coming here. She never gave up."

Keir's hand gripped Alison's free hand underneath the table.

"That's lovely, Mr. Gilroy. We'll tell her just that," said Alison.

Alison thought for a few moments and then scratched down a verse.

There had been a change within me; all my thoughts were churning,
But you were ever constant as the rise of the north star,
Oh, how I've longed for you, the love within me burning,
To hold your lovely face and learn of all the joys you are.

Strelka whistled. "That'll do it. You're a lucky man," she said to Keir, who let go of Alison's hand in surprise. But seeing Strelka's smile, he reached his arm around Alison's shoulder.

"I know," he said.

Mr. Gilroy took the poem from Alison and copied it into the illustration of the school, slowly forming each letter with a degree of precision that seemed improbable given the size of his hands. The finished product was a work of art.

"She's going to love it," said Alison. Seeing the image, she was struck with a sudden idea. "Say, Mr. Gilroy. Have you ever considered doing commissions? I've been playing with the idea of making a book out of my poetry, and with these illustrations, it really could be something special."

Mr. Gilroy's eyes lit up. "All I've wanted since I got back was to find a way to stop working in the forge. I'd be happy to help you, Ms. Lennox. And you can call me Weyland."

"It's a deal," said Alison, shaking his hand. "When will you take it to Lady Sibba?"

"This very afternoon," said Strelka. This was news to Weyland, but he slowly nodded with Strelka's encouragement. "And I'll be sure to make things right with Mezec at the same time. I appreciate your discretion."

"And your help," said Weyland.

Alison smiled. "The pleasure is mine. Actually, there's one thing you could help me with as well."

"Name it," said Weyland.

"I lost Gwenla's machete in the woods when I went to meet the spriggan. I was hoping to get another one for her and a second for myself." Even with the vine retreating, there was still a hedge maze to maintain.

Strelka held up a single gloved finger, and then she headed to the back and opened a chest. "This is where I keep the good stuff. The stuff I make for myself to hone my craft."

She produced two blades. They were quite unalike, but both were skillfully crafted. One had a handle made of a darkened wood turned in a complex knotted pattern. The other handle was inset with mother-of-pearl, and the spine of the blade had been crafted with file work in an elaborate, curved design reminiscent of the elvish style.

"They're magnificent. I've never seen their equal," said Alison. "I can't possibly take them."

"Of course you can. You're giving me an excuse to make more." Strelka clapped Alison on the shoulder.

With the blades sheathed, Alison and Keir bid the pair adieu. Once they were safely out of earshot, Alison shared with Keir Weyland's draft of his love poem. It had quite the effect Alison had hoped for: he laughed so hard for so long that passersby looked at him in alarm.

Chapter Twenty-Two

THE LORD OF MERELOR

On the walk home, Alison spotted something familiar over the river near the inn.

"It's the postal carriage!" she said. "Come, let's
see if Rinka has replied to my postcard."

Keir was reluctant, but he allowed himself to be dragged
over the bridge and to the post office. A small crowd had
gathered there, including Gwenla and Alison's neighbor,
Aras.

"Oh, Alison, I'm not sure how he's going to take it,"
whispered Gwenla. She shot a furtive glance toward Keir.

"Take what?" Alison asked, but she couldn't stop to hear
the reply because the postman was waiting to hear from her.
"Alison Lennox," she said to the postman.

"Got one for you here, Ms. Lennox."

It was a letter from Rinka. Letter in hand, she allowed
Gwenla to pull her to the side.

"It's the Lord of Merelor. The Senior Mr. Ainsley. He's due to arrive any day now."

Alison felt the color drain from her face. "He's coming here?"

"Aye. And he's bringing a dwarven industrialist to see the town. They're hoping to open manufactories all over Wilderise. There's talk of a dam in Fossholm."

Alison looked at Keir, who was waiting for her by a lamppost. He had that same anxious look he always had around crowds, but the fact that he had come at all was an improvement. Alison knew that this news would break him, would send him back into his hole, and he might not emerge again during her visit.

"How can I tell him?" she asked Gwenla. "He's just finally come around."

"Perhaps it would be best for him to stay out of the way for a little while. The duke can be a hard man, and cruel. Take him back to Orchard Lane first. It'll be better for him if he doesn't hear it here."

Alison nodded and thanked Gwenla for the heads up.

"Come on," she said to Keir, taking him by the arm.

"You're not going to read your letter now?" he asked. Most of the townspeople tended to stand around and read their letters near the postman. It was one of the primary sources of gossip, and something Alison would have enjoyed being part of on a different day.

"No, I'd prefer to take it home so that I may answer straight away. Besides, it's only from Rinka. While I'm happy to hear from her, I only saw her a bit over a week ago. There can't be that much news to share."

None of this was exactly true, but it was the kind of lie that amounted to little and would be easy to correct later.

They had almost made it over the bridge and onto Orchard Lane when they crossed paths with Mr. Corbett. "I'm sorry to hear the news," he said to Keir. "I know there's a strain on your relationship."

Keir looked at him quizzically. "I don't know what you mean." He looked to Alison, but there was no strain there of note.

"Thank you, Mr. Corbett," said Alison, and she tried to pull Keir along, but he did not budge.

"Mr. Corbett, please explain," he said.

Mr. Corbett looked at Alison. She tried to plead with him with her eyes, but either the Halfling misread her, or he didn't realize her concern.

"Why, the lord's arrival, of course. Any day now, they're saying. Unless I was mistaken about your relationship. If so, I do apologize."

Keir stood stock-still. The only movement was the tiniest twitch of his left brow. "You say the lord is arriving any day?" His words were unnaturally calm and slow.

"Yes, sir. It was in the post just now. I thought you would have heard."

Keir looked to Alison with recognition. And then betrayal. He freed his arm from hers. "You knew?"

Alison's chest tightened, the breath catching in her throat. "I was going to tell you just as soon as we were out of the view of prying eyes. I didn't know how you would react."

He nodded, his lips pressed into a flat line.

Mr. Corbett, finally picking up on the tension of the situation, explained that he had to be off to see to a pot he was boiling and scurried away before either of them could protest.

Keir took several long strides alone down Orchard Lane, avoiding all other eyes as he crossed through the intersection with the high street.

"Keir, I–"

"Don't. I'm not angry with you." His voice was clipped and thick with anger in spite of his words.

"But–"

"Alison. Please. Give me a moment." The words were forceful but not cruel. Alison could see the fear in him.

Painful though it was, she allowed him to rush away from her. She stood there alone in the lane, trying to come up with a way to help him. She imagined the horrible mixture of emotions he must be feeling–guilt over the episode that estranged them in the first place, anger at having been abandoned, grief for the loss they had shared and the lives it had cost them. She wanted to take it all from him. To find a way to spare him from this pain forever.

And yet she knew that he would never be free of it. Even when his father was gone, it would haunt him still. It was a part of him.

"You can follow," he spat back at her. Alison's heart lifted somewhat. Though it wasn't delivered kindly, she took the invitation to accompany him, even at a distance, as a positive sign.

Keir did not stop his relentless march until he was safely inside his own cottage. Alison, who had kept pace with him from a few yards back, found his front door swung wide open. She gently pulled it closed behind her.

He was in the kitchen, pacing. Alison crept up and took a seat at his kitchen table. He did not seem to see her. She watched him for several tense minutes, muttering and having a conversation with himself. Finally, he slammed his hand against the back door, rattling it in its hinges.

"Why now? Why come back here now?" He said it out loud, but he looked out the window as he spoke.

Alison wasn't certain he was addressing her. Still, she figured she ought to say something. "How long has it been?"

"Six years since I've seen him. He's been at court for three, maybe four, from what Gwenla told me. So why now?"

Alison had the answer to this question. She hoped he wouldn't be angry with her for keeping it from him. "He's bringing a dwarven industrialist. They're considering building a manufactory somewhere nearby. And possibly a dam in Fossholm."

Keir laughed bitterly. "Of course. I should have known."

"What do you mean?"

He pounded a fist onto the table. "All he cares for is that bloody estate. 'His solemn responsibility, his noble duty.' Everything is coin to him or a means to secure it. Of course he would want to bring manufactories to Wilderise. He sees no value in this land other than the coin he can make from it."

Alison could hear the disdain in his voice, but she had harbored similar feelings to his estranged father until very recently. "All I wanted from the cottage was the coin it could bring. Maybe he just needs to see it here again. He's been gone a long while."

"You don't know him. He lived here all his life. He knows these lands better than anyone living. If he hasn't seen anything else by now, he never will." He tapped his fingers on the table in an increasing rhythm.

"You will be the lord someday," said Alison.

"After he's dead, and he's burned down the forest and razed the fields."

"Keir, surely if you talked to him–"

"You aren't hearing me," he said sharply. "It won't matter. He will not listen."

"Can you take him to court? These lands are yours by right when he's gone. Surely he can't–"

"Alison, enough!" He turned away from the table and back towards the door.

"I was only trying to–"

"I know," said Keir. His eyes softened, and he sighed. "I didn't want you to see me like this."

But he had asked her to follow, which meant some part of him did want her there. Perhaps he wasn't looking for her to give him a solution to a problem that had none. He was simply looking for the comfort of her presence.

She stood and joined him by the door. He avoided looking at her, but he didn't refuse her when she reached out and took his hand.

"I'm sorry," she said softly. "I know it's difficult for you."

They stood there, still, for a long moment. Finally, he turned away from the door and led her by the hand to sit together at the table.

"Did I tell you anything of him? Any of the stories from our childhood?" His voice had the same unnatural steadiness from earlier. An effort to keep his emotions from overwhelming him, Alison guessed.

"No."

"My brother. Hmm," he said, lifting his head to the ceiling and breathing deeply. "My brother Danny was a force of nature. He was three years younger, but he did not follow in my footsteps the way younger children often do. He ran circles around me. But when he was very little, shortly after our mother had gone, he was a sensitive child. He had a favorite toy, a doll that had been our mother's. She called it Charlotte and brought it out to play with me while she was with child; it was her way of getting me used to the idea of being an older brother, I suppose. Charlotte was meant to have been Danny's name. Once Danny was born, my father told her to put the doll away, but she refused him. She was the only one that could. She let Danny sleep with the doll, and when he was old enough to walk, he carried it around by the hair. He carried it everywhere for so long that the hair stood straight up like a gnome's hair in the end."

Keir cracked half of a smile at the memory.

"After she was gone, my father hated looking at it. He hid it several times–Danny would cry for days on end–but the servants kept bringing it back. Until finally, one day I caught him in the nursery with a hammer. He smashed in its porcelain face. Our mother's doll, the only thing we had left of her, in shards on the floor. I crept from the room before he could see me. Hours later, Danny came running up to me, bashing his tiny fists against my chest. Father had told him I was the one who smashed it. I knew I'd pay for it if I told him what truly happened, and so I told Danny that I had done it. That dolls were for girls, and he was too old for them, anyway."

"Keir," said Alison, reaching for him across the table. "That's horrible."

"There's a version of that story for every major holiday, every occasion since my mother died. I dreaded birthdays, anniversaries, and any kind of celebration. There were other incidents, but he saved the worst for the big moments. By the time of the first anniversary of Danny's death, I had become so accustomed to his torment that I was convinced I was immune to it. And I figured there was nothing he could say to me that was worse than what I already thought of myself. I was wrong."

Alison gave his hand a squeeze.

"He went through a phase after Danny died of telling me that I wasn't his son. I think he meant it just as a jab, at first, but eventually he started to believe it. There was a part of me that hoped it could be true, but my governess pointed out that I looked exactly like him. I screamed at her when she said it–I still feel awful about that to this day–but she was right.

"The month of the anniversary of Danny's death, we had my mother's sister and her family staying with us. Father was always on his best behavior when company was around. And so that night, he came into my bedroom while I was sleeping. I woke with my face covered by my pillow. I couldn't breathe. 'This is what happened to him,' he said.

'This is what it felt like under the water. It should have been you. You killed my son. My only son.'"

"Oh, Keir." She got up so abruptly the chair fell backwards to the floor. She left it there; all she wanted was to be near him. She stood next to where he sat and pulled him into her, pressing his face into her chest as she held him. He pushed her away at first, flinging away a tear from under his eye with the same disgust as shooing a biting fly.

But she pulled him back to her, and finally, he sighed heavily and wrapped his arms around her hips. He released a single sob and then swallowed hard, trying to push it back down.

She gently pushed him forward so that she could look him in the eye. She wiped another tear from his cheek. "You don't have to hold back. You don't have to hide anything from me."

"It was long ago. I am a fool, crying about it all these years later. What good will it do? It won't change what he was to us. It won't bring Danny back. If my father saw me like this, he'd spit in my face and tell me I'm no man at all."

"What utter nonsense. Why does one of the worst men who's ever lived get to decide what it means to be a man? What gives him the right?" Alison had met this kind of man before. Her father had viewed them with utter contempt. "My father was the greatest man I've ever known, and he cried all the time. He cried when I hurt my arm playing at school. He cried at my graduation. Sometimes, he'd cry just from reading a particularly sad book. He had no shame in it. He thought that true cowardice lived in the people who were too afraid to face their feelings, not in those that let the power of their emotions–even the bad ones–take hold of them, if only for a little while."

Keir's response was interrupted by a frantic knocking on the door.

"Keir! Alison! Are you in there? Come quick!"

Chapter Twenty-Three

THE LIES THAT BIND

Gwenla was frantic. Her face was beet red, and she had to prop herself up against the doorframe to keep standing.

"My Gods, Gwenla, what's the matter?" Alison walked under her outstretched arm and held her upright, helping her into Keir's sitting room.

"It's the vine," she said through gasping breaths. "It's back and worse than ever. I've never seen it grow so quickly. I don't know what to do."

After she helped Gwenla onto the couch, Alison went to the window. The path was unrecognizable less than an hour after they had last traversed it. All the work and withering of the past few days had been undone.

Then she looked at Keir. She could see the wheels turning in his head.

"We'll come at once," Alison said. "I lost your machete in the woods, but I just got a replacement for you from Strelka. Keir, you can take this one. Keir?"

He had backed up to the bookshelf beside the fireplace. He was looking somewhere far in the distance, dazed. "Of course," he said. "It's me."

"What?" asked Gwenla. "What do you mean?"

"I'm the cause of the vine. I don't know how I didn't see it before. It's tied to me. It came along so long after Jack that I convinced myself it wasn't me, but it was. It was the old magic that I tried."

Alison evaded his glance. She tried to turn back to the window, but it was too late. He had seen her.

"You knew," he said, shocked. "You knew." The second time, his voice was cold as ice.

"Keir, you're talking nonsense," said Gwenla. "The vine is back to defend the town. Think about it. Your father wants to drown us all, and it's fighting back. But we can't let it hurt anyone. Alison, tell him."

"I don't–I–"

"What did the spriggan tell you? Why did you lie to me?" Keir shook against the bookshelf.

"I didn't want to lie to you. But the spriggan said there might be another way. And he said you weren't ready, so I couldn't see why you needed to know before–"

"Stop it. Stop lying." His voice was knife-sharp.

"I'm not–"

"Alison, I don't understand," said Gwenla.

"So that's why it tried to kill me and not you," said Keir.

"It tried to kill you? The spriggan?" asked Gwenla.

"Yes, but he told me that you could stop it, only you weren't ready yet. I was going to tell you–"

"When, Alison?" He slammed his arm against the bookshelf, shaking several books loose to the floor. "After someone got hurt? After someone died? When were you going to tell me I am the cause of all of it? After I confessed everything to you? After I shared with you my darkest memories? When?"

Alison tilted her head towards the floor. Her heart pounded so loudly in her ears she could scarcely hear herself speak. "I don't know. I'm sorry, Keir. I thought if you knew that you'd separate yourself again–not just from me, but from everyone. I thought that if I waited until you were ready–"

"How were you to know when I'm ready? What does that even mean?"

Gwenla reached over to him, but he jerked away from her. "Keir, I think she was just trying to–"

"Get out. Both of you. Get out of my house." He did not yell. His words were careful, measured.

"Keir–"

"Now. Don't return."

Alison wanted to ignore his words. To stay and to keep talking to him until he listened. She needed to make him understand why she had done what she had done. She was trying to protect him, trying to carry the burden of knowing for him until he was ready to take it on himself. He had come so far in being able to talk about his past, his memories, his pain. With a little more time, they could have worked through it together.

It was Gwenla who pulled her away. She sighed and lifted herself from the couch slowly.

"Come on, Alison. Let's go, love."

❧⚮❧

Gwenla cleared the vines for them on the way back to her cottage. Alison followed closely behind her, but in reality, she hadn't left Keir's living room. Her mind was still there. And her heart as well.

"Come, sweet girl." She led Alison to her kitchen table and prepared her a cup of tea. "Tell me everything."

It took Alison a minute to find words. "Don't we need to take care of the vine?"

"We do, and we will, but I need your help, and you're in no state to help at the moment. Have some tea and a biscuit. Tell me what's happened."

Alison took Gwenla through it–the day they found the spriggan, its attack, what it said of Keir and the vine. And then what had happened after, how she'd been hopeful that he was getting better and that eventually the vine would go away on its own. "And it seemed like it had gone away. But now, with the duke's return–"

"Well, we had a good run," said Gwenla. She was looking at an empty chair at the dining table rather than Alison.

"What?"

"Oh, sorry dear. I still talk to her from time to time. I knew her so long and so well, I can hear her part in my head. She'd say, 'You can't stay here.' And I'd argue with her about the house and the garden, but she'd just say it again, gently,

'You can't stay here.' And I'd nod because she'd be right. She always was."

"Because of the vine?" asked Alison. It hadn't sent Gwenla packing in all those years. And now, right when they were close to an answer, she was giving up?

"The vine, yes, but mostly the dam. Do you know what happens to towns upstream of a dam when a dam is built?"

"Oh," said Alison. Of course the dam would alter the natural flow of the waterway. She had seen lakes behind dams on postcards from the far west of Loegria, but she never stopped to consider what had been there before. "But there's an entire village here. What of the people? The duke doesn't own all of this land. I own a piece of it, and you own a piece too. Small pieces, but pieces nonetheless."

"It doesn't matter. They'll take it from us by law. We'll be paid for it, but we'll have to leave. All of the town will."

Alison could not believe what she was hearing. Gwenla loved this town and her home here, maybe more than anyone. She couldn't believe she would give up on it after all this time. "Where will you go?"

"I have a niece in the mountains. I don't know if I can bear to be underground again though after all this time. Lady Willana and I talked about a cottage by the sea once. Her people were seafarers long ago. Maybe whatever they give me for the land will be enough."

"You're sure there's nothing we can do?"

Gwenla sighed and shook her head.

Alison still couldn't accept it. "If you're giving up on the town, why are you still fighting the vine?"

"I just don't want to see anyone hurt until we're out of here. Look, maybe it's for the best. I've never seen the vine go near water. Maybe the flood will kill it."

"But what of Keir?" It hurt Alison to say his name. She could still see the betrayal in his eyes. "What if it follows him wherever he goes?"

"I suppose it will. But what are we supposed to do about it? You can't heal what's wrong with him by force. As the spriggan said, he has to be ready to help himself.'

"I know that you're right." She took a big sip of tea and held the warm mug in her hands.

Gwenla smiled. "But you're going to try anyway."

"Yes," said Alison. "Does that make me a fool?"

"A fool in love. But who isn't?"

Chapter Twenty-Four

THE LORD RETURNS

Gwenla and Alison spent the evening slashing away at the vine and warning the town. When they stopped by the town hall, Alison took the chance to ask Mr. Corbett if he had done any reading on old magic of a personal nature.

"Oh yes, the old magic can have quite an affinity for certain individuals. There are many stories of wishes gone wrong or spells that backfire and leave the caster cursed for all eternity." He led her downstairs into the basement. Gwenla stayed behind; she needed to reserve her strength for the vine.

The basement walls were lined with books and scrolls and stacks of papers reaching to the ceiling. Mr. Corbett, who could reach halfway to the ceiling at best, dragged a ladder on wheels around from shelf to shelf, pulling several large volumes and a stack of ancient scrolls.

He spread everything he gathered onto a table near the staircase. "Right, so personal magic. Here's the story of a woman who wanted a child. She cast a spell, but instead of the child, she was given a bean. When she planted it, it grew so many beans that it crushed her house."

"That's awful. What's the moral of that story supposed to be?" asked Alison.

"No moral. This is a true account. It happened in southern Loegria some two hundred years ago according to the elf who recorded it."

Hearing about the misfortune of others who had tried old magic, often long after the initial spell was cast, made Alison wonder if the spell she had tried had backfired in some horrible way that she didn't yet know about. "Are there any tales of people who have overcome the darker aspects of the old magic? Who stopped the spell in its tracks?"

"Hmm," said Mr. Corbett. "Not many. Let's see here."

He opened a book that was nearly as big as he was. The smell of old paper–dust and a hint of mildew–filled the air as he turned the pages.

"Ah, here we are. This sad man was turned into a duck after he tried to bring back his love who was lost at sea. It turned out the man had feared the water all his life, and so even as a duck, he would not approach the river or the pond. But one day, he decided that the spell had worked after all; it had given him what he needed to find his love. So he conquered his fear and went out into the ocean. The story ends there, but the scholar notes that there were sightings of a duck onboard a sailboat that went from port to port for many years after."

"Of course. 'The old magic has something he needs…'" The answer was there in what the spriggan had said. The vine was the key to overcoming Keir's own wounds. Alison wasn't sure how yet, but the answer was close.

She thanked Mr. Corbett, who not only didn't seem to mind the late hour, but who also seemed overjoyed that someone had a need for his work. And then she returned upstairs to meet Gwenla.

"Did he have an answer for you?"

"Maybe," said Alison. "I need to make one more stop before I call it a night. I'll meet you first thing to continue our fight against the vine?"

"Of course. But if you're going to see him, I'll help you clear the way."

⚜

The path to Keir's house was once again overwhelmed. But there were signs of movement from within, and the path around the back had been recently cleared.

"Thank you, Gwenla." She pulled the dwarf into a hug after they'd made it to the front door.

"Be careful, dear. A wounded animal is a dangerous thing."

"I will," said Alison.

Once Gwenla was halfway down the path, Alison knocked on Keir's door. She knew he wouldn't answer, but she wanted to make sure he was close enough to hear her.

"Keir, I know you don't want to talk to me. I'm sorry for lying to you. I was trying to help you, but I should have trusted you enough to tell you what I knew. I'm here because there was something else the spriggan said, something I forgot about until I just spoke to Mr. Corbett."

There was a crashing sound from within as if he'd dropped something. Alison took that to mean he was listening.

"Don't worry. I didn't tell Mr. Corbett who was connected to the vine. But he found a story about how the old magic gives you what you need, even if you don't realize it, and it reminded me that the spriggan said the same thing. Of course, there was also a story about a woman being crushed to death by beans, so I can't say for certain, but it feels like the vine has some kind of answer for you, if you're ready to hear it. I don't know what that means either–being ready. But you invited me in and cared for me when you could have easily turned me away. I don't know if that makes you ready for what the old magic has in store for you, but it must mean something. It means something to me."

She pressed her ear to the door. Silence.

"I meant what I said earlier. I'm here for you. Whether you're ready or not. Whether you find the answer or whether the vine follows you for your entire life. If you'll have me, I'll go with you. I promised the spriggan that I would. That if we couldn't solve the problem, we'd go somewhere far away from anyone. And I meant that. You said you'd follow me anywhere. I'm making you the same offer. I understand if you don't want me after what I've done. But if you can find it in yourself to forgive me, I'll be there. Come and find me at the cottage. Good night, Keir."

She followed the path back to Orchard Lane. For a moment, she thought she heard the door crack open. But when she turned back, it was shut as firmly as ever.

❧

In the morning, the vine had so overwhelmed Alison's cottage that she was forced to hack at it from the windows before she could get the door open. Dinah and Willow were scratching to be let out, but Alison had no choice but to keep them confined indoors.

"I'm sorry, Willow. The vine is running rampant. Give me an hour to clear you a path."

Willow understood. Dinah, on the other hand, was less sympathetic. She tried to dart out the moment Alison opened the door a crack.

"No, Dinah. Come back here," said Willow. "Maybe a fishy distraction will help?"

Alison smiled. Many of Willow's plans involved canned fish in some capacity. But she did as she was asked, and the distraction did work to keep Dinah inside, at least temporarily.

Outside her cottage, the vine was as bad as on the first day that she arrived. It was both depressing and disorienting, as if no time had passed and the entire previous week had been a dream. And the result after making the initial cuts around the cottage was even worse. By the time she had freed the path to the well, the vine was creeping along the ground to the door once again.

"Come on, Keir," she whispered to herself as she caught her breath from the exertion. "I know you can figure something out."

Gwenla had joined her in the cottage by the time she'd finished the morning chores.

"We've got to get down to the village. The duke's carriage has been spotted in Fossholm. They'll be here within the hour. And the vine has reached the common. Everyone will gather in town to meet their lord. We've got to keep them safe."

Alison wasn't sure she should go to see the duke's arrival. She struggled to imagine meeting him without giving him the hard slap across the face that he desperately deserved. And yet, she couldn't let down Gwenla. Regardless of what the duke had done or was about to do to the town, the villagers needed their protection.

Gwenla and Alison cut through the woods–the vine still avoided them–and followed the stream to the common, where Lady Sibba had brought the schoolchildren to play. In any other town, a dwarf and human wielding machetes would have been a cause for alarm, but in Herot's Hollow, the villagers were used to it.

A little hobgoblin child played dangerously close to where the vine had grown over Aras's eastern wall. Alison dashed over, waving her arms. In his fright, he nearly ran into the vine, but at the last minute, he turned back to the schoolhouse.

As Alison and Gwenla hacked at the vine, the church bells rang. The stomping of hooves and the rolling of wheels followed, taking the high street into the town square. Alison stopped slashing. As much as she despised the duke for what he had done to Keir, she could not resist the temptation to see the man in the flesh. To put a face to the specter of evil that existed only in her mind and in Keir's memories.

Gwenla came along beside her. "Go see him, if you're curious. I'll hold down the fort."

Alison walked through the common and up the lane by the churchyard as if she were in a trance. Here was the real cause of the vine, the real enemy of the town. The man whose selfishness, greed, and neglect had soiled the very lands he was sworn to protect. Could he possibly live up to the image that she'd made of him?

In short, he did not. He emerged from the carriage, which was black with gold leaf and very fine, first. Keir had been correct: he did greatly resemble his father. The duke's hair was gray where Keir's was dark, and his cheeks were far more hollow, but they had the same brown eyes, the same strong jaw, and the dusting of stubble even formed much the same shape on their necks and faces. He was around the same height but broader of shoulder than Keir, and it gave him the impression of being top-heavy, as if he'd fall over with one good push. Alison had an intense urge to provide that push, to see his face smeared in the mud of the streets.

From the carriage behind him came the dwarven industrialist. The first word that came to Alison's mind when she saw him was, *round*. The broadness of the duke's shoulders was echoed in the dwarf's midsection, and the dwarf's silk shirt seemed to reach the man's chin, no neck in sight. The wild gestures of his short arms gave Alison the distinct impression of a spinning top.

The duke pointed to the woods Gwenla and Alison had just left, muttering something to the dwarf beyond Alison's hearing. And then he turned to address the small crowd of villagers that had gathered.

"Thank you, everyone, for the warm welcome. It's been far too long. I've brought with me today a titan of the manufacturing industry, none other than Lathaz of the Mynan Mountain dwarves. Lathaz owns an astounding twenty-nine manufactories around Loegria–"

The duke's speech was interrupted by a blood-curdling shriek. The sound was higher and shriller than humans were capable–a wild, fairy scream.

"Help! Help us!" A pair of fairies darted into the square, flying faster than a pigeon on a delivery and carrying something between them.

"What is the meaning of this?" asked the duke. He attempted to reassure his guest, but the dwarf, like the crowd and Alison, was far more interested in the fairy spectacle.

Gwenla followed behind the fairies and took Alison by the arm. "It's happened. The vine got him."

"Got whom?" said Alison. She couldn't see what the fairies were carrying over the crowd that had gathered around them.

"Aras. Mezec and Lydiach found him in the field. He was trying to keep the vine away from his sheep."

Alison pushed her way through the crowd. On the ground, the tiny apothecary and tailor were tending to their father. His skin had gone the same inky shade of deep purple as Alison's dress had, the color of the night sky. Mezec shook his father's body, but Aras did not move.

Alison kneeled to the ground. "What happened? Where did it get him?"

"I don't know," said Lydiach. "I found him like this. I don't know if he's alive." She collapsed into tears on her brother's shoulder.

"What's going on here?" said Lathaz, the dwarven industrialist. He and the duke had pushed their way through the crowd as well.

"I'm sure it's nothing. Mr. Rainey, be a good man and fetch the doctor," said the duke.

Mr. Rainey looked up at him in surprise. "Are you sure, sir?"

Alison watched the recognition cross the duke's face: he was summoning his son. The duke had actually forgotten who the doctor was in this town.

But he couldn't backtrack now in front of Lathaz. "You heard me," he growled.

"Mr. Rainey, wait," said Alison. "Why don't we take Aras to him directly?" She could not resist shooting a cold glance to the duke, but he misinterpreted her. He mouthed her a thank you, and Gwenla had to pull on Alison's arm to stop her from protesting.

"He thinks I did that to help him," she said to Gwenla. "As if I ever would!" she said loudly, hoping the duke heard.

"Come now, it won't help anything," said Gwenla. "Let's hope Keir will be willing to see Aras. If there's anything left of him to see."

Alison carried Aras while his children followed behind. He was such a small thing, no larger than a human infant.

In her arms, she could feel the slow rise and fall of his chest–
he was breathing.

"He's alive!" shouted Alison.

"Wonderful!" said the duke. "Now, as I was saying–"

But the duke was cut off again.

"What's that?" asked Mr. Corbett.

Alison followed Mr. Corbett's finger to the lane near the
common. The vine was stretching up the lane with such
enormous speed that Alison could hardly see it. It looked
like a dark blur.

"My Gods," said Gwenla. "Everyone run! To the woods!"

"I've seen quite enough–" said Lathaz, but he was pushed
to the ground by the stampeding crowd.

"Gwenla–we have to help Keir–" said Alison.

"We will. Through the woods. Come on!"

Alison carried Aras and ran up the hill to the woods
across from the forge. She turned back to see the duke helping the dwarf up and into the carriage, the vine inches away
from the horses. She heard as they startled and broke into a
run back down the high street. *Good riddance*, she thought.

The vine had entered the woods, but it grew more slowly
there, and it had not yet reached the stream.

"Stay on the other side of the stream," yelled Alison to
the villagers. "Gwenla, see if Weyland and Strelka have anything they can spare. Knives, swords, axes, anything. You've
got to be ready if the vine makes it across."

"Alison," said Gwenla, grabbing her by the arm. She
looked exhausted, and for the first time since Alison had
met her, terrified. "Do you think he can stop this? What are
you going to do if he can't?"

Alison could not bear to think of it. "He must stop this. He can. I'm sure of it."

And she ran off into the woods, following the stream back to the place where she'd met him.

Chapter Twenty-Five

MAGIC, NOT MEDICINE

Alison had no choice but to hand Aras back to the fairies in order to clear the path beyond the stone circle. Though they could fly, they couldn't stay above the vine's reach for long while bearing their father's unconscious body between them. Thus the fairies had no choice but to follow closely behind Alison, the vine tangling behind them almost as soon as they had passed.

It had overtaken most of Keir's yard, but there was a short path from his back door to his shed that had been cut very recently. Alison led the fairies there and into the back door. There was no time to bother knocking.

"Keir, it's Alison," she called. "Aras has fallen to the vine. We need your help."

A door upstairs slammed shut. Alison helped Mezec and Lydiach carry their father onto Keir's kitchen table.

"Hold on," said Alison. "I'll talk to him."

Alison ran up the stairs and pounded on Keir's bedroom door. "I know you're in there. Aras is downstairs with Mezec and Lydiach. Please come take a look at him. I'll wait outside if you don't want to see me."

The door opened just as Alison lifted her fist to knock once again.

"I can't help him. It's old magic, not medicine." Behind Keir in the bedroom, a pair of great trunks were full to the brim with his clothes.

"You're leaving?"

"Yes, and not a moment too soon. Once I'm gone, the vine should go too. Perhaps he'll even wake."

"You can't possibly know that. What if the vine continues to spread all along the way? What if it never stops spreading? Don't run away from this, Keir. You can stop this."

Keir pushed past her and ran down the stairs. "I don't know how, Alison!"

Alison hurried after him. "Please, just take a look at Aras. Then you can go if you feel that you must." She caught him in the sitting room among a pile of books being sorted on the floor. She leaned over him. "Keir, please. There has to be something you can do."

Keir grunted and pushed himself back to his feet. "If it will get you to leave me alone."

Alison reached for his hand to lead him to the kitchen, but he snatched it away.

Undeterred, she brought him to the kitchen table. "He's still breathing," said Alison.

"We tried everything to wake him," said Mezec. "Smelling salts and strong tea, peppermint, and lemon oil. Lydiach even stabbed him with a sewing needle. He does not stir."

"The blood on the end of the needle was black," said Lydiach. "Our blood should be blue."

"I know the color of fairy blood," said Keir. "Back away."

Keir stood over Aras's tiny body and examined him without a great deal of delicacy. He poked and prodded, lifting limbs and wings alike. Then he shook his head. "It's the sleeping sickness."

"The one that took Jack?" asked Alison.

"The same," said Keir. "I'm afraid there is no cure," he told the fairies. "We can keep him alive for a time, but eventually he will perish. I'm sorry." There was no kindness in his voice, no emotion at all.

"There must be something–" began Mezec.

"There isn't. Now, please leave me. I'm rather busy at the moment."

The fairies looked at Alison, pleading. "Keir, look outside," said Alison. "Where are they to go? We had to fight our way through the vine to get here, and we barely made it. The entire village is trapped in the forest with Gwenla. Your father–"

"I don't give a damn about my father," Keir said sharply.

"–isn't with them. He's gone. He left when the vine broke into the town square. The vine causes the same sleeping sickness that killed Jack. There is something here for you. Something you have to do."

"Do what, Alison?" His voice broke on her name. "Cut it back? I've tried. Save the fairy? How? What am I supposed to do? Repeat the same old magic that caused the vine in the first place?"

"He caused the vine, and you brought our father here?" asked Lydiach, betrayed. "How could you?"

"He's the only one who can stop it," said Alison. "Please don't go."

Mezec had flown to Keir's door, flinging it open. "We'll take our chances. Come on, Lydiach."

The pair lifted their father and flew out the door. Alison ran after them into the tiny gap among a wall of vine. "You'll never make it! I'm sorry I didn't tell you. Please!"

But the fairies were gone from Alison's view.

"You need to leave too," said Keir. He had followed her outside, bringing the machete she'd left on his table.

"I won't," she said. Her mind was forming around an idea. It was insane, but it also seemed inevitable at this point. The vine was inescapable. Even if she managed to get back through it unscathed, there was no guarantee that she or anyone else could keep away from it forever. The only way out was through.

"Keir," she said. She moved in front of him, close enough to touch him but not daring to. "Listen to me. You are more than the worst things that ever happened to you. You can stop this. You are strong enough, I know it. I meant everything I said to you. I'm putting my life in your hands."

She reached for the vine. It was close at hand, twining a dark streak on the ground between them. Near the end, there was a thorn as large as a thumbnail dripping with inky black venom. The thing she'd spent the entire week fighting, the entire week narrowly avoiding.

"Alison, what are you talking about–No!" Keir leaned forward, trying to wrestle it from her grasp, but she pushed him away.

"See you on the other side," she said, and she pricked her thumb with the thorn.

Chapter Twenty-Six

DREAMING, DARKLY

The first thing Alison noticed when she woke was how hot she was. She was lying in the grass, and her back was wet with sweat. She rose and peeled the dress from her back, whipping the fabric back and forth against her to air it out.

The sun shone brightly, burning the skin of her bare arms pink. Except for her left thumb. It was a dark purple, nearly the color of iron gall ink after it dried. That was odd, but it didn't seem that important.

What mattered was getting out of these sweaty clothes. Alison rose and turned around in a circle. Behind her was a manor house–a sprawling country home of tan stone, ionic pilasters, and dozens of windows arranged in two neat rows. She shuddered at the sight. Nothing good came from there.

To her left was woodland, or an approximation of it; the rows of trees were too neat to have been placed there by nature. To her right was a dirt road twisting and turning down a steeply sloping hill.

In front of her was the answer: the river. The grass lawn stretched right out to the bank. She ran through the grass–it was warm and soft on her bare feet–and stopped on the sandy shore. She dipped a toe into the water. It was perfectly cool.

She pulled her dress over her head, fighting with the heavy fabric. Then she waded into the water in her undergarments.

The water moved slowly here, but it felt glorious nonetheless. It was so clear that she could see her feet as she walked along the smooth stones on the river's bottom. The sky overhead was a dazzling shade of blue with not a cloud in sight.

Alison played there in the water for what felt like only minutes, but when she looked up, the sky was tinged with scarlet.

"What are you doing? Come out of there."

There he was on the shore, coming to spoil her fun. Keir.

"Five more minutes," she yelled.

"No, come out of there right now."

"You'll have to come and get me," said Alison. She spotted a rock not too far away. It would be a fun game to climb on it and make him come and get her there.

She took off, half swimming, half hopping along the bottom until she reached the rock. He was yelling all the while, but she paid him no mind.

"You can't get me," she called to him in a sing-song voice.

"Get away from there. You're too close to the falls." He had followed along the bank of the river. He stood now beside a great old willow whose branches skimmed the surface of the water.

"Are you coming?" asked Alison. "I'm not going back inside unless you come and drag me in."

"If you don't come back here this instant, I'm telling Father," said Keir. His face twisted as he said it: something wasn't right about that.

Alison felt a jolt of fear pass through her. He wouldn't really tell Father, would he? "No, you won't."

"I will," said Keir. "You have until three. One. Two…"

"Alright, alright. You're no fun." Alison slid off of the rock. The sky was getting darker now, and even if Keir didn't tell Father, he would send someone for them soon, anyway.

She took a reluctant step towards the shore, but her foot didn't touch the bottom. It was whipped downstream by the current. Then her other foot slipped beneath her too.

"Help!" she cried, but her head was pulled under the surface.

She couldn't make out his response over the rush of the water.

One of Alison's feet collided with a rock; she wedged herself on it to keep from being pulled forward. "Keir, help! The water is too fast."

"Hold on," he yelled. Alison's head bobbed above the surface just long enough to see him kicking off his shoes and wading into the water. "Don't move. I'm coming."

"Keir!" The rock Alison had been braced against slipped beneath her. Her feet were free once more.

"Hold on! Danny!"

The last thing Alison thought as she fell over the edge was, *Who's Danny?*

⚜

The first thing Alison noticed when she woke was how hot it was. That, and the buzzing sound near her head.

She swatted at the noise violently.

"Alison, it's me. Aras," said a voice. Whatever was buzzing and flying about, it was very large. Bigger than any bee she had ever seen.

"Ow! Alison, stop hitting me!"

It was a fairy. It was wearing a little farmer outfit, its white wings poking out between the straps of its overalls. Alison found it rather cute.

"Oh, hello, Mr. Fairy! Have you come to play with me?" Alison asked. She hoped it liked to play hide and seek. It would be especially fun considering it could fly.

"Alison, wake up. We're in some kind of dream state. It keeps repeating. I didn't remember who I was the first few times either. We've got to find a way out of here."

"Do you like to swim? It's so very hot today. I was thinking of going for a swim," said Alison.

"No, that's not–"

"Oh, can you not swim with your wings? How rude of me. What other games could we play?" Alison hoped she'd still have time to swim after playing with the fairy. She really wanted to get into that water.

"Keir, over here!" cried Alison. She had spotted him across the lawn. He was in the shade of a big tree. "There's a fairy! He wants to play with us."

"Later," said Keir. "I'm reading."

He was always reading. It was ever so boring. Alison couldn't see the point in reading about climbing trees when you could be out climbing them yourself.

Something about that last thought didn't ring true to Alison's mind, but she ignored it. "Come on," said Alison to the fairy. "Let's go play by the river. If you don't want to swim, you could throw rocks into the water, and I'll try to catch them."

"Don't go into that water, Alison. I watched you the last time. You're going to go over the falls and drown. Then the whole thing starts over."

"I won't drown," said Alison. "I'm a good swimmer."

The fairy had his hands on his hips. He was trying to look angry, but really he just looked adorable. "You must not go into the water."

"I bet you can't catch me," said Alison, and she was off. Her bare feet pounded into the grass. She yanked her dress over her head and threw it onto the shore and dove into the river.

The fairy had not chased her.

"Hey!" she shouted. "You were supposed to chase me."

"I'll see you next go 'round, Alison," said the fairy. He flew away towards the woods.

Well, he was no fun. Alison spent the rest of the day playing on her own in the river. She tried calling to Keir, but he didn't hear her.

She played a dozen games by herself. Pretending the fish and the dragonflies were her enemies that could only be defeated by catching them, which she never did. Pretending she was a korrigan, singing a beautiful song and luring men to the water where she would drown them. Pretending she was a fish herself, swimming up and down stream, opening her mouth and closing it under the water until it made her cough.

Keir finally found her there when the sun had dipped below the trees.

"What are you doing? Come out of there."

"Five more minutes," she yelled, but she was struck with a feeling that she'd said it before.

"No, come out of there right now," said Keir, but Alison said the last words along with him. She had heard this too.

The next words were there on her lips, but she didn't want to say them. The words, however, seemed to have a mind of their own. "You'll have to come and get me."

Alison felt the pull of her body towards a rock further downstream. It was very close to the falls, she realized. The fairy had said something about the falls. She tried to resist the urge to go to the rock, but she found that her body would not move in another direction.

"You can't get me." The sing-song voice had come from her before she could fight it. There was another word in her mind–Alison. Her name was Alison.

"If you don't come back here this instant, I'm telling Father," said Keir. He was talking to her as if they shared a father, but they didn't.

"No, you won't," she said. And he wouldn't. Alison's father was dead.

"I will," said Keir. "You have until three. One. Two…"

"Alright, alright. You're no fun." Alison slid off of the rock. She looked up into the sky: it was growing darker by the minute. Downstream, to the east, it was deepening to a dark purple. A color that was both familiar and disturbingly unnatural, a midnight sky at dusk.

She tried to strike out for the shore, but her foot didn't touch the bottom. It was whipped downstream by the current. Then her other foot slipped beneath her too.

"Help!" she cried, but her head was pulled under the surface. It was just like the fairy had said. She was going to drown here.

Alison thrashed desperately until one of her feet collided with a rock; she wedged herself on it to keep from being pulled forward. "Keir, help! The water is too fast." But he wasn't going to help her.

"Hold on," yelled Keir. He was kicking off his shoes and wading into the water, but he was going to be too late. "Don't move. I'm coming."

"Keir!" The rock Alison had been braced against slipped beneath her. Her feet were free once more.

"Hold on! Danny!"

This was how Danny died. She felt the terrible pull of the water, dragging her over the edge, and then the terrible lurch down, down into the abyss.

⟡⟡⟡⟡

The first thing Alison noticed when she woke was how hot it was. That, and the buzzing sound near her head.

It was Aras, her fairy neighbor who had been pricked by the vine.

"Now do you remember?" asked Aras.

"Yes," said Alison. "Although I can't remember how I got here."

The fairy fluttered to Alison's thumb. The dark spot where she had been pricked–of course, she had been pricked by the vine too–was spreading down her hand and onto her arm, a dark blotch of purple.

"Your skin isn't purple," said Alison. The fairy's skin was its usual grayish tan. "When they brought you to us, your entire body was this color."

"The spot spread on me with each repetition until you arrived. I was in your place when I first got here, going over the falls."

"How did you break free?" Alison had no interest in going over the falls again.

"I didn't," said Aras. "You arrived, and I woke up in the woods instead with no compulsions of any kind. Do you still feel drawn to the water?"

"I do," she said. "It's like I'm being pulled there. When I try to consider something else, my thoughts shift until they arrive back at the river."

"I see that," said Aras. "You're walking there right now."

She had crossed twenty yards without realizing it. "Bloody hell," said Alison. "What is this magic?"

"The old magic," said Aras. "My kind were once steeped in the stuff. But we turned from it long ago when we chose to live among the people. There were so many modern solutions to the problems the old magic solved that it didn't seem like much of a loss. Especially considering how wild and unpredictable the old magic can be." He gestured around him.

"It certainly has a remarkable power," said Alison. She had sat herself down on the grass and refused to get back up. The old magic tugged at her, urging her to tumble forwards and roll through the field into the river if she had to.

"There's Keir," said Aras. "I tried talking to him near the tree, but my words didn't reach him."

"They took a while to reach me, too. Maybe he's back to us now. Come on," said Alison.

"Alison? Look where you're going," said Aras.

She was walking towards the river again. "Argh!"

She forced her foot to go towards the tree. It was as if it weighed three hundred pounds, but it did finally take a step in the right direction. "Look! I'm doing it," said Alison.

"Only a hundred more strides to go," said Aras, flitting around her head.

"How long has Keir been here?" Unlike herself or Aras, Keir was playing himself in this farce. Perhaps he or some version of him had been here all along.

"He arrived moments after you. When I was alone, I said my side of the conversation to no one. It was extremely baffling. I only fully made sense of what happened when I saw you go through it."

"Are Mezec and Lydiach here as well?"

The fairy flew in front of her face. "No. I don't think so. Should they be?"

Alison grimaced. "I'm not sure. They carried you away back in the real world. I wasn't sure they'd make it over the vine."

"Why did they do that?"

"Because I took you to Keir for help, but I didn't tell them that Keir was the reason for the vine's existence. When they found out, they fled."

"Ah," said Aras. "Well, I'd worked that out myself a long time ago."

"What?" Why hadn't the fairy said something?

"I told Gwenla, but she didn't believe me. This was years ago. When you arrived and he took such a liking to you, I figured there was a chance it would go away. It seems like I was wrong." He repeated his gesture to everything around them.

"Maybe not," said Alison. "I brought us here. Or I brought myself here, and he followed. There's something he has to do here. Once he does it, I think we'll be free, and the vine will be gone."

"Maybe it's a change you need to make. I don't see why the old magic would let us have any freedom in this world unless it wanted us to use it. Anyway, I'm going to go look for my children. If I find them, I may spend a few go 'rounds with them, snapping them out of whatever state they wake up in."

Alison had almost made it to Keir. "Thank you, Aras," she said as he flew away.

"Keir," she said.

Keir was sitting under the tree. She had spotted him here from a distance, but up close she was struck by how young he looked. He was still fully grown, still had the same wrinkle between his brows and stubble on his chin. But his posture was different. He had the casual air of a child, the way they sat with their limbs sprawling everywhere as if it was a chore to keep them confined to one place.

"Go away, Danny. I'm reading."

"Keir, it's me, Alison. It's not Danny. We're in a dream."

Keir looked up from his book. "Is this one of your silly games? You know what Father will say if he hears you pretending to be a girl again." His face was harsh, but his scowl turned to a smile in spite of his words. "I do like the dress."

"Keir." Alison knelt before him. "We have to get out of here. There's something we need to do. That you need to do. I don't know what yet, but I need you to remember who you are so we can figure it out together."

There was a flash of something in his eyes. A hint that something wasn't right.

"You're supposed to be playing in the river," he muttered. "And I'm meant to go there later. This isn't right."

"Yes, it isn't right at all. Hold on to that feeling," said Alison. "I'll go to the river." That wasn't what she wanted to say. She had meant to say, "I'm not going to the river," but the old magic wouldn't let her.

"I'll see you there later," said Keir.

Alison resolved to plant herself there in the ground unmoving until the sun set and the next iteration began. But the compulsion to the river was strong, and soon her mind was making excuses. Maybe alerting Keir to the situation had been the necessary change. Maybe now she just needed to let the loop play out the rest of the way.

She couldn't fight it any longer. Soon she found herself in the clear waters.

And then, right on cue, Keir arrived. The scene played out exactly as before: the swim to the rock, the teasing call, the threat to tell Father. All the way until the point where Alison entered the water again.

"Keir, help! The water is too fast."

"Hold on," yelled Keir. "Don't move. I'm coming."

"Keir!" The rock Alison had been braced against slipped beneath her. Her feet were free once more.

"Hold on! Alison!"

Alison. That was different.

⌘

The first thing Alison noticed when she woke was how hot it was. And rather than the buzzing of wings, there was someone lying in the grass beside her.

"Keir!"

Alison threw her arms around him but withdrew them once she remembered the tension that still existed between them. He sat up in a daze. As he pushed his hands into the grass, Alison saw that his right hand was stained dark purple.

"What happened? Where are we?"

Alison shared with Keir what Aras had told her and his suspicion that there was something they needed to change. If Keir was still angry with her for her deception, he didn't show it. In fact, his mood only seemed to improve the more she spoke.

"Of course," he said when she had finished. His eyes were bright. "I'm here to save Danny."

Alison considered it. Wasn't it exactly what she would think if she was forced to relive her father's death? That maybe there was something–anything–she could have done to change his fate, and that maybe the old magic was giving her that chance.

But something about that idea, and especially Keir's optimism about it, didn't feel right to her.

Keir stood and paced. "I've thought about this a thousand times over the years. What if I'd gotten in the water earlier? What if I'd made him get out before he swam to the rock? What if I'd had a rope or a willow branch to extend to him? I suppose we'll have to try them all."

"You don't think the old magic is going to bring him back though, do you?" asked Alison. Surely that wasn't possible after all this time. Would he be able to handle the disappointment if it didn't happen?

"I don't–" Keir's sheepish expression told her he had considered it. "It seems preposterous. But who knows what the limits of the old magic are? It made this place, this shared dream, and brought us here. It's not the house in Herot's Hollow where I treated Jack. It's Weldan House, the place where I grew up, on Danny's last day. If there's something that I need here, something that will bring me peace, surely it's saving Danny."

He had a point about the setting, but there was something wrong with his logic. "If you're meant to save Danny, why isn't Danny here? Why am I playing Danny?" The prospect of reliving Danny's death a dozen more times filled Alison with dread.

"Maybe the old magic is just using what it has. Now, the real question is what do we try first?" Keir noticed Alison's discomfort and hesitation for the first time. "Alison, I'm sorry to have to ask you to go through this with me. Can you feel it? The end?" His voice choked on the final word.

"Not the very end," said Alison. "But everything leading up to it. The pull of the water, the sensation of falling, the terrible fear. It's…horrifying."

He reached for her but stopped short, placing his hand on her shoulder. "I can't ask you to do this. There must be another way. Perhaps if you don't go into the water at all."

"I've tried, but the old magic compels me in. It won't let me stay on the shore."

In fact, they'd walked halfway there already.

"I don't feel the same compulsion. I'm pulled to the shore. That's what I'll do. I'll keep you on the shore with me. By force, if I have to."

Alison nodded. She wanted to go back into the water, but the wish was not her own. Her mind held both the terror and the pull of the river simultaneously. It was exhausting.

"Come here and sit with me," said Keir. He led her to a spot in the grass overlooking the river, but her body would not sit down.

"I can't," she said.

"Do you mind?" he asked. He held his hands out over her shoulders.

"Not at all," said Alison. The thrill of his touch overwhelmed her, even in their perilous situation.

Keir gently pushed on Alison's shoulders, but her spine straightened in an involuntary response.

"I'm sorry. Let me know if I'm hurting you."

He put his hands on her hips and pulled her down onto the grass. His body hovered over hers. He brushed a strand of hair from her cheek. "Are you still being drawn to the river? Or would you rather stay here?"

It was both at once still, but her body's response to their position was making it easier to ignore the call of the river. "I want to stay here," she said.

"Good," he murmured. He shifted his weight beside her, keeping his head and shoulders over her chest. His body was a cage, but it also had a pull of its own. His voice was shy and choked with regret. "Alison."

He took a moment to compose himself. Alison reached and placed a hand on his shoulder, and he didn't pull away. "I'm sorry for the way I reacted when I realized I'd caused the vine. You were right about it. And about me. I'm sorry that I made you feel like you couldn't tell me. You've been nothing but kind to me, and I've repaid you with anger and childish outbursts. I hope you can forgive me."

"There's nothing to forgive," said Alison. She shifted her body towards him. "We are here now, together. I'll do anything to help you. I'll replay this moment a thousand times until we get it right. You aren't alone in this."

"Alison," he whispered.

And then he kissed her, pressing his body against her and pinning her to the ground. It was the sweetest prison that ever was.

They stayed there together until the sun had fully set, and the sky above them turned to black.

Chapter Twenty-Seven

LETTING GO

The first thing Alison noticed when she woke was how hot it was.

Keir was already sitting up next to her. "Well, that didn't work, but I can't say that I regret trying." He kissed her softly on the cheek. "Should we try it again?"

It was tempting. But the stain had spread down Alison's arm and onto her chest, and it was mirrored on Keir's body as well. "I don't know how many chances we'll have at getting it right," she told him. "Try saving me this time. Don't keep me from the water."

"Are you certain?" he asked. "I may fail."

"I'll be alright," she said.

In truth, returning to the river offered some relief. The nagging compulsion was satisfied, and she was free to enjoy the refreshment of the water. Keir watched her from the shore, entranced.

When the sun began to set, she felt the old familiar pull. "It's starting," she said to Keir. "I'm heading to the rock."

Alison watched out of the corner of her eye as Keir climbed into the willow tree. He returned with several branches, which he braided together into a rope. "I still feel a strong compulsion to stay on the shore. I'm going to try throwing you the rope once you're off the rock."

She was ready. When Alison left the rock, she fought to keep her head above the water. She spotted the rope as Keir threw it. When she reached the stone on the riverbed that kept her from going over, she grabbed hold of the rope.

"I've got you!" said Keir. Alison held on tight as he pulled her in. Her arms shook from the effort of holding on, and she coughed up a lungful of water as Keir held her on the shore. He was elated. "I've actually done it. The thing I've dreamt of all my life. The vine has given me a gift. A most wondrous gift."

The sky turned black, and they were gone.

❧☙

The first thing Alison noticed when she woke was how hot it was.

"You've got to be kidding me," said Keir, pushing himself from the ground. "That felt so right. It was the only thing I've ever wanted, the chance to redo that day and get it right. So why are we still here?"

The purple stain had reached his face and neck and continued down the other side. "We're running out of time," said Alison.

"Maybe if we reverse it. Maybe I'll go in the water in your place. Or I can go in after you and pull you to the shore, even if it means I go over."

Keir continued musing, but Alison did not hear him. She had felt the plans of saving her were wrong from the beginning, and that feeling was growing more acute with their failures.

"Keir," she said. He stopped his pacing and looked down at her. "I'm compelled into the water. And you are compelled onto the shore. But at the very end, you always get in the water. What if you stay on the shore instead?"

He didn't understand. "Then you'll go over, the same as before."

"But it won't be." The more Alison thought about it, the more certain she felt this was right. "You always try to save me–to save Danny–but you can't. The point isn't to save us. It's to let us go."

"But I do let you go, each and every time but the last two–"

She stood and took his hand. "No, you don't. You always try to keep us safe. But it wasn't your responsibility. You were a child too, Keir. It wasn't for you to save him. It wasn't your fault that he died. Your father was wrong, and Jack's father was wrong too. You can't save everyone, Keir. It's enough that you tried."

It was a lesson that Alison had once struggled to learn herself. Though she could not have saved her father from his illness, in the years that followed his death, she had ex-amined and re-examined every moment that led to it, looking for something she could have done differently to change the outcome.

But it was fruitless. What had happened had happened, and no amount of wishing or praying or begging could change it. And no amount of guilt or blame or self-flagellation would bring Danny back.

A tear slid down Keir's cheek. Alison gently wiped it away and took his face in her hands, pulling him close to look into his dark eyes. "But now it's time to let him go, to let them both go. To let me go over the falls. The first time we met, you tried to save me. And you've done everything in your power to keep me safe since. And I love that about you. I hope you never stop trying. But sometimes things happen that are beyond your control. Let them go, Keir."

He collapsed into her embrace, sobbing into her shoulder until the fabric of her dress was wet with his tears. She held him there for a long while, stroking his back and murmuring words of comfort into his ear. "It's okay," she said. "I'm here."

Alison slipped into the water for what she hoped was the last time. When it was time to go to the rock, Keir called to her from the shore. "I don't think I can do this. To just watch you fall and do nothing."

"You can," she called. "You did what you could. It didn't save him, and that's okay. It wasn't your fault. Just let it go, Keir."

She watched him pace as she entered the water. Though the panic hit her when she lost her footing, she resisted the urge to call out to him for help. She knew that if she did, he would come, and they'd be right back where they started.

"Keir," she called when her foot caught on the stone. "It's going to be okay."

Her foot slipped from beneath her, and then the other one did too. She heard the rush of water and felt the sickening drop as the world fell out from under her.

And then she was under the surface. She had never been this far before, never felt the sting of her lungs–Danny's lungs–as they ached for air. She was pushed down to the bottom, over and over, until everything darkened and the sound of the water in her ears went quiet.

But then something was pulling her, dragging her up to the surface. The air filled her lungs in a violent gasp, and she blinked her eyes open, but it was too dark to see.

Somewhere in the distance, she heard a song.

Chapter Twenty-Eight

NEW BEGINNINGS

The first thing Alison noticed when she woke was how cold she was.

She was lying on the path in Keir's backyard. A cool breeze blew over her, raising gooseflesh bumps on her bare arm, arms which no longer bore the stain. The sky above was full of stars.

As she pulled herself up, her mind registered what was missing: the vine. Even in the darkness, its absence was conspicuous. Her eyes caught the shimmer of ash on the ground, piles of it, and a few yards away, she spotted Keir gently stirring.

She ran to him. He jolted upright at the sight and met her in a tight embrace. He breathed her in, arms wrapped around her like they would never let her go again.

"You did it," she whispered in his ear. "I knew you could."

He pushed her away gently to look at her in the moon-light. His gaze was warm and soft. "No, Alison. It was you. I could never have found the strength without you." He grasped her hands in his and pulled them between them, between their hearts. "You are my strength."

A long moment passed as they held each other. Alison knew that working through grief was a long process, that what they'd gone through together was just the beginning, not the end of it. She knew he would not be healed over-night, that there were parts of him that may never be whole again. But she also knew in her heart that he was still worthy of her love, just as she was worthy of his. And that together, they could face anything.

The moment was finally broken by a voice in the dis-tance–Gwenla.

"You've done it! You've actually gone and done it!" She ran up the path as fast as her short legs would take her. Be-hind her fluttered Aras, Mezec, and Lydiach.

Gwenla hugged Alison first, then Keir, and then back to Alison. Mezec flew over to Alison and held out his right hand.

"My father told us what happened in there on the way over. Thank you," he said. Alison took his hand between her thumb and forefinger and gave it a shake.

"Come on," said Gwenla. "Everyone else is already at the inn."

Alison held out her arm to Keir.

He was reluctant. "Did you tell them it was my fault? Are they angry?"

"They were frightened at first," admitted Gwenla. "But once we'd come through it, Mr. Corbett piped up with his theory that the vine was protecting the town from the dam and the manufactory. Mr. Smalls did an impression of the dwarven industrialist on the run that earned quite a laugh, and by the end of it, everyone was hailing the vine as the town's savior. I couldn't see any reason to argue. The only people who know the entire truth are right here."

"I told them that you both entered the vine's world to save my life at great personal risk," said Aras. "That's the truth. It's the only truth that matters to me." He offered his tiny hand to Keir's to shake.

Keir's eyes were soft as he shook the fairy's hand. And then they opened wide as he registered just how strong the fairies were.

"Let's go," said Lydiach. "There's a thimbleful of mead with my name on it."

⚬◠◡◠⚬

A carriage waited outside the inn. Though it was black, it wasn't the fine black carriage that had brought Lord Ainsley and the dwarven industrialist to town. It belonged to the King's Constables, and Tirrin and Lord Wexenas were climbing inside.

"I take it they found their culprit, then?" asked Alison innocently.

"Oh, yes," said Aras. "It was the funniest thing. I had completely forgotten that I stopped by for some inks to mark my sheep. My satchel had a hole in it, and I dropped one without realizing it. I'm going senile, you see. And Mezec here forgot that he told me I could take as many as I liked."

"Completely slipped my mind," said Mezec. "We apologized profusely for wasting the good constables' time. They were very understanding."

Alison smiled. If Aras was senile, she was a knocker's uncle. But she didn't doubt their ability to fool Lord Wexenas. And DCI Tirrin was probably grateful for the reduction in paperwork.

As usual, the entire town was inside the inn. Mr. Smalls spotted them entering and stopped the lively tune he'd been playing abruptly. "The heroes of Herot's Hollow!" he cried.

Someone put their arm around Alison's shoulders as they cheered. Keir was pulled into a number of hugs and handshakes, his ears bright red. Strelka rescued them from the excessive attention by strong-arming everyone else who tried to come close.

"I thought you'd want to see this," she said. She led them to a table near the back, near enough to see but not be heard.

The table shook as Weyland Gilroy banged his knees underneath it. Beside him was Lady Sibba. He had taken her delicate brown hand in his giant red ones and was whispering something to her that made her laugh.

"When he brought her the poem, she didn't know how to take it. I think she was just surprised, but Weyland was terribly disappointed. And I was too. But then today when the vine took off, he rescued one of her students on his way to the woods with the axes. He stayed by her side until it withered and didn't let those kids out of his sight. Afterward, she took his hand, and I haven't seen her let it go since."

Weyland spotted Alison then and waved her over. "I've got something for you," he said. He reached into his pocket and produced a small scrap of paper.

On it was a portrait of Alison and Keir done in black ink. Alison thought he'd made her a little prettier than she truly was. In the portrait, her face was sweet and heart-shaped, not round and full as she pictured it, and her nose was more delicate than it appeared to her in the looking glass. But the likeness of Keir was true down to the stubble on his chin, and she supposed many people gave themselves less grace than they granted to others. She thanked him sincerely.

Keir led them to a table in the corner. She doubted he would ever be fully at ease in such a crowd, but he'd handled their recognition admirably.

"I feel guilty," he said to her, leaning over the table and keeping his voice low. "Not just because they don't realize we saved them from a problem I created, but also because they think my father will give up after this setback. He won't."

"Change is going to come to Wilderise eventually. The manufactories aren't all bad. Without them, my parents would never have been able to give me the life that I have. And have I ever told you about the marvel that is the modern flushing toilet?"

He grinned, slightly.

Alison took his hand and gave it a squeeze. "Maybe there's a way to do it right. And maybe there's a way you can be part of that. The town needs an advocate. If you feel you owe them something, maybe it can be you. I know it would be asking a lot. Standing up to him won't be easy. But I believe in you."

He leaned forward and brushed his fingers along her cheek, cupping her face in his hand. "With you at my side, I could move mountains."

"I'll settle for the toilet," she said.

And there was his real smile. It was radiant.

⚜

Back in the cottage–her cottage–the next day, the pot whistled on the stovetop. Alison stayed at her desk; Keir would take care of it.

In front of her was a letter received days earlier but forgotten in the mayhem that followed.

My dearest Alison,

It seems that I have nothing but ill tidings to share in response to your lovely postcard and the most excellent book of poetry that you were so kind to send me. You see, that awful Lord Arleas has raised the rent once more! Rather than the six gold increase he promised, he has raised it by ten. Ten! The gold you left me will only cover it for…I don't know how long. You know I can't crunch numbers. But it won't be very long at all, and unless you've been very successful in your endeavor to rent the cottage, I'm afraid we're simply going to have to let the flat go.

I've written to my mother, but I don't think they can take me. I've been scouring the ads in the papers, but there's nothing even remotely livable. I'm afraid at this rate we may be cast out of the city of Arcas Dyrne for good.

I do hope you're finding the cottage enjoyable. Is there perhaps an extra room?

All my love,
Rinka

Alison took her time with her reply. She heard a commotion in the kitchen: Keir yelling at Dinah to stay away from the stove, Willow yelling at Keir for yelling at Dinah, and Gwenla yelling at all three of them for disturbing Alison while she was trying to write her letter. She smiled and lifted the pen once more:

My dearest Rinka,

I'm appalled but unfortunately not shocked to hear of the latest exploits of that dastardly Lord Arleas. But perhaps all is not lost.

You asked if there was an extra room here, and indeed there is. In fact, there may be an entire extra cottage soon.

You see, I've rather fallen in love with the place. And not just the place, but the people, and perhaps with a particular person. He's tall, dark, and handsome, sure, but he's also protective, kind, and brave. I'm afraid I've become quite an idiot in his company, which I've been assured means I'm in love.

It is truly wonderful here, Rinka. And they're looking for a butcher! But if you'd prefer a different vocation, perhaps you can be a fortune teller, for you got it just right about the cottage. I hope you'll come as soon as your affairs are settled. I'll be sending for the rest of my things soon. Safe journey.

All my love,
Alison

She sealed the letter with a drop of red wax and then walked into the kitchen to join her friends.

Epilogue

In the vine's place, they planted a garden for all the seasons. White lace alyssum and pink peonies, forget-me-nots and daffodils, a thousand different roses, and a gently weeping willow by the pond. Under its branches, they placed a stone. *Danny,* it said, painted in white letters. And on cold nights, Keir lit a candle to keep him warm.

About the Author

Amy Yorke is an author of light and cozy fantasy and lover of all things magical and romantic. She is half English, half American, and she offers her sincere apology to readers of both languages for her idiosyncrasies in word choice. In her spare time, she enjoys gardening, playing video and tabletop games, and chasing after her cats.

Join her mailing list to receive news, updates, and promotions, including free advanced reader copies prior to new releases: https://www.amyyorke.com.

Read on for a preview of *The Bright and the Blue*,
Book Two of the Wilderise Tales

Chapter One

TALKING TO STRANGERS

Rinka

Sure, there was more blood coming from Rinka's nose than was ideal, but at least she had made it. She was on board the rail-wheeler and on her way to join her friend Alison in Wilderise.

The day had started well enough. Rinka had packed everything she owned into the largest trunk she'd been able to find and had lugged it to the station an hour before her rail-wheeler was due. She had spent the time since pacing the platform, checking her maps and watching the passengers coming and going, wondering how they could be so nonchalant about the whole thing.

Rinka had never left the city of Arcas Dyrne before. Her family left the orcish strongholds for the city generations before she was born and never looked back, her mother insisting that the orcs who remained were "uncivilized" and "barbaric." And while most city dwellers took at least the occasional holiday to the coast, Rinka's mother found those people to be "lazy" and "unscrupulous."

Truth be told, Rinka's mother was a judgmental old hag.

Rinka had freed herself from her mother's house two years earlier when she moved in with a human number-cruncher named Alison Lennox. Their flat had been small but comfortable, and it had been a short walk to Rinka's job at a butcher shop. A job she hated, but along with Alison's salary, it brought in enough to pay the rent.

Until one day, it didn't. With their landlord's latest rent increase, they were priced out of Arcas Dyrne for good. And thus Rinka had a choice: move back in with her mother, or join Alison in a land she'd never set foot in, a wild and dangerous land she'd only seen at the picture show.

She chose the latter.

Morning light flashed from the open windows of the rail-wheeler as it rounded the final curve into Arcas Dyrne's North Station, the great black engine billowing smoke and pulling a dozen red cars behind it. A crowd had formed on the platform, primarily human and dwarven families heading out for one of those "unscrupulous" early holidays. Rinka lifted her trunk with ease despite its size, planting it and herself just a step from the platform's edge.

The rail-wheeler slowed. Rinka could not resist the urge to take one final look at her maps and the letter from Alison with instructions on each step of her voyage, even though she'd had them memorized for weeks. She reached into her leather satchel, but when she removed the papers, a sudden gust of warm wind from the rail-wheeler swept through the platform, sending them into the air.

"No!" cried Rinka, snatching with her strong grey arms. She came away with only one of the documents: the map of her home country, Loegria. The one she needed the least.

Rinka pushed through the crowd as they inched closer to the platform's edge in anticipation, elbowing a dwarf in his ear ("Watch it!") and nearly tripping over a tiny Halfling child as she followed the papers, which swirled and flapped in the breeze as if they were birds in flight. She caught the corner of Alison's letter just as she reached the part of the platform where the first-class passengers waited, shouting an apology that frightened a lady elf in a fine silken dress back into her partner, who huffed in Rinka's general direction.

The rail-wheeler had pulled to a stop, and the platform grew even more crowded as the overnight passengers from Landsend pushed through the outgoing travelers on their way from the station. A human man in a hurry batted the final paper—the most important one, the map of Rinka's destination, Wilderise—out of his face and down to the concrete of the platform floor, where Rinka lost sight of it as it tangled in the legs of the passengers.

She grabbed at something on the ground, coming away with a folded and yellowed object that greatly resembled the worn map Alison had sent her, but it was only a human newspaper. The crowd thinned as the passengers began to board. Finally, Rinka spotted the map caught on the armrest of the last bench before the end of the platform. She sighed with relief as she tucked it back into her satchel, content to have everything back in its rightful place.

Her joy was short-lived.

Turning hastily to make her way back to the third-class section, she crashed face-first into a cart of luggage pushed by a human valet.

For a moment, everything went black. And then stars danced in her eyes as she blinked to refocus them. She smelt something metallic and felt a warm drop of liquid slide from her nose to the top of her lip before she felt the pain.

"I'm sorry, miss, but you should watch where you're going," yelled the valet. He had not stopped to see the damage; Rinka doubted the elf he accompanied would have allowed it if he'd wanted to.

Her nose hurt, badly. She wiped at her face and came away with a surprising amount of blood on her hand. She reached into her satchel for her handkerchief, staining her maps with her own blood.

"Pixie's britches," said Rinka to no one in particular.

There wasn't anyone to speak to.

The platform was nearly empty now, the waiting passengers having finished boarding during her struggle. Ignoring the blood streaming down her face and the throbbing of her nose, she sprinted back to her abandoned trunk, the rush of air pulling tendrils of her auburn hair loose from its bun.

"All aboard!" shouted the conductor.

"Wait! Wait for me!" yelled Rinka as the rail-wheeler's wheels squealed into motion.

Rinka tossed the trunk up the stairs of a third-class car just as it began to move away. But when she reached out her hand to grab the railing and pull herself on board, she came back with empty air.

The rail-wheeler was picking up speed quickly. Rinka's reflexes were normally excellent, but the pain had sent tears into her eyes, obscuring her vision and making it hard for her to find the stairs to the next carriage as it rushed past.

"Look, Mummy," said the Halfling child Rinka had nearly trampled earlier from the approaching stairwell, tugging on his mother's sleeve and pointing to Rinka. The Halfling's mother, a human woman, shook her head at the child and muttered something about the impoliteness of staring, offering no help whatsoever.

As Rinka turned to the final stairway, her teary eyes caught the motion of a figure sprinting across the platform. She couldn't quite make him out, but he appeared to be as tall and broad as an orc. He certainly moved like an orc, covering the gap between the platform and the moving rail-wheeler in one great leap.

"Please!" yelled Rinka. She had just one last chance to get on the rail-wheeler before it carried everything she owned away to Landsend, leaving her behind.

The stairwell would be in front of her in seconds. This was it. She had to time the jump just right—

"Grab on," said the stranger. Rinka blinked away the tears—he was standing in the stairwell, reaching out to her.

She didn't think, she just thrust her hand into his. The stranger pulled with incredible strength as Rinka fired the muscles in her legs as hard as she could.

It was enough. Almost too much, actually. Rinka very nearly knocked the poor man over.

"I'm sorry," she said as she pulled herself up slowly, being careful not to lean too far back into the open air behind her as the rail-wheeler cleared the platform. From the top step, the stranger extended an arm again, and Rinka gratefully accepted. "Thank you for helping me," she continued, but her voice was muffled by the blood in her nasal passages.

"My Gods, are you alright?" asked the stranger.

Rinka saw herself reflected in his dark eyes—crimson streaks running down her face and onto her pretty green dress, eyes filled with tears, and, worst of all, her hair was a total mess. It was so pathetic she couldn't help but laugh.

"My father always said it's not a party if no one's nose is bleeding." Rinka's father had a number of sayings that were in no small part responsible for her parents' divorce, at least according to Rinka's mother. But Rinka always found them charming, and in this case, surprisingly appropriate.

The corner of the stranger's mouth twisted a bit in bemusement or perhaps bewilderment. "Looks like it's a party, then." It was clear that her first guess had been incorrect—he wasn't an orc—but there was something strangely familiar about him.

She studied his face as he fumbled in his pockets for something, trying to guess at his background to give her a clue as to where she might have seen him before. Humans could be as large as orcs, sometimes even larger, and they were frequent patrons of her (now former) employer. But there was something about his face that wasn't quite human. While his eyes had the almond shape of traders from the Far East, the rest of his features were sharper and thinner, more like the elves from the high mountains of Loegria.

His ears, which would have given her more of a hint, were unfortunately hidden behind his dark hair. She couldn't quite place him, although she did have a guess.

"Have you ever been in a picture show?" she asked him as he held out the object he'd been seeking: a handkerchief.

He furrowed his brow and looked from her—no doubt wondering just how much injury Rinka had sustained to ask such a question—and then to his clothes, which were tattered and stained. "No, I can't say that I have. I've never even seen one."

"Never?" asked Rinka. She pulled the handkerchief to her face and was surprised by its pleasant floral scent. The fabric felt fine in her hands: silk maybe, or a very fine cotton. She nearly asked the stranger where he'd gotten it, but as she looked from his ragged clothes to the handkerchief, she realized it must have been stolen.

Rinka wasn't one to judge. She'd seen enough of life in the city to understand the difficult choices that had to be made at times, and the stranger had been kind enough to help her when no one else would.

The bleeding had slowed to barely a trickle, but Rinka was grateful to be able to clean herself up. As she wiped the blood from her face, the soothing touch of the fine fabric seemed to wipe what was left of the pain away.

Rinka followed him into the carriage. There were no seats left together, but as the two of them approached the first row, a Halfling gentleman in overalls stood abruptly to offer his seat, his face registering alarm at the disheveled man and the orc in bloodied clothes.

"Poor fellow," said Rinka. "My trunk is in another carriage. I'll have to get changed quickly before I scare away the rest of the passengers."

"Never mind the passengers," said the stranger as he gestured for Rinka to take the seat by the window. "Are you sure you're alright? May I ask what happened?" His voice was warm and deep with a bit of a rasp, as if he'd spent too long by the fire or had smoked one too many pipes.

"Just a mishap with a luggage cart. I'm Rinka, by the way." Rinka held out her hand to shake.

"Drystan," he said.

"Just Drystan?" Rinka asked. Humans tended to have surnames, and elves were almost all nobility of some kind, Lords and Ladies of ancient lands Rinka knew nothing about. Drystan sounded like an orc's name, or maybe a dwarf, but he resembled neither of those.

"Drystan Droswyn," he said. "But you can call me Drystan."

That was curious, too. Humans preferred to be addressed by their surnames unless you were closely acquainted.

Still, Rinka could hardly see the point in arguing with a stranger about their own name.

"Nice to meet you, Drystan," she said.

Rinka leaned back into her seat and sighed in relief. She had made it on board the rail-wheeler, her maps and instructions safely in her satchel, her trunk safely on board (if a few carriages further away than she would have liked), her nose no longer hurting, and all was well.

"It's a beautiful day to travel, isn't it?" she asked Drystan as she looked out the window at the great buildings of Arcas

Dyrne shrinking in the distance. The landscape beyond the city quickly transitioned into fields of green and yellow and brown, some growing high with the last of the winter crops and others freshly planted and ready for the warmer weather to come. Rinka had seen it all before, but only in the grey tones of the picture show. It did not prepare her for how bright and blue the sky could be beyond the city's smog, for the way it reflected on the water, the perfect mirror images of cotton candy clouds in the stillness of a lake. For the gentle ripples that danced on the surface as the rail-wheeler rushed past.

Rinka turned back to Drystan when he didn't respond. He was looking at her incredulously.

"Oh, my clothes," said Rinka, guessing at his confusion. "Excuse me for a moment—I'm going to go see to my trunk and change into something a little less alarming."

Rinka made her way to the carriage where she'd thrown her trunk, ignoring the stares and frightened comments of the passengers. She retrieved a clean dress, a pretty yellow number she'd made herself after admiring a similar one in a shop window.

After she had changed in the water closet, she retrieved her sewing kit from her trunk. Mending Drystan's clothes would give her something to pass the time, and it would repay him for his kindness.

"That's better," she said when she returned. His eyes lingered on her, but there was no hint of mockery in them. "Now, off with your trousers."

"Excuse me?" Drystan's face registered genuine surprise.

"Your trousers," repeated Rinka. She shook the sewing kit in its biscuit tin, the notions and needles rattling.

Rinka studied the torn trousers as he considered her offer, assessing where to start. But there was something odd about them. There were rips and small holes, but not in the places you would expect. Rinka had mended enough of Alison's trousers to know that the fabric usually wore along the cuffs and the seams, and sometimes at the knee. The imperfections in Drystan's trousers were in the good, strong parts of the fabric that rarely caused Alison trouble. It was almost as if they'd been placed there on purpose.

Almost like a costume.

There was something about him that didn't make sense. The clothes and the bag at his feet were too exaggerated in their humble appearance to have belonged to someone truly down on their luck. And Rinka had known few of even the lowest stature in society who did not take some pride in their appearance. Especially rare were those who would take the trouble to shave their faces but not wash their hair. "You're sure you're not from the picture shows? What about the theatre—"

"Tickets!" Rinka's line of inquiry was cut off by the ticket taker's arrival in the carriage. Luckily, Alison had prepared her for this possibility. Rinka reached into her satchel and withdrew her ticket, frowning at the bloodstain.

Beside her, Drystan tensed. He didn't reach into his pockets or make a move at all.

He didn't have a ticket, she realized.

Rinka knew she should be suspicious of him. He had jumped onto the rail-wheeler without a ticket, and the handkerchief he'd offered her was likely stolen. She knew exactly what her mother would say: *"He's an unsavory sort, and King Derkomai's finest will see that he gets what's coming to him."*

But Rinka didn't want to see the only person who had helped her thrown off the rail-wheeler. And if that made her naïve, so be it.

"I know," she whispered to him. "We'll just say that you lost your ticket when you were helping me onboard."

"That's very kind of you," he said. He smiled at her. "But I'll handle this."

Rinka didn't have time to imagine what he meant before the ticket-taker had arrived.

"Tickets, please."

Rinka handed over her ticket. "Sorry about the blood," she began, but the ticket-taker had already marked it and returned it to her.

She held her breath as she watched Drystan slip something to the ticket-taker she could not see.

"Of course, sir," said the ticket-taker, winking at Drystan. "Have a good day."

"What was that? What did you—"

Drystan pressed his index finger to his lips. A bribe, perhaps? But if he could afford to bribe the ticket-taker, why not just pay for a ticket?

"Who are you?" Rinka whispered, only it came out so loudly half the carriage turned to look. "Are you a criminal?"

At this, Drystan laughed. "Do you always ask suspicious men if they're criminals?"

"Only if they're behaving like criminals."

He turned to her, his shoulder blocking her view of the aisle. "Is that really your best theory? An actor or a criminal?"

Rinka stared at Drystan for a long moment, failing to understand his meaning.

Then it hit her.

"You really are someone else, aren't you?"

He shrugged a single shoulder as if to say he could neither confirm nor deny it, but there was a playful intensity in his eyes that gave him away.

She was right—there was something else to him.